Then He Kissed Me

Then He Kissed Me

LAURA TRENTHAM

St. Martin's Paperbacks

This is a work of fiction. All of the characters, organizations, and events portrayed in this novel are either products of the author's imagination or are used fictitiously.

THEN HE KISSED ME

Copyright © 2016 by Laura Trentham.
Excerpt from *Till I Kissed You* copyright © 2016 by Laura Trentham.

All rights reserved.

For information address St. Martin's Press, 175 Fifth Avenue, New York, NY 10010.

ISBN: 978-1-250-07764-6

Our books may be purchased in bulk for promotional, educational, or business use. Please contact your local bookseller or the Macmillan Corporate and Premium Sales Department at 1-800-221-7945, ext. 5442, or by e-mail at MacmillanSpecialMarkets@macmillan.com.

Printed in the United States of America

St. Martin's Paperbacks edition / July 2016

St. Martin's Paperbacks are published by St. Martin's Press, 175 Fifth Avenue, New York, NY 10010.

10 9 8 7 6 5 4 3 2 1

For Steve

Acknowledgments

I don't think any of my books would be what they are without music. Growing up in Tennessee, I rebelled against the country music that was the standard fare so close to Nashville. I listened to pop, but also discovered U2 and REM and Tori Amos. Then, my senior year of high school, Garth Brooks came out with his first album, and I slunk off to buy the tape(!), hoping no one would recognize me. I still can't not sing along to "Friends in Low Places." Talk about a great song to inspire a book! Over the years, I've evolved and listen to everything, but when I started writing southern-set small-town books, I rediscovered a love of country music and have come to really appreciate the mini-stories in each song.

I have a playlist put together for the entire Cotton-bloom series, but this book in particular had some stand-out songs . . . Sam Hunt's "Take Your Time" inspired the scene where Tally and Nash meet again as adults. Chase Rice's "Gonna Wanna Tonight" inspired their trip to the top of the water tower and Nash's list. As far as non-country, Ed Sheeran's "Photograph" inspired the thread of past photos in the story. Wishing everyone happy reading and many inspiration songs!

Chapter One

Nash Hawthorne ducked into the tall reeds by the water. The stream widened farther down and joined up with the Mighty Mississippi, but behind his house in Cotton-bloom, Louisiana, it burbled along, shallow enough in most places to wade.

That's what he'd do. Wade all the way to the Mississippi and take to the river like Huck Finn. He checked his pocket for his inhaler. It was the only thing he really needed.

Everyone was up at his house. They tried to smile around him, tried to keep the whispers confined to corners, but he knew exactly what was happening. He was ten years old, not an idiot.

His mother was dying.

She'd spent the last three years dying. Almost as far back as his memories went. He had vague recollections of her swinging him in the air, her dark hair thick and lustrous, her cheeks round and full of color. Now her hair grew in sparse patches over her mostly bald scalp, and she looked like a character in her own black-and-white comic. Pale papery skin and dark shadows.

His father worked an oilrig out in the Gulf, and he'd

heard his aunt Leora saying it would be touch and go whether he made it back in time.

Back in time. He wished he could turn everything backward like one of the characters in his comic books. Back to when his mother could get out of bed to make him a peanut butter and jelly sandwich. Back to when his father smiled.

Or maybe he would shrink to the size of a ladybug and hide in the grass until it was all over. Sit on a blade of grass and watch the river flow by and the sun circle the earth. They'd just finished studying about planets in science, and he envied the stars up in the sky, cold and beautiful.

He toed off his sneakers and stepped into the cool water. Instead of heading toward the freedom of the Mississippi, he waded upstream and sent out telepathic messages for Tallulah. He knew that sort of thing was make-believe, like Santa and Superman, but he wanted to believe. Wanted to believe his mother would get better.

As he drew closer to the Fournette's house, a girl rose out of the reeds, a breeze tangling her long, dark hair around her shoulders. His heart swelled until it was painful. Maybe there was hope.

His tongue froze, and he didn't know what to say. She saved him by throwing her arms around him and giving him a hug. He dropped his forehead to her bony shoulder and took a deep breath. She smelled faintly of oranges.

She pulled away first and scrabbled back up the bank to sit cross-legged under the drooping limbs of a willow tree. He followed, sitting so they both looked out over the water.

"Mommy's dying. It might even happen today." The wobbly way he'd said "mommy" heated his face. He was too old to cry, especially in front of a girl.

"I know. I heard Daddy talking this morning when he didn't think I could hear."

"No one up at the house will say anything in front of me, but I can feel everyone waiting for it to happen."

"Where's your dad?"

"Still out on the rig. Bad weather is keeping him there." Nash stripped the leaves off a thin green branch, his gaze down. "They want me to go sit with her."

"Don't you want to?"

He would never admit his shame to anyone but Tally. "She's not my mother. Not anymore. I don't understand what she's saying. I think they've given her a bunch of drugs. And, she smells funny."

"How so?" As he expected, no judgment, only curiosity lilted her voice.

"Stale. Like I imagine death would smell." He risked a glance at her, but her attention was on poking at a piece of moss. "You know the comic where the police commissioner dies? And, he's all pale and stuff? That's her."

She abandoned her stick, pulled a cloth bag with her name embroidered on the front closer, and took out two oranges. She handed him one and dug her thumb into the peel of hers, a burst of orange scent surrounding them. He did the same, and they were quiet as the pile of discarded peel grew between them.

"Is your dad going to get a job on the mainland . . . after?" She bit into a slice, squirting him with juice.

He wiped his cheek, dropped to his back, and stared into the newly sprouted leaves. The breeze rustled them and sunlight dappled the twirled ends. "I heard Aunt Leora say something about taking me to her house."

"But . . . but that's in Mississippi? Miles away. What will we do?"

He was relieved to hear the panic and outrage he'd been unable to voice at the time, considering he was eavesdropping on an adult conversation. Somewhere along the way, his mother had taught him that was a no-no.

"We both have bikes. Maybe we could meet in town."

"But it won't be the same. Who's going to go fishing with me?"

Even though he was wondering the same sorts of things, he said, "At least you have two parents and your brothers."

She looked over her shoulder, first at him and then her house. "It's not the same. I don't belong in this family."

"What do you mean?"

"Mama and Daddy go together like a pair of gloves. Cade and Sawyer are whip-smart. And, I'm . . . I'm just . . . here."

"You're smart."

This time the look she shot him was dire. "They're talking about holding me back. I would never be able to set foot in that school ever again."

He popped up on his elbows. "If they hold you back, let's run away together. We can head toward the Mississippi and find somewhere to live. You can fish for our food, and I can . . . I don't know, find work somewhere." As the idea took root, a shot of excitement made his breathing ragged. He fumbled his inhaler out of his pocket and took a pump.

"Are you serious?"

"Sure, why not? Huck Finn did it."

"Yeah, about a hundred years ago. Don't be silly."

Her words smarted, but he pressed on. "Wouldn't living out there be better than me living with crazy Aunt Leora or you getting held back?"

Her mother's voice, singsongy and strong, called from up the hill where her house sat. "Tallulah! Come on up for ice cream before your brothers eat it all."

His breathing fractured again, but an inhaler wouldn't help. It was the kind of hurt medicine wouldn't fix.

She took his hand and squeezed. "We can decide whether or not to run away together later, right?"

"Sure," he said vaguely and turned his face away so she wouldn't see the sting of tears in his eyes. Why would she leave her family? Two brothers who teased her, a mother and father who exasperated her, but even so, warmth and love seemed to pour out of her whenever she talked about them. He wished he could collect the feelings to study alone in his room.

She stood and brushed the dirt off the back of her shorts. He pushed up too, awkwardly stomping his feet, suddenly aware his T-shirt had a strain from his morning chocolate milk along the bottom. He hoped she didn't notice.

He turned back toward the river, but she grabbed his hand, hers slightly sticky from the orange. "Will you come back later . . . afterward?"

"If I can get away from everyone."

Going downstream should have been easier, but his feet felt heavy, numbed by the cool water. He climbed up the bank to find his aunt Leora standing in the middle of the backyard, scanning the river. When she saw him, she gave a little sob and ran forward.

He stood still, but she was there too quickly. Her words buzzed around him like gnats. His mother had died sometime while he was eating oranges and talking about running away. No tears came. His aunt guided him toward the house even as every part of him longed to throw himself back into the river and run toward Tallulah's house where he could pretend nothing had changed.

The rest of the day was a blur of neighbors hugging him and dropping off food. The mingling food smells upset his stomach to the point he couldn't eat any of it. His father arrived sometime during the night, the commotion waking him. His mother had been taken away in a shiny, black hearse, and his aunt had already washed the sheets and disinfected the room as if what his mom had was contagious.

The funeral was somber and long, drawing a large crowd. He sat on the red cushioned church pew and picked at his fingernails until they bled. The organist played "Amazing Grace," the music vibrating through his chest.

The next days passed in a haze, and he was kept home from school, even though he'd rather be learning about Galileo than staring at their fruit bowl–covered kitchen wallpaper.

Whispers between his aunt and his father drifted out of the kitchen.

". . . tragic. And, leaving those three children parentless and on their own. That uncle of theirs is a ne'er-do-well. Can't ask him to take three children on."

Since they weren't talking about him, he felt safe enough to step through the doorway. "Who are you talking about?"

His father glanced up from his coffee and the newspaper, his eyes bloodshot and two days growth of beard on his face. "The Fournettes up the river. Parents were killed by a drunk driver last night."

His father flipped the page, and his aunt took a carton of eggs out of the frig. Nash backed out of the room, pulling his inhaler out and taking a puff, his heart pounding like a kick-drum. He ran outside and grabbed his bike, peddling like mad.

Like his house of a week ago, cars lined the front and somber women with casserole dishes drifted inside. As if they had some psychic connection, Tallulah poked her head out of a second-story window. She disappeared, and he waited, wondering what he should say.

She ran out the front door toward him, her eyes red and swollen, her hair a tangled mass around her head. "They're gone." She sounded shocked and hurt.

"I know. I'm so sorry."

Someone from the house called her name, but she didn't look over her shoulder. "I have to go. Will you come back?"

He swallowed, the words getting stuck like taffy in his throat. "Daddy's going back to the rig. I'm moving across the river to Aunt Leora's."

"When?"

"Soon, I think." Desperation drove his question. "Will you run away with me?"

"Nash . . ." She shook her head.

Somehow, she seemed older and infinitely wiser than him even though only a few days had passed since she'd held his hand with her orange-scented sticky one.

"I can't. My brothers need me."

I need you too, he wanted to say. "Of course. I'm being dumb." He started to roll his bike backward, still straddling it, his feet on the ground.

"I'll see you in school though, right?" she asked.

"Aunt Leora is moving me to the elementary school on *that* side. She said it's because the schools here stink. She thinks I'm gifted or something." Even as young as he was, he understood the river marked more than a physical separation between Louisiana and Mississippi. The social divide between well-to-do 'Sips and the blue-collar swamp rats was a festering gash that stemmed from a long-ago dispute.

"Oh, Nash." She stepped forward and hugged him, the handlebars of his bike between them. Her lips brushed his cheek, moving with her words. "I don't think I can do it without you."

Considering she was the strongest person he'd ever met, he knew she would be fine without him around. But he wasn't so sure how he was going to make it on the wrong side of the river without her. He tightened his hold, and she returned the ferocity of his hug. Someone called her name from the house again. This time she pulled away, her hair falling around her face, but not before he saw her tears. Helplessness overcame him.

His world was changing too fast. Last summer, he remembered running from the river holding a tadpole in water he'd cupped in his hands, but by the time he'd made it to the house, the water had leaked through his fingers and the tadpole had died. Everything and everyone he cared about was slipping through his hands like trying to hold water until he was left with nothing.

Chapter Two

Eighteen years later . . .

Tallulah Fournette sat at the bar of the Rivershack Tavern, debating whether to head home. Three episodes of *The Bachelor* waited on her DVR. Even under the threat of torture, she'd never admit to watching the show, but the desperation oozing from the contestants fascinated her.

Her phone beeped and she glanced at the incoming text, muttering a curse that would have her mother clutching her pearls in heaven. A small amount of fear shaded the edges of her frustration, and she flipped her phone facedown as if that could shut her ex-boyfriend up.

She nursed her beer, feeling a little in limbo, not wanting to stay, but not wanting to go home to an empty apartment either. Cade and Monroe were probably somewhere making googly eyes at each other, and Sawyer was so busy getting the newly named Fournette Brothers Designs set up and planning the Labor Day crayfish festival, he didn't have time to hang out with her.

She swiveled on the bar stool and exchanged smiles and waves with several men and women who were members of her gym. It was Friday night and all she had waiting for her at home was accounting work for the gym and episodes of *The Bachelor*. She might as well adopt a litter of cats.

The heavy wooden front door opened as she was turning back to the bar. From the corner of her eye, she saw a man enter. She glanced over her shoulder and whipped her head back around to stare down at the scarred bar top. It was Nash Hawthorne. Her heart skipped like a third-grader seeing her crush. Under the guise of taking a sip of her beer, she stole another glance.

She'd seen him at Cade's welcome home party a couple of weeks earlier, and the same shock and zing of awareness stripped away the restlessness that had plagued her all evening. She'd beat a hasty retreat from Cade's party, the reasons as murky as the river.

When he'd moved to Mississippi when they were young, it was like he'd hopped into a different river that had taken him in the opposite direction than her. While she'd barely squeaked through high school, he'd gotten a PhD and would be teaching history at Cottonbloom College come fall.

Unable to help herself, she looked his direction again. He still stood inside of the door. Calls from a pool table in the back went up, and he smiled and waved. Not only was she surprised to see him at the Tavern at all, apparently he'd become a regular. Tonight he fit right in with his olive green cargo pants and black T-shirt.

If she'd known professors like Nash existed, she might have attempted college after all. He had an old-school Indiana Jones vibe. Although scholarly with his black-rimmed glasses and perpetually rumpled brown hair, danger permeated the air around him nonetheless, like he would risk his life to save some ancient scroll or might rappel into a tomb seeking the Holy Grail.

It didn't hurt that the man was jacked. Not in an artificial way like some of the men who lifted weights in her gym, but in the lean, defined way she much preferred. She had no idea what happened to the brilliant, skinny, short, acne-covered kid of her childhood. It's like he'd been in a cocoon and emerged as a brilliant, built, tall, handsome man. Nerdy Nash Hawthorne had turned into Cottonbloom's most eligible bachelor—and that included both sides of their peculiar little town.

His gaze swept the room. Maybe he had a hot date. She'd heard rumors the single-ladies Bible study at Cottonbloom Church of Christ had nearly come to blows trying to decide who was going to take him a "Welcome to Cottonbloom" basket.

She turned back to her beer before he could catch her staring and watched the foam bubbles pop around the edges. A warm body took the seat next to her, and she was enveloped in a wholly masculine scent that muted the halos of cigarette smoke around them. Seeing his big hands link together on the bar and the dark hair that peppered his forearm settled a weird knot of nerves in her stomach.

Nash had never made her nervous when they were kids. She'd trusted him above all others back then, even her brothers. But that had been a lifetime ago. In fact, those days seemed to belong to someone else. The days before her parents had died. Before things got hard.

Nash had been gone a long time, and once he'd moved to Mississippi after his mother had died, they'd barely seen each other. His aunt Leora had kept him close, claiming his asthma made it difficult for him to be outside. Although it hadn't seemed to bother him all the time they'd spent wading and exploring the river as kids. She fingered the end of her braid.

She screwed up her courage and turned to him. "Hey, I don't know if you remember me, but I'm—"

"Tallulah Fournette. How could I ever forget you?" He swiveled toward her. His carefree, charming smile struck her mute.

She had the tendency to hang out with rough-and-tumble men who'd followed the same path she had. Street smart and tough, the difficulties of life forcing them to be serious and defensive. Those were her people, the ones she felt comfortable around.

Nash's optimism and easygoing nature was in his smile and in the way he held himself. His body language was foreign, yet unusually appealing, and she found herself smiling back. "Everyone calls me Tally these days. Except for my brothers when they're trying to annoy me. I'm not sure what my parents were thinking saddling me with a name like Tallulah."

"Maybe they were thinking, here we have this unique baby girl who is going to do great things in the world, so we should give her a great, unique name." His voice had matured along with the rest of him. Deep and a little husky, it projected like a professor's should.

"Or maybe they were thinking, let's pick the most embarrassing name possible so our daughter learns to deal with bullying at a young age."

The bartender stopped in front of them, wiping his hands on a bar towel, a smile parting the hair of his long dark beard. "What'll it be, Nash? The usual? Or would you like something special?" He leaned in as if imparting a secret.

"Special? I'm intrigued. Surprise me, Clint."

"You want another beer, Tally?"

"No, I'm good. Thanks." She waved Clint off while still staring at Nash. "You've been hanging out here a lot, I take it?"

"Little bit." He pointed to where Clint had disappeared

through a short curtain into a storage room. "We discovered a common appreciation of Scotch whiskey."

Clint returned with a heavy tumbler and an inch of amber liquor. Nash went for the side pocket of his cargo pants, but Clint waved him off and stayed to watch Nash take the first sip. He closed his eyes, leaned his head back and hummed. Tally couldn't tear her eyes away from the happiness on his face. "Perfect."

Looking extremely pleased, Clint rattled off the name and vintage before being called away to the opposite end of the bar.

"Scotch whiskey, huh? Is Jack not good enough for you?" The amount of flirt in her voice surprised her. Flirting was not in her wheelhouse.

"I did my postdoctoral work at the University of Edinburgh and developed a love of their whiskey. Jack will do in a pinch, though." He winked, and something fluttered around the nervous knot in her stomach. She did her best to ignore the feelings, but found herself smiling at him nonetheless.

"As in Scotland? Are you kidding me? That is so cool." Now that he mentioned it, a foreignness lilted through some of his words. A Scots brogue mixed with a Southern drawl was intriguing and surprisingly sexy.

"I'm not going to lie. It was cool. My research emphasis is medieval history. Americans think anything from the Civil War is old. That's nothing compared to Hadrian's Wall, for instance. Built a hundred and twenty years or so after Christ's crucifixion."

"And it's still there?"

"Miles and miles of it. You can touch stones placed by hands that are long gone."

His enthusiasm was intoxicating. Her heart was pounding a little faster, and she leaned closer. Close enough to see the shaving nick on the edge of his jaw, close enough to see the yellow flecks in his brown eyes framed by the black rims of his glasses, close enough to see the tattoo that peeked out of the sleeve of his black T-shirt.

Before she could stop herself, she pushed the sleeve up a couple of inches. His biceps flexed, and she pulled back as if bitten. Geez, you'd think she'd never touched a man before. She cleared her throat. "What's your tattoo of?"

He pulled his sleeve to the top of his shoulder, exposing a stylized cross on a shield. "The symbol for the Knights Templar."

"Oh my God, are you on the hunt for the Holy Grail? In Cottonbloom?"

He threw his head back, his laughter coming deep in his chest but morphing into a cough that had him hunched over and covering his mouth. Finally, his laugh-cough subsided, and he took a sip of the whiskey. "No Holy Grail in Cottonbloom to my knowledge. The Knights Templar stood for bravery and discipline. I guess that's what it means to me."

"Bravery and discipline, huh? Not bad things to stand for." She took a sip of her warm beer to have something to do besides stare at his defined arm.

"Would you like to dance?"

"Dance?"

"There's a dance floor in the corner." He pointed somewhere behind her. "And music playing. Dancing's not so far-fetched an activity, is it?"

She looked over her shoulder. The corner consisted of a small square of planked flooring she'd never noticed. Maybe because she'd never seen anyone actually dancing in the Rivershack Tavern, unless it was a drunk girl's mating call in the middle of the pool tables.

"Yeah, I don't dance."

"That's not what I remember."

"What are you talking about?"

"You used to take ballet. You put on a recital for me in the middle of your backyard."

"I can't believe you remember that." She turned toward him.

He looked into his whiskey as if he could divine the future, a half smile on his face. "I've not forgotten a minute that we spent together. Don't you remember?"

Emotions she didn't understand grew a lump in her throat. Of course she remembered. Every second. Next to her parents, Nash had been the most important person in her life. Above even her brothers back then. The fact he remembered filled her with hope and despair.

"Why in the world did you come back to Cottonbloom, Nash?"

Nash suppressed another coughing fit. All the cigarette smoke hanging in the room like fog was making his usually well-controlled asthma act up. Friday and Saturday nights were definitely the worst as he discovered over the past two weeks of coming in regularly. He took a too large sip of the excellent, aged Scotch to soothe his throat. Not the way such fine liquor should be savored.

He wasn't at the Rivershack Tavern for the Scotch or the company—although he'd surprisingly enjoyed both—he was sitting in the smoky bar for Tallulah Fournette. As soon as he'd heard she was single again and a semi-regular, he'd found himself there night after night, waiting.

It's not like he'd moved back to Cottonbloom for her. A multitude of reasons drew him back to his hometown. His aunt was getting older. Cottonbloom College, while not as prestigious as an Ivy League school, offered something none of those schools could. The chance to build an outstanding history department from the ground up and the promise of early tenure. He was excited for the challenge.

But more than familial obligations and a job drew him home. Cottonbloom lived in his memories like an old tome he struggled to translate and interpret. When he dreamed of Cottonbloom, the negative recollections leaked out as if his memory was a sieve, saving only the good stuff.

The days before his mother got sick, catching lightning bugs in the summer, the walks along the river with Tally. He ignored the bad stuff—his mother dying, bigger boys pushing him down, calling him a freak and later Nerdy Nash, the constant ache of loneliness.

If reconnecting with Tally had crossed his mind more than a few times while he had been debating the job offer and move . . . well, it wasn't something he was willing to admit to her.

"Is Cottonbloom not on *Conde Nast*'s top destinations list?" He kept his voice light, hoping to coax out another of her smiles.

"Not yet, but it will be if Regan and Sawyer have a say."

"Ah, yes. Regan is rather passionate about her tomato festival."

"Try obsessed. My brother has bought stock in antacids. Not that he's any better. He wants to win the competition so bad, he might have sold his firstborn to the devil." Her smile was a combination of tease and sarcasm.

"You don't think"—he cleared his throat and side-eyed her—"Sawyer had anything to do with the gazebo fire?"

Her smile thinned and her eyes narrowed. "Absolutely not. Who said he did?"

"No one. Well, no one besides Regan thinks he did it."

Nash had a hard time believing someone as smart and level-headed as Sawyer would torch the gazebo, but then again, the man had planned to drop a half-dozen rabbits into Regan's mother's prize tomato garden. Regan had caught Sawyer in the act.

"Regan's motivations are more personal than professional, if you ask me," she said with more than a hint of antipathy.

Nash would have said the same of Sawyer, but he kept his opinion to himself. Tally looked ready to defend her brother to the death. "Say what you will, but the woman can get things done. Businesses on the Mississippi side of River Street are booming. And she has a solid plan for the contest money from *Heart of Dixie* magazine if she wins."

"So does my—" A text buzzed her phone on the bar between them. She glanced at the screen, her forehead crinkling.

"Is that your escape text?"

She set the phone back on the bar, facedown. "What are you talking about?"

"I thought all girls had some system in place if some weirdo dude was hassling them. You know, your friend calls or texts you and all of a sudden something very important requires your attention somewhere far, far away."

"Are you a weirdo?" The worry cleared from her face, her smile making her green eyes sparkle.

"I do get ridiculously excited about *Star Wars*."

"Really? I pictured you as more of an Indiana Jones fan."

"Why's that?"

She raised her eyebrows and harrumphed. "Knights Templar, Holy Grail. I can only imagine what percentage of your classes are female."

"Professor Jones was an archaeologist." He took another sip of his Scotch and shook his head. Now that she mentioned it, a good eighty percent of the classes he'd taught as an associate professor at Edinburgh had been female. He stilled. Was she insinuating women signed up for his classes because they might find him attractive? Did *she* find him attractive? Embarrassment followed by a wave of longing incinerated his insides and triggered another spate of coughing.

Her eyes flared before she burst into laughter. This was the laugh he remembered, and he tumbled back twenty years.

"Ohmigod, you don't even realize, do you?"

"Realize what?"

"Better if you don't know." She grinned.

Her cheeks were flushed, and dark hair that had escaped her braid wisped around her face. Unlike most of the women in the bar, she wasn't wearing a skirt or heels. Her simple blue T-shirt emphasized lean curves, and her dark-wash jeans were tucked into a pair of black motorcycle boots. Smudged black eyeliner emphasized the only thing about her that was soft. In her laughter, her intense green eyes shed their wariness and turned warm and welcoming.

He smiled back and propped his chin up on his hand, leaning in closer. "I can assure you I am stodgy and boring."

"Really?" Her voice dripped sarcasm, but she mimicked his stance, so they were only a few inches apart, their elbows nearly touching on the bar. "What do you do for fun?"

"I like to explore creepy, cobwebby catacombs full of dead people."

Her smile faltered. "Are you serious?"

"Yep."

"I'm pretty sure Cottonbloom is fresh out of dead-body-stuffed catacombs. How are you keeping yourself entertained? Are you dating anyone?"

"Nope. How about you?"

She glanced at her phone. "Not at the moment."

Even though she'd voiced a denial, his spidey sense tingled at her slight hesitation. A woman as tough and beautiful and smart as Tally probably had men crawling all around her. Had he missed his window already? Or had she and Heath Parsons gotten back together? He forced his voice to stay light and teasing. "What would you suggest for entertainment?"

"You could pull up a chair with the rest of us to watch these festivals unfold. Ten-to-one odds that they'll get us on the national news—and not in a complementary way. More like a point-and-laugh-at-the-rednecks kind of way."

"That's not good. I'll be implicated if someone starts digging for dirt."

"How so?"

"I might have been involved in the bunny kerfuffle last month."

She blinked at him a couple of times before bursting into husky laughter. He couldn't help but smile back. She'd turned into a beautiful woman, if an intimidating one. He'd had to screw up his courage to walk across the bar and take the seat next to her. She seemed to have some sort of force field around her that repelled men. The vibe alternated between "back off" and "you are beneath my notice."

He held his hands up. "Are you laughing at me?"

"I'm not . . . Yes, I am, but not in a bad way. I like the way you talk. It's cute."

"*Cute?* Geez, next you'll be putting ribbons in my hair." "Cute" was the word any man of legal age dreaded hearing from an attractive woman.

"I didn't say *you* were cute, you're . . ." Her gaze drifted over him.

"I'm what?"

"Definitely something other than cute."

The way she said it made him think it was meant as a compliment. "What else is there to do?"

"Let's see . . . Uncle Delmar and some of his buddies play bluegrass out on River Street the occasional Saturday evening in the summer. Turns into a kind of block party. They built that new movie theater up by the college. An ice cream shop opened this spring on the Mississippi side. And, there's this charming establishment." She presented the bar like a game show host presenting a prize.

"Wow. You're really stretching for entertainment."

"God, I know. You're going to regret moving back."

"I doubt that," Nash said before throwing back the last of his Scotch.

The front door opened and a breeze gusted around the bar, curling smoke around them. Bands were tightening around his lungs, and he forced himself to breathe slowly. Call it prideful or just plain foolish, but he didn't want to pull out his inhaler in front of her.

"You could come down to the gym. You look like you're in good shape. Do you spar?" Her eyes flashed over his body again. Was she checking him out? Or assessing how easily she might kick his butt? Deciphering the ancient scrawls of monks was effortless compared to reading women.

"A little." Gaining early admittance to college at sixteen had made him an easy target for teasing. The fact he'd been a gawky late bloomer who looked closer to twelve than sixteen put a bull's-eye on his back, and he'd taken a martial art class at the urging of his counselor.

Martial arts had given him friends and confidence—two things he'd never had in abundance. When he'd moved to Scotland for graduate school, he'd taken up boxing, finding the workout and regimen more suited to his energy levels. It was an outlet for his generally sedentary work and a way he kept a handle on his asthma.

"Why don't you come down one day after your last class and I'll put you through your paces."

"I'm not teaching this summer, actually."

"You're not working?"

"I didn't say that. I'm finishing up a paper on Charlemagne for publication in a trade magazine and catching up on my reading—both academic and for pleasure—and planning for my fall classes."

Her gaze dropped to the floor, and she sat up straight on the stool, swinging her legs back around to face the bar. She toyed with her still half-full beer glass, but didn't take a sip. An awkwardness had descended, but he wasn't sure why.

His nervousness grew in the silence. He'd worked hard over the years to control his ingrained shyness when it came to the opposite sex, but Tallulah was different. He wanted her to like him, dammit. He didn't want to take her home—not yet anyway—he just wanted a chance to get to know her now that they were grown. The closed-off look on her face made him wonder if he'd already blown it.

"Do you still go down to the river?" He choked off another coughing fit.

She side-eyed him, but didn't turn to face him again. The connection that had been knitting itself together had frayed. "Not so much anymore. Sawyer bought a house that backs up to the river farther into the parish, but"—she shrugged—"it lost its magic somewhere along the way."

He coughed again and his hand slipped into his pocket. He wasn't going to make it much longer. "Listen. I have to head out." He stifled more chuffing coughs as he slid off the stool. "I'm going to take you up on your offer though. When's a good time to drop by the gym?"

"Right after lunch is our slow time. Hey, are you all right?"

Squeezing his lips together to stem another round of lung-scraping coughs, he backed away, nodding. He hit the front door and launched himself outside, taking big gulping breaths of humid air. Not caring who saw him now, he fumbled with his inhaler and took a hit.

The medicine coupled with the clean air offered immediate relief. He slid into his imported Land Rover Defender and banged his forehead against the wheel a couple of times. No doubt, Tallulah Fournette thought he was the biggest weirdo on either side of Cottonbloom.

Chapter Three

Tally stared at the door half-expecting Nash to bound back inside. His exit had been abrupt. Had she said something to scare him off? Or maybe it was her in general. She didn't exactly excel at small talk, although with him she hadn't even been trying and their conversation had flowed as naturally as the river through town.

Until he mentioned how he was spending his summer reading. Of course he spent his free time reading. The man was a genius to hear his aunt Leora talk. Considering Nash left Cottonbloom for college at sixteen, the woman wasn't bragging.

The Nash she remembered was a sweet, skinny kid who waded upriver to her house every chance he got. He'd become an integral part of her life and her best friend. She rarely allowed herself to dwell on that time, because of the mish-mash of emotions it invoked. She'd gone from being the revered and protected baby girl to a student failing in school to a parentless child struggling to survive her grief, all over the course of one year.

Nash was wrapped up at the core like a spool holding all her memories together. But then both their lives fell apart. His mother finally succumbed to the breast cancer that had spread through her body, and her parents were killed by a drunk driver. By the time she'd emerged from the comalike state of grief, his aunt had whisked him away to her stately gingerbread Victorian house on one of the oldest, richest streets of Cottonbloom, Mississippi, and enrolled him in the elementary school across the river.

With Nash gone, she began a slow retreat into herself, acting like her struggles with reading and near-failing grades didn't bother her, but each cutting comment by a teacher or classmate was another ding to her self-confidence. It didn't help that both her brothers were near-geniuses themselves, even though Cade had been forced to drop out to take care of the family. The constant comparisons to Golden Boy Sawyer had grated.

She had drifted in with a group of tough kids who smoked weed, partied hard, and generally rebelled against anything resembling authority. But between her parents and Cade, right from wrong had been drilled into her, and while the other kids kept to the path that would land most of them on the wrong side of the law, Tally could see beyond high school. She dreamed big—just like Cade and Sawyer—and like them, she was a risk-taker.

Her phone vibrated, and she tapped her finger on the back, but didn't turn it over. Nash hadn't even asked for her number. Did she want him to ask for her number? Why? So they could hold hands and sing "Auld Lang Syne"?

She slid off the stool. Her lips twitched up thinking about Nash's lopsided grin. The night hadn't been a complete waste after all. Would he actually come to the gym? Her stomach tumbled with a combination of anticipation and nerves. She tucked her phone into the back pocket of her jeans and headed toward the door.

A man holding a pool stick stepped into her path. "What's up, Tallulah?" He said her name as if he were making a joke. "My boy's been looking for you. Wants to talk."

Bryce was her ex's butt-kisser and an all-around jerk. They had been fraternity brothers at Ole Miss until they'd both flunked out. It would be easy enough to flip the stick up and rack him in the balls. But she didn't.

"I've said all I have to say to him. Next up is a restraining order if he doesn't leave me alone. How about passing that tidbit along?" She kept her voice low.

Bryce glanced over her shoulder toward the door and chuckled before dropping to take a shot, the balls clinking off one another but none falling into a pocket. The back of her neck burned and her heart jumped around in her chest like a rabbit on speed.

She turned to find Heath standing inside the door, effectively making sure she had to go through him to exit. His hair was dark, his eyes flinty, his biceps huge. After two months of dating, she hadn't discovered a goocy center underneath his frowny, tough exterior. Although he had been born a 'Sip, after Ole Miss sent him packing, he settled over the line in Louisiana, working a variety of blue-collar jobs. Most of his time, energy, and money went into training for amateur MMA fights with the hopes of making it big.

She approached him, attempting a serene, unaffected expression. "Excuse me, I'm heading home," she said in a honeyed voice her brothers had learned long ago signaled danger.

"I'll walk you to your car."

She wanted to tell him no, but they had already become the center of attention. The buzz of voices in the bar had diminished, and a glance around showed a fair number of people looking their way. She didn't want to give anyone fodder to take back to Sawyer or, even worse, Cade. In his eyes, she would always be his ten-year-old little sister who needed his protection.

After Cade took off when she was nineteen, she'd handled things herself and didn't like to rely on anyone. She'd made decisions and dealt with the fallout, in her business and personal life. It had taken two months of pep talks and internal negotiations for her to call Cade and ask him for a loan to start the gym. Her business success only highlighted her string of personal failures, Heath being the pinnacle.

"Fine. Come on then." Tally walked into the night, the sound of bullfrogs and bugs drowning out the music of the bar the farther they moved into the parking lot. When she'd arrived, the sunset had been orange and brilliant, and she hadn't given a thought to where she'd parked. Unfortunately, a broken bulb topped the nearest light-post, leaving her car in deep shadows.

Heath didn't try to touch her, but anxiety kept her on edge. Her past relationships had ended on a whimper. Either she or the guy drifted away, neither one of them invested or heartbroken. The animosity brewing with Heath was foreign.

"You have to stop calling and texting and stuff," she said.

"Give us another chance. I can change."

Even if she didn't recognize his statement as a plati-tude, she wasn't remotely tempted to give him another shot. A brain transplant wasn't a viable option.

"It's not you. Really. I'm superbusy with the gym and not interested in dating anyone right now." She had no problems keeping secrets, but the outright lie squirmed her stomach. Instead of pacifying him, he bowed up, the muscles of his arms jumping, his entire body reflecting his agitation.

"Then who was the dude at the bar? Bryce said you were practically eye-fucking each other."

How had she ever been attracted to him? Maybe a better question was why did she attract men like him? She needed to hang out somewhere besides dive bars and her gym. Try internet dating. Audition for *The Bachelor*. It offered better odds than Cottonbloom.

"You are being juvenile and jealous when you have no right to be."

"What's his name?" He grabbed her upper arm in a too-tight grip and pulled her between two cars toward a bank of pine trees that lined the lot. Unease rippled through her, leaving her knees wobbly.

"What is wrong with you?" She kicked his ankle with the toe of her boot, but he didn't flinch or slow down.

"What's his fucking name, Tally?"

Heath had been annoying since she'd dumped him, bordering on intimidating, but she'd never been truly scared of him. He had been like a constantly buzzing gnat. Now she realized he had a stinger. She could hold her own with most men, but he had spent a considerable amount of time training in her gym, and she wouldn't stand a chance if things turned physical.

As she debated on how big a hit her pride would take if she called for help, a voice rumbled out of the darkness. "Unhand the lady."

Tally looked over her shoulder. Nash stood between the cars at the bumpers, not ten feet away. Relief at someone coming to help mixed with worry over how Heath might retaliate, along with a dash of entirely inappropriate humor at Nash's gentlemanly declaration. Heath turned, keeping her in his grasp, so she was forced up against the door of one of the cars.

She squirmed, trying to break his hold, but he was a grappler in the ring, and holding her was child's play.

"Nash, go and get the bouncer. His name is Butch." Her voice wavered and she hated that both men could recognize her ingrained fear.

"No need for that, is there? Do you want to end up in jail? Because that's where I see this headed in a hurry." Nash held his hands up like a peacemaker, his voice full of appeasement, and took a step toward them.

Tally could feel Heath's hesitation, yet he didn't release her. "Holy shit. Nerdy Nash Hawthorne." Heath's laugh was like a rusted axle trying to move in a socket after years of disuse.

"Heath. It's been a while, yeah?" Nash stepped closer, sounding like they were being introduced at church.

"I'd heard you'd moved back. Are you and my girl old friends or something?" Finally, his hand loosened. She pulled free and walked toward Nash.

"I think she'd beg to differ on being called your girl based on what I witnessed."

When she came within a couple of feet, she recognized the anger, not reflected in his stance or voice, masking his face. It hadn't crossed her mind that Nash might have had a history with Heath too, but they would have been in school at the same time in Mississippi.

"Are you all right?" His lips barely moved, his gaze on Heath as he slipped off his glasses and handed them to her.

She nodded and took the glasses automatically. He pushed her behind him and closed the distance between him and Heath. Grabbing onto one of Nash's biceps, she attempted to tug him away. He didn't budge. "Nash, let's go, please."

"She's thinking about rekindling things with me, so I'd appreciate it if you'd get gone." A taunting confidence threaded Heath's voice.

Nash made a tsking sound, shook his head, and

took another step forward. "Sorry, mate. Not going to happen."

Heath threw the first punch, a slow, lumbering cross that Nash ducked. He answered with a well-placed, hard jab to Heath's forehead. A tiny split in his eyebrow trailed blood into his eye, but he was seasoned, and instead of wiping it away, he rushed Nash with a bellow.

She was knocked backward, losing her balance and landing hard on her butt and hands. His glasses snapped. Scrambling up, she hollered for Butch while the two men rolled around on the gravel, neither one getting a hit in.

Butch ran over and worked to pry Nash and Heath apart. His yells brought a few more men over until between them, they pulled the two men apart. Heath sought to escape the hands like a wild animal in a trap. Nash shrugged out of Butch's hold and dusted himself off. Heath seemed to have gotten the brunt of the beating, but Nash hadn't escaped without a few welts, and his T-shirt was ripped along a side seam.

"Calm down, Heath, or you're going to force me to call the police. What the hell was this about?" Butch paced, spittle flying.

"It was just a silly fight, Butch." Tally took Nash's forearm and guided him to the passenger side of her car. "Heath'll calm down with us gone. No need to call the cops."

Butch didn't argue with her, only chucked his head and concentrated on keeping Heath at bay.

"My truck's on the other side." Nash thumbed over his shoulder, his words sounding strained.

"I'll bring you back by later. Right now, let's get out of here. Give Heath a chance to cool down. And you need someone to clean you up." Her tires spun on the gravel as she hit the blacktop.

"Have you got my glasses?"

She was still clutching the pieces, and opened her hand between them. "I'm so sorry. I fell on them."

He took them between two fingers and slid them on. The nosepiece was bent, one eyeglass sitting well above the other, and an earpiece dangled down his cheek. Scratches obscured one of his eyes. He grinned. "What? Not a good look?"

Laughter born of relief sputtered out of her. "Are you insane?"

"No, but fairly blind. I guess it's a good thing you're driving since I can't see. Where to?"

"My place unless you have any objections."

"Actually, I do. I assume he knows where you live. Maybe best not to stay there tonight. Let's go to my place."

At the crossroads where she needed to decide, she headed across the river into Mississippi. "You're staying with your aunt, right?"

He nodded and a dread like getting called on by a teacher welled up. Ms. Leora treated Tally like a dirty, used piece of gum stuck on the bottom of a favorite pair of shoes. When she was a kid living downriver from Nash, she hadn't understood the disdain.

"Will your aunt ask a bunch of questions or get upset?"

"I'll tell her we're having a sleepover for old time's sake." The flashing from the streetlights of Main Street illuminated his smile. Half of his upper lip was puffy and a few scratches along his cheek oozed blood.

She couldn't summon anything resembling a smile. Things could have been worse. Much worse. Twisting her hands on the steering wheel in a death clutch, she looked straight out over the road. "Thanks, Nash. You stepping in like that . . . I'm not sure what Heath was thinking."

"Were you really looking to get back together with him?"

"Goodness, no!" The denial reverberated through the car. She swallowed. After putting himself in harm's way for her, didn't he deserve the truth or at least a portion of it? "We dated for a couple months over the spring until I realized—" She bit the inside of her lip, not even sure what to say.

"Doesn't seem like he's changed much over the years."

"I didn't even think about you knowing him."

"Once they jumped me two grades, we were in classes together." He stared out the passenger window, his voice distant and unforthcoming. Considering she was the poster child for withholding information, she didn't press him.

Her headlights brushed his aunt Leora's house and her palms slipped on the steering wheel. Not many people intimidated Tally, but his aunt happened to be one of them. She parked and closed her car door as quietly as possible. A confrontation with his aunt would really top the evening off in a spectacular fashion.

The house was dark, the porch swing swaying slightly in the breeze, the chains warbling a squeak with each pass. She ran her hands down the legs of her jeans and didn't move away from the car. Nash was halfway up the driveway when he turned to wait for her.

The prospect of heading to her apartment and trying to sleep in fear of Heath battering down the door outweighed her fear of a judgmental old woman. She locked up her car and joined him, but instead of heading to the front door of the big house, he led her through the fence gate and toward a guesthouse at the back of his aunt's sizable garden.

In a nod to the main house's classic gingerbread-style

architecture, whoever had built the addition had taken it to the extreme. Swooping scallops, heart cutouts on the shutters, faded pink paint on the clapboard. In the moonlight, it looked like a magical, oversized dollhouse.

She grabbed him, somehow ending up with his hand in both of hers, and tugged him to a stop, keeping her voice at a whisper. "You're staying out here?"

"I'm close enough to help Aunt Leora if she needs me, but enjoy a modicum of privacy. Good thing I'm secure in my manliness, right?"

Nothing seemed to faze the man, and after the events of the night and drama of the past few months, she appreciated his calm confidence.

Her eyes were level with his smiling lips, and her breasts pressed into his thick, hard biceps. She was aware of her femininity in ways she hadn't been in a long time.

His rumpled brown hair curled up at his nape, a wave falling over his forehead. He smoothed it back, running his hand all the way to the back of his neck. He nudged his chin toward the front door. "Come on. My head is killing me."

A round of stomach-churning guilt assailed her, for both the incident tonight and fear that he'd be Heath's target in the future. "I'm so—"

"Don't say it." Without dropping her hand, he guided them up three short steps to a narrow porch and opened the unlocked door. When he shut it, he turned the deadbolt and secured the chain. "He's the one with the mental imbalance, not you. Anyway, you didn't ask me to come charging to your rescue. When I saw you walk out with him . . . I don't know, I had a funny feeling something was wrong."

"You're giving me too much credit. Have you considered that I'm the one who's mentally unbalanced?"

His chuckle reverberated off the walls. A staircase

was directly in front of them while an arched doorway stood on the left, soft light permeating the shadows of the small entryway.

"What were you still doing in the parking lot anyway? You left a good ten minutes before I did," she said.

"Catching my breath."

His odd answer was forgotten when she stepped under the arch and into a big, airy room. A galley kitchen off to one side looked as if it had been added as an afterthought. Floor-to-ceiling bookcases took up eighty percent of the wall space. The rest of the room was taken up by lamps, a couch, and comfortable-looking chairs.

She'd never seen so many books except in a library. They were stacked on most of the horizontal surfaces. Extras were shoved on top of the neat rows in the bookshelves. The table closest to her held a particularly thick book with an embossed leather binding. She stared at the cover, willing the ornate letters to take their places in her head. Fancy script always gave her dyslexia more trouble than block letters. *The Life and Times of Charlemagne*.

He disappeared into the narrow kitchen. When she joined him, he was drinking a glass of water. A bottle of pain pills sat on the counter. He set the glass in the sink. "Can I get you something? I've got water, OJ, beer. No tea, I'm afraid, unless you would like a cup of the hot variety."

She fake-gasped. "Are you telling me you betrayed your Southern heritage and converted to English tea?"

"No choice. The withering look I got the first time I asked for iced tea made me want to crawl under a table. Ice in general isn't the norm, much less the blasphemy of watering down good tea with the stuff." He pulled his smile up short and dabbed the taut, swollen skin with his fingertips.

"Have you got a first aid kit or something? Go lie down and I'll clean you up."

"Should be one in the cabinet." He pointed to the cracked door by the sink on his way out.

She gathered everything she thought she'd need while she waited for hot water from his tap. Balancing everything in her arms, she joined him. Sprawled on the couch, he rested his head on the armrest, face to the ceiling and eyes closed.

She set the first aid supplies on top of a stack of books on the floor and kneeled next to him. Surely he hadn't fallen asleep in the few minutes it had taken her to get organized? Taking her time, she studied him.

The years had been kind, maturing him into a man that could disintegrate the staunchest of panties. He didn't even realize how sexy he was, which only made him about a million times sexier.

A piece of hair curled over his forehead. She fisted her hand under her chin in a moment of indecision. Finally, she gave in to the urge and pushed the hair back with her fingertips. Once she touched him, it was a compulsion she couldn't control. She threaded her fingers deeper into the thick mass of brown waves. He needed a haircut, but she imagined that sort of thing took second place to Charlemagne.

She dabbed a warm washcloth along a red, painful-looking welt along his cheekbone. Her fingers found his lips, soft and slightly parted, before she cleaned the area. She wet her own lips, her mind wandering dangerous paths. He was only an old friend. An old friend who stoked a fire in her blood.

How many years had it been? Too many. This man didn't seem a stranger. Her soul recognized him, yet . . . the books surrounding them seemed to press closer. She and Nash were nothing alike. It would take her a week and a half bottle of ibuprofen to read even one of the books on his shelf.

A long-buried memory resurfaced. Nash on his bike, waiting in her front yard, soon after her parents were killed. Somehow, she'd known he would come in spite of his own grief. Whatever they'd said was lost, but she remembered his hug. Their final hug. Although at the time, she hadn't realized what the death of his mother and her parents would mean. If she had, she would have hung on harder, tighter. She wouldn't have let him go. Nash represented the last remnant of her childhood happiness.

Even with the years and distance and heartache that had separated them, she hadn't forgotten.

Chapter Four

Nash opened his eyes when he felt her retreat. Her tender hands in his hair and on his face had made him want to do foolish things. Like pull her close and kiss her. Insanity.

Her gaze glanced off his, her green eyes misty. She chewed on her bottom lip and busied herself with the first aid kit. Her braid fell over her shoulder, the tail brushing the tip of her breast. Her body language now was starkly opposite of the confident, take-no-shit woman in the bar. Which was the real Tallulah? Or was she too complicated to be classified so easily?

"Do you remember when I asked you to run away with me?" He wasn't sure what prompted him to ask, knowing the memories it would dredge up would be painful.

She stilled for a moment before wetting a cotton ball with hydrogen peroxide. "I remember." At the first touch of the cotton ball, he flinched. She brushed his hair back while dabbing the scratches, keeping her gaze averted. "After you moved across the river, I thought about packing a bag and coming to see if the offer was still open." No hint of laughter or tease lightened the seriousness of her face or voice.

"I would have gone with you. Things here were hard."
An understatement. The loneliness had been suffocating.
While he hadn't exactly been the most normal kid in
Cottonbloom, Louisiana elementary school, he'd had
Tally as his best friend and that had made everything
bearable. He obtained official freak status in the Cottonbloom, Mississippi elementary school. Heath and his
friends had made him an outcast, which drove him further into his books.

"Oh, Nash." Her gaze finally scooted up to meet his.
"Things got hard for me too."

He waited, hoping she'd elaborate, but she only said,
"Do you want a Band-Aid or not?"

"I'll pass."

She turned her attention to reassembling the first aid
kit. "I'm sorry you got mixed up in my problems. I'm
sure dealing with my jealous, possibly insane ex was not
on your radar. Bet you wish you had stayed home tonight."

Considering the events had brought her back to his
place for the night, he wouldn't take any of it back. Even
the almost paralyzing shot of fear he'd experienced when
he realized it was Heath Parsons dragging her away.

Suddenly, he'd been twelve again and in the middle-
school locker room before gym, forced to change clothes
in front of everyone. His boney chest and knobby knees
stuck out in a sea of boys cresting their first wave of
testosterone.

Most kids ignored him, which was fine, but Heath,
who'd started shaving by sixth grade, took delight in
shoving him into lockers or giving him wedgies or stealing his street clothes. In front of teachers, he kept his bullying confined to whispered taunts or the occasional
trip.

It wasn't that Heath physically intimidated him any

longer, but the younger, wimpier, insecure Nash who lived somewhere in his psyche had been scared. He hated the feeling. Tally didn't need to know any of that.

"I'm glad I was there for you," he said simply.

She sighed, nodded, and disappeared into the kitchen with the first aid kit. When she returned, she stood in the center of the room, rocking on her feet as if ready to deliver an oration. "So . . ." She drew the word out. "You want me to take the couch for the night?"

Tally wasn't an Amazon, but she wasn't petite either and would have to crumple herself to fit on the short couch. "I have a bed upstairs in the loft." She stiffened, her feet ceasing their nervous shuffling, but before she could make excuses, he stood up. "It's a king. Plenty big for both of us. You can build a pillow fort down the middle if you're worried you might accidently touch me and get cooties."

He'd kept his voice light. Once he'd found his groove in academics, the pain of being bullied had diminished. In his world, he was valued for exactly what had made him a target for teasing as a child.

"You know, if it makes you feel better, Heath flunked out of Ole Miss and never finished college." She cocked her head, somehow seeing behind his joke to the little kid who'd cried himself to sleep more times than he could count.

"I would have to be pretty petty to admit that it does." He half-grinned, his lip throbbing with the pull. "Apparently, I'm *extremely* petty."

She laughed, and as he watched her face light up he wondered when and what had changed her into a serious, closed-off woman. Was it because of men like Heath or had it happened long before?

Although he'd only moved over the river—a few miles as the crow flies—it was like he'd been transported to another world after his mother had died. The only news came from the local paper and from eavesdropping on his aunt's quilting circle.

"Are you ready to go to bed?" Although it was earlier than he normally went to sleep, with a headache pounding his temple, lying in a dark room on cool sheets sounded fabulous.

"I guess. Are you sure your aunt isn't going to have a stroke when she sees my car out front? Should I move it down the street?"

"I am approaching thirty years old. I love and respect my aunt, but if me having a female friend over gets stuck in her craw, then . . . frankly, she can choke on it."

"Nash Hawthorne, you old dog." Her tone was teasing and reminded him of the hours they spent under the willow tree talking and laughing about everything and nothing.

He grabbed her hand like they were still kids and pulled her toward the stairs. Besides the floor-to-ceiling bookcases, the loft was his favorite part of the cottage. It faced the backyard, and skylights opened panoramic views of the stars on clear nights. Even better were rainy nights when the rivulets of water down the glass turned hypnotic and soothing.

The bedroom wasn't a disaster, but a couple of drawers stood open, dirty clothes were piled in one corner, books were stacked haphazardly on the nightstand, and his bed was half-made. He shoved the drawers closed and kicked a dirty shirt under the bed. "Sorry for the mess. Wasn't planning on bringing anyone home tonight."

"Glad to hear it," she muttered, but he couldn't decipher her tone. In a louder voice, she asked, "I don't suppose I could hop in the shower? I hate going to bed smelling like bar smoke."

"Go for it." He gathered her a towel, a washcloth, and

one of his old T-shirts in case she wanted something clean to wear to bed. "There's an extra toothbrush in the medicine cabinet, I think. If you need something else, give a shout."

She disappeared into the bathroom, the running water providing white noise. After shedding his socks and shoes, he paced a couple of minutes before scooching back on the pillow and picking up a book. He pulled a spare pair of glasses out of the drawer of his nightstand.

The water turned off, and he couldn't remember anything that he'd read. He stared at the bathroom door. Finally, she emerged and he popped off the bed. Her long dark hair was out of its braid, still damp and hanging midway down her back. Her face was scrubbed clean of the smudgy eye makeup, her cheeks were pink, and she wore his T-shirt, a red one with a huge Superman emblem over the front. She was every comic-book nerd's dream girl.

"Thanks for the shirt." She shrugged, and it listed to one side, revealing the curve of a shoulder. No bra strap was visible.

"No problem. I'm going to clean up now." He thumbed toward the bathroom and backed into the door, his heels taking a painful knock.

He took a quick shower, debating whether to masturbate before joining her in bed. Perhaps it was general horniness, but he had a feeling it was all due to Tally in that shirt and imagining her not in that shirt. How freaked out would she be if she noticed that he was desperately, embarrassingly attracted to her?

In the end, he flipped the tap to cold until things were under control. He pulled on a clean pair of boxer briefs, even though he normally slept in the nude. Hoping the lights were off and her back was turned, he shuffled out of the bathroom. No such luck.

She was propped up on a pillow on the far side of the bed, the sheet tucked under her arms. Her eyes were wide and wandered his body, negating the effects of the cold shower. His blood flowed south, and as quickly as he could he tuned the lamp off and slid under the sheet, hoping he wasn't pitching a tent.

He laced his hands behind his head and let out a slow breath. The night was clear, and the stars were visible through the skylights. They seemed closer and brighter tonight. The confrontation with Heath had nothing to do with the remnants of adrenaline pumping through his body. The pulsing energy was because Tallulah Fournette was in his bed. It didn't seem to matter that nothing was going to happen.

The silence stretched a long time, so long, he assumed she was asleep. His body calmed, even though his mind was still active. When she shifted toward him, he turned his head. On her side with her knees drawn up and her hands tucked under her cheek, she stared at him.

"I came here once when we were twelve or so. It was November, right after Thanksgiving. Rode my bike all the way in the cold. Could barely feel my fingers." Her voice had a tentative quality that made her sound younger and less secure.

"I didn't know. Where was I?"

"Here I think, but your aunt answered the door. Mother taught me how to be polite, how to introduce myself. But I'll never forget the way she looked at me."

The same protective impulse that sent him across the parking lot bowed him up now. He turned on his side and propped his cheek in his hand, ignoring the burn of his scratches. "How so?"

"Like I was something below the scum off a pond. Like poverty was something she could catch by me breathing on her. She told me to skedaddle and to not come back. Said you were happy and didn't want to be my friend anymore." Her voice broke on the last two words.

His lungs emptied and strained for air, not in the way of an asthma attack, but the way of reflected pain. Anger at his aunt's high-handedness burned low and slow. He didn't know if Tally needed or even wanted comfort, and without letting himself consider it, he trailed his callused fingers over her soft skin and into her hair.

"I never told her that. You know that, right? I missed you more than I can even express. You were my only friend, and I lost you in a blink." His hand formed a fist in the silky strands as if physically holding on to her now could rewrite their history.

A moment passed. Neither of them moved. The shadows were too deep to see her eyes, but the Fournettes had the gift of night-sight, every single one of them, Tally included. Whatever she saw in his face sent her rolling toward him. She hugged him tight, her face in his neck.

He kept one hand in her hair and returned her hug with the other, breathing her in. His shampoo and soap smelled different on her, more feminine and sensual. Her hands brushed over his back. Her breasts were soft against his bare chest. He shivered, but not from cold. He let her go and lay on his back before she could take note of his rock-hard erection. That not-so-little problem occurred in about two seconds flat. Instead of Superman, maybe he needed to adopt The Flash's emblem.

She settled shoulder to shoulder with him, the sheet drawn up to her chin. "Why does your aunt hate me? Is it because I'm a swamp rat?"

The disparaging way she'd said the nickname given to anyone born on the Louisiana side of the river surprised him. As kids they'd been proud to be swamp rats. "Considering my mom—her sister—married one and

I am one and a good number of the ladies she quilts with are swamp rats, I don't think it's that."

"Then it's me in particular she hates. What did I do to her?"

Nash didn't know that to say, because his aunt had always shown a marked dislike for Tally. In fact, a mention of any of the Fournettes would be sure to draw a lemony expression to her face. Her disapproving glances when he'd high-tailed it upriver as often as possible hadn't bothered him as a child, but knowing she'd driven the final wedge between him and Tally was unsettling.

"Does it matter anymore? We're grown and don't need anyone's approval to be friends."

She chuffed a laugh. "I suppose not. Your aunt can still make me feel like I'm about ten though, and like she caught me doing something *really* bad."

"Like drinking unsweetened, hot tea?"

Silence reigned for a measure of beats before her laughter peeled. "That is sacrilege, Nash Hawthorne."

"Scotland turned me pagan. Although, I never got used to eating kippers and black pudding for breakfast. Give me grits any day of the week."

"I hate grits." Tally made a gagging sound. As minor as it was, he'd learned something new about her. How much didn't he know and how much had changed? Before he could formulate a list of questions, she asked, "So what did you do for fun after your aunt moved you up here?"

"I read. A lot. More than was healthy probably. Got even more into comic books. None of the kids on the street wanted to play with me, so I took to wandering down to the river."

"That's a long way from here."

"It was my only form of rebellion. One Saturday, I went too far down river before turning back, and it was dark before I hit the road to town. Chief Thomason picked me up. I got grounded for two months. Not that it really mattered, since I had nowhere to go but school anyway. That was the extent of my excitement. What about you?"

"What about me?"

"What kind of trouble were you up to?"

"I'm not sure I want to tell you."

"Geez, now you have to tell me or I'll make up crazy stories."

"Like what?" Laughter lilted her voice.

"Let's see . . . you ran off and joined a troupe of travelling clowns for the summer. You attempted to learn their trade, but never made it beyond making a balloon weiner dog. You came home depressed that your lifelong dream of clownhood had been dashed."

Her laughter vibrated the mattress. "You are ridiculous."

"Anything you actually did will never live up to my imagination, so spill it." He waited. The moment took on an importance beyond whatever stories she had to tell. A thirst to know everything about her plagued him.

As she fiddled with the edge of the sheet, her laughter trailed off. "Pretty typical teenage stuff, I suppose. I stopped trying to be the good girl and started hanging out with a rougher crowd. The ones who cut classes on a regular basis to drink and smoke pot. Cade was strict, but he worked odd shifts. It was easy to sneak out. I'd finally found something I was good at."

Along with residual amusement, bitterness edged her words. He imagined her climbing out of her back window and into the hostas that grew around her house. "I always imagined you as homecoming queen or something. A tiara and everything."

She barked a laugh. "Football games and homecoming were not my thing."

"What about prom? Did you go?"

"I got asked."

"But?"

"We didn't have the money for a dress and hair and stuff, so another girl and I drank some beers we'd filched from her dad and watched old movies. What about you? You go to prom?"

He huffed. "Let's see I was a sixteen-year-old senior who puberty bypassed. I was a foot shorter than most girls, my voice was still cracky, and my face could have been the before shot for an acne commercial. Even with all that, I somehow got up the courage to ask the head cheerleader to go with me."

Her gasp was half surprise, half laughter and she propped her head on a hand to face him. "What did she say?"

" 'No.' Actually, I think it was closer to 'Hell no.' After she finished laughing, of course."

"That must have been mortifying."

"Little bit." Vast understatement. He'd pretended to be sick the next three days. He forced a nonchalant tone. "No regrets, right?"

"*That* I can't say."

"What do you regret?"

"Doing stuff that would have made things even harder for Cade if I'd been caught, but doing them anyway."

"What kind of stuff?"

"I never turned down a dare. I drank liquor, smoked pot, skipped school. I once climbed the water tower over on this side to paint graffiti."

"I remember that. They thought some delinquent boys did it."

"Nope. It was me." Regret or not, he could hear a sliver of pride in her voice.

"What else?"

"Stole a car."

"How old were you?" He popped back up on his elbow, facing her.

"Fifteen. One of the quilting ladies left her keys in her giant Buick. I drove it about half a block down River Street one Saturday afternoon. I thought I heard sirens, parked it at the curb, and took off running. I was so scared I nearly wet myself."

"I never heard anything about it."

Her giggles turned into laughter. "That's what was so funny. It was Ms. Candace. She stared at the empty spot for a while, then bee-bopped down half a block and drove off. I'm pretty sure she thought she'd just forgotten where she parked it."

He laughed too, but it faded into a sense of melancholy. Her long dark hair cascaded around her shoulders to pool on the bed. He itched to touch it again. "I feel like I missed out on rites of passage or something."

"If you want we can crash the next high school kegger." A teasing speculation was in her voice.

"Har-har."

"You could go play beer pong with a bunch of football players at the college or something." Her teasing turned more contemplative. "Actually, why not relive your youth?"

"I'm about a decade too late for that."

"For the high school kegger, yes. But we could get a little bit wild. Do things that scare us a little. Might be fun."

"Like what?" He wasn't sure he liked where she was headed, but knew he'd follow her anyway.

"We could climb the water tower, go floating down the river with a cooler of beer, stay out all night, steal a car."

"I'm a professor and you're a business owner. If we get caught—" He shook his head.

"We can skip the felony carjacking if you want." The laughter lightening her voice reminded him of the old Tally.

The dim shadows made it difficult to get a read on her. Was she serious or teasing him? Sketching a list of pros and cons in his head, he determined the cons way out-numbered the pros, but one pro outweighed everything: getting to spend more time with her.

"Have you ever been skinny-dipping?" he asked.

Her intake of breath was audible, and on the exhale, she said, "Once or twice. A long time ago in a galaxy far, far away. Have you?"

Her *Star Wars* reference might have amused him if he wasn't picturing water streaming over her naked body. "Nope. But I want to." And suddenly, desperately he did. As long as it was with her. He didn't want to give her a chance to say it was all a joke. "How about this? We both make a list of stuff we never got the chance to do. Then, we'll tackle the lists together."

"I wouldn't have anything to put on a list." Her voice was wary. "I thought this was for you."

"Come on. At least, come up with a couple of things so I don't feel like a complete loser. You didn't go to any school dances, right?"

"Good grief, Nash. You are the opposite of a loser. You have a PhD for goodness sake. I barely got my high school diploma. If we're comparing, I'm the loser." In stark contrast to her tough-girl, wild exterior, a vulner-ability wove through her words.

This side of her destroyed his common sense and

tapped into his own insecurities. Unable to help himself, he wrapped his finger around a swath of her hair that had fallen forward over her shoulder. "You were a genius with numbers. You had to help me a time or two with my long division if I'm not mistaken."

She plopped backward, her hair passing through his fingers like silk. "I'm no genius. I used to wonder if I was adopted or something."

He dropped his head to his pillow, but stayed on his side, facing her. Reaching out, he tipped her face toward his with a finger. "Don't sell yourself short, Tallulah."

She took his hand and tangled their fingers, letting them rest on the covers between them. Neither of them spoke again, but Nash watched until her eyes drifted shut and her breathing deepened before allowing sleep to steal him away.

A man with rumpled hair and brown eyes trailed his mouth down her naked body, planting himself between her legs. She arched her back and tried to move her legs farther apart to give him better access.

Her leg was trapped. Bright sunshine danced stars behind her eyelids. Had she fallen asleep outside? Where was her mystery lover? She tensed and her eyes shot open, blinking to clear the fog of her dreams.

A stack of comic books on a messy nightstand was in her field of vision. Dust motes played in the sunbeams shining through the skylights. Memory flooded back. She was in Nash's bedroom. Her head was pillowed on one of his arms while his other was draped over her waist. His hairy, heavy leg had caged her in. Dear Lord, they were spooning. Even more alarming, Nash had been her sexy dream man.

Her breathing hitched. She couldn't deny that Nash had turned into a handsome man, and neither could she deny that when he'd walked out of the bathroom wearing nothing but a pair of boxer briefs, all her female parts tingled.

But Nash was the total opposite of the type of man she usually went for. For one thing, he was smart—really smart. For another, he seemed nice—adorably nice. Chivalrous even. Maybe that was something he'd picked up studying medieval knights or maybe it was his Southern DNA flaring to life in the humidity.

The way he'd swooped in last night to get her away from Heath had made her want to throw herself into his arms. And the way he'd insisted they come back to his place so she'd be safe made her heart flutter.

But, it was *Nash*. Her best friend. Until he wasn't anymore.

What time was it? Birds trilled and called to one another. Probably still early then. She should get up and leave, but she had nowhere to be until noon. Reed Garrison, her second-in-command, was opening the gym that morning. Nash's chest moved against her back with deep, slow breaths. As soon as she moved, he would awaken and the moment would be lost. A few more minutes wouldn't hurt.

His hand was splayed on the bed in front of her. As kids, they'd held hands while wading the river. She'd watched him catch frogs and tie slipknots for rabbit snares. His hands had been small but his fingers dexterous.

Now his hands were huge, his palms broad and his fingers long. They looked completely unfamiliar. Gently, so he wouldn't wake, she tilted his hand up a few inches. A white scar traced from the meaty part of his thumb around to the base of his index finger.

A rusty fishing hook had sliced him while he was casting around in the muddy reeds for crayfish. Blood had poured out, and she had hollered so loud both her parents had come running. Her mother took over, pressing a dishtowel over the wound while her father had called Nash's house. By that time, his mother was already sick. His aunt Leora sat with her most days while his dad worked on the oilrig.

Her daddy drove him to the doctor in his old truck, and she had sat in the middle of the bench seat holding Nash's uninjured hand, telling him he'd better not die. Ten stiches and a tetanus shot later, Nash was strutting around, proud of his battle scar, but he'd squeezed her hand hard while they waited for the doctor.

"Morning. Glad no rampaging ex-boyfriends found us last night." His sleepy, rumbly voice startled her, and she shifted around to see his face, but didn't drop his hand.

His brown eyes were half-lidded, his hair even more rumpled than the night before. And . . . yep, that was definitely a hard-on brushing against her hip. Her body didn't recognize Nash as off-limits and responded in kind. Her nipples pebbled, and she was afraid if she glanced down to see how obvious they were, it would only draw his attention to her inappropriate reaction. At least, he would have no idea how damp her panties were from her erotic dream starring him. Her body was in full rebellion.

His hand twitched before he curled his fingers over hers. "I've never forgotten how nice your parents were that day. Your mother had popsicles waiting when we got back."

Even though her parents had been gone for many years, the void they'd left would sometimes open and swallow her. She nodded, cursing the lump of tears in her throat. She never talked about her parents. Not even with her brothers if she could help it. Any mention of them was a trigger to change the subject.

"I still miss them." The surprise at what had popped out of her mouth unleashed more. "Sometimes I get so mad, I have to open the gym so I can beat up on one of the body bags."

"I miss my mom, too. Or more like, I miss the idea of a mom. There were so many things she was too sick to do."

Still pillowed on his arm, she turned her head so they were face-to-face. What she saw in him poured understanding into the void. He truly understood. He wasn't spouting platitudes.

Being with Nash made her feel exposed and raw yet protected at the same time. The conflicting emotions tore through her. She pushed up and swung her legs over the side of the bed. Away. She needed to get away to figure things out.

"I've got to head out. Thanks for letting me crash here last night." She grabbed her smoky-smelling jeans from the night before and yanked them on. Working her bare feet into her boots was a little more challenging.

He rose and stretched. A sunbeam from the skylight emphasized the muscles of his chest. Hair a shade darker than on his head covered his chest, her gaze following the line that disappeared into his waistband of his boxer briefs. She dropped her gaze to what was barely hidden. After fumbling with her laces like a kindergartner, she stood up fast, her head swimming, unable to tear her gaze away from the bulge in his underwear.

A garbled noise welled out of her throat. He muttered a curse, grabbed a pillow, and held it in front of his hips, shuffling so his back was against the bathroom door. A red flush had spread up his neck and into his face. Heat radiated from her too. Embarrassed, yes, but something else as well. Something that made her want to rip that pillow out of his hands and fall to her knees.

"Sorry. Mornings . . . beautiful woman in my bed . . . nature taking over, I guess." His sleep-roughened, sexy voice only made things worse.

"Understood. Not a . . . big deal." She choked as the Freudian slip exited her mouth. It *was* a big deal, a huge deal, possibly even an enormous deal. Grabbing the shirt she'd had on the night before, she held it in front of her chest, hiding her traitorous nipples, and backed to the loft stairs. "I've got to get to the gym so . . . I'll see you around."

She ran down the steps, tripped on her poorly tied laces, and stumbled over the last few stairs. Not exactly a smooth exit. She ran across the wet grass of the back-yard and through the gate. A middle-aged male jogger ran by and glanced in her direction, but otherwise the street and sidewalks were deserted. Why did she feel guilty? It's not like anything actually happened except for some handholding and unintentional cuddling.

But Lord have mercy, she'd dreamed about doing things to Nash and him doing things to her. Naughty, dirty things. Things she might have been able to shove back into her subconscious until she'd seen the bulge in his underwear. Her naughty, dirty thoughts got exponentially naughtier and dirtier.

She fumbled with her key fob, unlocking her sensible four-door sedan and sliding behind the wheel. Even at this time of morning, heat had built up inside, forcing her to turn the air conditioner to max. Did he really think she was beautiful? A glance in the rearview mirror showed a woman with bedhead, no makeup, and shocked, wide eyes.

She pulled up to her apartment building and inspected the parking lot before getting out. No sign of Heath, and no crazy messages or texts on her phone either. The lack of contact should have settled her nerves, but instead her anxiety turned to a simmer. She let herself into her apartment and relocked the door. Everything was still. A sense of safety eased the muscles across her shoulders. She tossed her things onto the couch, toed her boots off, and headed into her bedroom.

She caught sight of herself in the full-length mirror. The oversized Superman emblem on the borrowed shirt made her smile. He still loved comic books and superheroes. Inside, he wasn't so different from the Nash she remembered after all. It was the transformation of his outside that was messing with her head.

After pulling on gym clothes and making a smoothie for breakfast, she was back in her car on the way to her gym. Her daddy's old truck was parked out front. Cade had commandeered it for his use when he'd returned. Every time she saw it, her heart leapt as if she'd shot back in time to before her parents were killed by a drunk driver. Yet, seeing Cade drive the old red-and-gray Dodge closed a circle.

She walked in to find both her brothers working out on weight benches, Sawyer spotting for Cade. She stowed her gear and ignored them. Reed waved from the back where he was sweeping. She pulled her laptop out of a desk drawer and opened her accounting software.

The columns and rows of numbers soothed her frazzled nerves. Numbers didn't elude her like words. She understood them without trying. Over the next half hour, she greeted members as they entered and updated her spreadsheets with current expenditures and profit. Her plan to expand was making steady progress. Even so, a down payment on more exercise equipment was still months away. She sighed.

"You know I'd lend you the money. Hellfire, I'd give it to you." Cade's voice rumbled over her shoulder making her jump and delete an entire column with the click of a mouse. Thank heavens for undo buttons. If only life had one of those, she'd wipe Heath out of her life and memories.

"You did enough helping me get this place off the ground. I don't want to depend on my big brother the rest of my life."

"It's not like that. It's family helping family. Seeing you succeed makes me happy. So, really you'd be doing me a favor by taking my money." His voice lilted up like a question.

"Nice try." She turned on the stool to face him. He wiped sweat off his face. Looking into his eyes was like looking into a mirror. She got along better with Sawyer, but it was only because they were so different. She and Cade were too much alike not to rub each other like sandpaper sometimes, but he also understood her like no one else. "If I can't get the numbers to work by spring, I might take you up on your offer, if it's still on the table."

"It's nailed to the table." He leaned in, bussed her cheek, and propped a hip against the counter. The smile that came to his face lightened everything about him. She could only shake her head.

His transformation over the past month since he'd moved back home had been nothing short of miraculous. Her best friend Monroe had been the catalyst, but Cade had made a huge effort to mend things with both her and Sawyer.

Somewhere along the way, he'd shed the resentments toward Cottonbloom like a snake shedding its old skin, leaving behind a shiny, happy, optimistic Cade. While she was glad he'd moved back and found someone, his happiness only emphasized her crappy personal life.

Sawyer strolled over, a towel hanging around his neck, the sleeves long ripped off his grungy T-shirt. His sun-streaked dirty blond hair and twinkling eyes were in sharp contrast to Tally and Cade's darkness.

"How's my favorite sister?" Sawyer wrapped a damp arm around her shoulders and forced her face toward his armpit. She elbowed his ribs. He yelped and let her go.

"You are so juvenile."

Chuckling, he retreated to stand next to Cade, exchanging a glance with him. A sense of expectation set her on edge. Had they heard about the altercation at the Tavern last night?

"Cade and I were brainstorming some ideas for the festival. What can we offer that the 'Sips can't?" Sawyer chewed on his bottom lip and looked to the steel-beamed ceiling. She sagged on the stool, her shoulders rounding. They hadn't heard about Heath. Or Nash, for that matter.

"And, what did you come up with?" Relief made her sound more enthusiastic than she'd intended. No way had she planned to get pulled into WWIII.

Cade gestured around them with both hands. "Your place."

Her gaze darted between her brothers. "They've got gyms too."

"Not like yours. Not one where legit fighters train," Sawyer said.

One of the reasons she'd hired Reed was because of his experience in MMA fighting. He'd moved up the ranks in the professional leagues until an injury had forced him out. Now her gym attracted boys and men who dreamed of being paid to fight and win. "What are you thinking?"

Sawyer's voice edged with excitement. "Monroe is going to ask a couple of the girls in her group if they want to demonstrate some self-defense techniques. You could maybe lead a kickboxing set. I talked to Reed and he'd be willing to put on an exhibition fight with one of his buddies. Nothing too crazy, but something to grab people's attention and get them cheering."

"Reed!" She shot a glance toward her employee and friend. Maybe former friend.

He jogged over with a sheepish expression. "I'm guessing they told you."

"Yep." She crossed her arms.

Reed rubbed a hand over cropped dark hair. The offspring of a half-white, half-Iranian mother and a black father, Reed laughingly called himself the ultimate minority. He reminded Tally of an exotic sheik in hiding. Hypnotic tawny eyes blazed against his darker skin.

"You can't tell me we wouldn't attract a big crowd to watch. And, think of the promotion the gym would get," he said.

She huffed. It wasn't a terrible idea. In fact, done right, it could be a win-win. An undertaking that big would require capital outlay for signage and advertising. She could offer a discount on the first three months of fees if they signed up during the festival. While her profits might initially take a hit, the upside potential was immense. A risk, but a calculated one. Excitement had her bouncing her leg as she chewed on the end of her thumbnail, numbers stampeding through her head.

"My gut tells me it's doable and maybe even a good idea. Let me confirm." Sawyer fist-pumped like it was a done deal. She waved a finger at all three men. "The numbers have to support it. No promises."

Sawyer nodded and held his hands up, but there was a grin on his face. All three men retreated, and she attempted to focus on her columns of numbers, this time with the new proposal in mind. Instead, her traitorous mind wandered back to Nash and how it felt to wake up in his arms and how he filled out that pair of underwear.

She grabbed a gym brochure off the counter and fanned herself. If he didn't come by the gym as promised this week, she would bake him some cookies as a thank-you for helping her out with Heath. Geez, she was as bad as the church welcome committee. What if she couldn't get her hormones under control around him and did something truly wild and reckless?

Chapter Five

Nash leaned against the counter of the small kitchen, eating a bowl of Fruity Pebbles and staring at the blank wall. How royally had he screwed *that* up? He'd never had a morning after that awkward, and this one hadn't even involved sex. Although, if the night *had* involved sex, he might not have been tenting his underwear like some fourteen-year-old horndog.

It was all her fault. She had looked so adorably sexy in his Superman T-shirt, her nipples poking at the S. Actually, he'd pretty much fought the uncomfortable arousal all night, especially after she scooted her butt right into his pelvis. His dreams had only stoked the fires ensuring he'd woken with the biggest, most uncomfortable hard-on ever.

He wasn't sure what to do about her. No way was he letting her get away that easy. It was Saturday and all he had on his to-do list was to finish reading a biography of Charlemagne. His to-do list . . . He smiled.

Although, he'd been skeptical when she'd suggested re-creating milestone moments he'd missed as an adolescent, the idea had taken root sometime during the night and flourished. It would force him out of his comfort zone, which was a little nerve-wracking, but he'd be spending time with Tally, which he wanted more than anything.

He didn't think to get her number, but unless it had only been a convenient excuse to escape the monster in his underwear, she'd be at the gym. She had invited him by after all. A hard workout might relieve the sexual tension that even a solo session after she'd run out his door hadn't managed to alleviate.

While he tossed some clothes and toiletries into a gym bag, a hard rapping cut through the sound of birdsong and the tinkling of wind chimes. His aunt opened the door without waiting for an answer and stuck her head in the crack.

"Nash. Where are you?"

"Upstairs. Hang on, I'm coming down." He slung the bag over his shoulder and jogged down the stairs.

His aunt Leora was his mother's older sister by a dozen years. The irony of cancer taking his young, vibrant mother and leaving her soured spinster sister wasn't lost on him. His aunt had tirelessly and lovingly taken care of his mother in her final months, and when she'd died, his aunt had welcomed him with both arms. In fact, she'd insisted on becoming his legal guardian. His father had been relieved to get Nash settled. His job on the oilrig made caring for a young son impossible—unless he quit, and it was obvious he loved the life and the money.

Aunt Leora smoothed a hand down her flower-print dress, her hose sagging into a pair of low-heeled black pumps. Arthritis had swollen her knuckles and her shake was growing more noticeable, but she still joined her quilting crew to work a needle.

He tensed, expecting her to bring up his nighttime guest, but instead she asked, "Where's your truck?"

"Aw, hell." He rubbed his chin. His truck was in the Rivershack Tavern's parking lot.

"Nash Hawthorne. I raised you better than to use vulgarities." Her mouth pinched into a circle.

He barely refrained from bowing his head in childhood penance. "Yes ma'am, you did. Pardon me. I got a lift home last night and left my truck in town."

"I'm headed to the Quilting Bee for circle if you'd like a ride."

"That'd be great." He kissed her papery cheek, the scent of talcum strong but not unpleasant. Not everything about his childhood had been terrible. His aunt had provided as many books as he wanted on any subject. She'd never censored him, answered his questions with candor and honesty, and pushed him to dig even deeper for meaning.

She led the way out of his cottage, holding tight to the handrail. He offered her an arm on the uneven grass, and she took it without comment. As they approached her white Crown Victoria, he side-eyed her, wondering if he could wrest the keys from her hand and drive them. At some point in the near future, they would need to have a frank conversation about her driving privileges.

She dropped his hand to head to the driver's side. That day was not today. He slipped into the passenger seat and made sure his seatbelt was secured before she backed the car up in a series of jerks that had him feeling nauseous before she fumbled the stick into drive. They puttered down the street at a blazing twenty miles per hour.

"My Defender is over the river at the Rivershack Tavern."

She harrumphed but thankfully kept her eyes on the road. As they came into the main part of Cottonbloom, she slowed even more, nudging her head toward River

Street. "Martha might have to relocate the Quilting Bee or close it entirely."

The Quilting Bee had been a Cottonbloom staple for as long as Nash could remember. It sold sewing machines and fabric and quilting supplies, and was a gathering place for women who made quilts for babies and grandbabies, for children in the hospital and children in need.

"What's going on?"

"All of a sudden River Street has become trendy. It's all four-dollar coffees and ice cream flavors I've never heard of. What's wrong with a cup of black Folgers and plain old vanilla?" She waved where the floor of the new gazebo rose from the blackened ground. "I can't believe you agreed to help resurrect that thing."

"It'll be a nice addition. Tally mentioned something about her uncle's bluegrass band. They could play in the gazebo and families could bring picnics for the lawn. Enjoy music and the river. Maybe even sell beer."

"Beer?" His aunt said it as if he'd suggested a public orgy. "That sounds like a Louisiana thing."

"It could be a Cottonbloom thing. Not everything has to be divided. This town integrated black and white with hardly a peep of protest, yet can't seem to get beyond an arbitrary state line. You realize I was born on the side 'that must not be named.' "

His allusion to Harry Potter fell on uninitiated ears. "You came back from England talking a different language."

"Scotland."

"It's all the same, isn't it?"

"Yep. Exactly the same." The irony of his aunt not understanding the centuries-old rift between two countries separated by a land border made him look out the passenger window to hide a smile. In his aunt's view, the world revolved around Cottonbloom.

"I don't have anything against Louisiana. In fact, Effie lives on this side, and we get along fine. But, we don't need Delmar Fournette bringing his band over to play, and that's that."

The Crown Victoria's pillowlike suspension absorbed the bumps in the Rivershack Tavern's washed-out graveled lot. His aunt broke hard, tossing him forward and making his seatbelt catch. "I can't believe you came to this place last night. And, brought *that* girl home."

He was honestly surprised she hadn't mentioned his overnight guest before now. He could tolerate a high level of his aunt's snobbishness, but not when she acted like Tally was tainted. "Tallulah Fournette is a remarkable woman and my friend. I won't have you being rude or throwing dirty looks in her direction, Aunt Leora. Is that understood?"

Her hands squeaked over the faux-leather steering wheel as she clenched and unclenched them. Their roles were in a constant state of flux. Now, he played the role of disciplining parent warning a child to play nice. The cords of her neck were taut, a prominent blue vein in her temple highlighting the delicacy of her skin.

"Will she be sleeping over often?"

Damn, he hoped so. He squashed the thought. Last night had been about protection not seduction, no matter his physical evidence to the contrary. "I have no idea."

"The neighbors . . ." She fluffed her bottle-red hair.

"It's not the eighteen hundreds. I'm nearly thirty and although I study monks, I've no desire to live like one." Residual anger over Tally's story about being turned away by his aunt had him turning in the seat. "Did Tally come to the house looking for me when we were about twelve?"

"Heavens, I don't remember." Instead of looking him in the eye, she was focused on his seatbelt buckle.

"You told her I didn't want to be friends with her any longer."

"Nash, that was years ago. I'm sure whatever I said was done with your well-being in mind." There was no use in arguing. His aunt believed that's exactly what she'd done. Protected him from the bad influence of the Fournettes."Your father trusted me to raise you right."

"Speaking of dear old dad, I got another email. That makes the second one in two weeks. Any clue what's going on?" He pulled at his bottom lip. Months would typically pass between the brief emails confirming Nash was still alive and vice versa.

"Does he know you're back in Cottonbloom?"

"He does now."

"Maybe he's planning to come up here on leave to see you."

"Didn't say anything about it. If fact, he didn't say much of anything beyond giving me a weather forecast." Even when his mother was alive, his father had flitted in and out of their lives. When he was at the house, he'd seemed almost a guest. The oilrig was his home, and the men who worked on it were his family. Nash had long ago given up hope of connecting with his father in any meaningful way.

"Time will tell, I suppose." His aunt's voice was distant.

He got out, unlocked the Defender doors, and tossed his duffle in the backseat. His aunt's car hadn't moved. He rapped on her window, and she rolled it down.

"You okay?"

"I'm fine. Fine." Yet still she sat with her hands tight on the wheel. "The Fournettes . . ."

"What about them?"

"I used to think they couldn't be trusted." The furrows along her forehead deepened.

"Used to think?" He curled his hands over the window frame and ducked his head low to see her better.

"Maybe I was wrong to judge them all just because—" She cut herself by looking away and clearing her throat. "I need to be getting on to the Quilting Bee. The ladies will be waiting."

She rolled up the window, forcing him to let go and step back, and executed a wide turn in the deserted lot. He coughed in the resulting plume of dust and climbed behind the wheel before he had to pull out his inhaler. The AC blew cool air into the already hot cab. He tapped his fingers on the steering wheel.

The odd conversation had teetered on an almost-apology. While her shake had gotten worse and she occasionally forgot things, she was still sharp. He had no doubts that she remembered with perfect clarity Tally's visit and her subsequent brush-off. He also had no doubts that she had done it not out of spite, but to protect him. But protect him from what? The Fournettes were good people.

He pulled up to Tally's gym still chewing on the past. With his hand on the door, he hesitated. Was he pushing things? Considering she'd almost killed herself on the way out of his cottage, the look on her face somewhere between embarrassment and horror, she might go out of her way to avoid him.

Maybe he should leave it be, but he couldn't forget the feeling of being curled around her, breathing her in, her soft body pressed into his. Even with the evidence of his mortifying exhibition, the draw to her was more than physical.

Her fingers toying with his imparted a sense of comfort and closeness he hadn't felt in years. While their shared history was years ago, it had been an important part of his life, and he wanted to recapture it for a myriad of reasons.

He took a breath, the humidity making his lungs work for the oxygen, and stepped inside. An overhead bell tinkled. It should have been easier to breath in the cool air, but nerves kicked his breathing rate up a notch.

A tall, muscular man with tattoos along both biceps occupied a stool at the front desk, staring at the computer and clicking the mouse. He closed the window, but not before Nash saw an online chessboard. A couple of beefy men lifted with the free weights in one corner. No sign of Tally.

Damn. Not only disappointment but worry quickened his blood flow. What if her ex had been waiting in her parking lot or in her apartment? "Is Tallulah around?"

The man raised his eyebrows, and although he didn't smile, Nash sensed his amusement. "Yo, Tally!"

Tally came around a corner holding a rag and cleaning spray. She stopped short, shifted on her feet, and glanced over her shoulder as if she were thinking about making another run for it. Her braid swung to hang to the side of a breast. Her pants were tight spandex to right below her knees, her tank equally as snug, highlighting the lean curves of her body. Everything about her was beautifully unharmed.

His shoulders relaxed, and he found a smile. "Thought I'd take you up on your offer last night. I need to expend some energy."

She set the spray bottle and rag down on the front desk. "If the weather's nice, Saturdays can be slow, but if you're looking to spar, Reed can accommodate you."

This time a smile did cross Reed's face. Nash was in good shape, and he was an experienced boxer, but the big, muscled man behind the desk would pulverize him. Nash fiddled with the strap of his gym bag over his shoulder. "Another time maybe."

She chucked her head toward the ring in the back and walked away, obviously expecting him to follow. "I don't blame you. Reed's a former professional fighter. If you want to spar me, I'd be game."

He couldn't think of anything worse than hitting Tally. "I'm more of a boxer than a martial arts guy. I'd prefer to punch a bag and jump rope if it's all the same with you."

The hint of a smile crossed her face. "Worried you might get beat up by a girl?"

"That's a given."

"Fine." She took a step away, but he caught her arm.

"Any trouble this morning?"

"Only if you count my brothers as trouble." She patted his hand, and he let her go. "I'm fine. Heath was probably drunk last night. It was a one-time thing."

He wanted to believe her, but the sideways dart of her gaze transmitted her worry and her reticence to volunteer anything else. He'd hoped after last night, she would trust him with at least this problem.

"Is Cade back for good?"

She led the way to the nearest body bag. "Looks that way. He and Monroe are practically living together, and he's moving the R&D part of his business down from Seattle. He's even talked Sawyer into joining his venture—renamed Fournette Brothers Designs. They've both been working long hours getting things set up."

"Something with engines, right?" He tucked his glasses away, pulled out a pair of protective gloves, and slipped them on.

"He designs new engine technology, patents it, and then licenses the patents to the highest bidder. He doesn't throw his money around, but he's done well."

"Does he know what's going on with Heath?"

"No. Sawyer doesn't know either, and neither one of them are going to find out." Her mouth tightened and her tone could freeze water. "I can handle Heath on my own. Don't turn into an old gossip like your aunt now that you're back in Cottonbloom."

Her braid made a dark arc in the air on her turn. He cursed under his breath as she stalked away. The way she'd answered confirmed his fears. The woman was too independent and proud for her own good. He hit the bag until his arms burned, expending a portion of his aggression. Next was the rope, and he stripped his T-shirt off.

Jumping rope was a challenge with his asthma, but he'd learned how to regulate his breathing until he found a rhythm that was almost meditative. He wasn't sure how long he jumped, but by the time he stopped, sweat was trailing down his torso.

His chest heaved but he forced his lungs to fill and empty completely as slowly as he could. In the mirror, he could see her somewhere behind him wiping over the same weight bench a dozen times. Was she looking in his direction? Without his glasses, he couldn't be sure.

Perhaps her swift exit that morning hadn't been *entirely* in horror. Perhaps he hadn't been the only one who'd been fighting an inconvenient attraction. He grabbed a towel and approached her, rubbing it over his chest.

The closer he got, the more in focus she became. Her gaze was definitely on his body, not his face. He could translate the ornate script of Norman monks and decipher the spindly, small letters in ancient books, but reading women, especially this one, seemed like it would take a lifetime of study.

Spending his formative years as a comic-book nerd and with musty books as his most recent companions, he would never qualify as "suave." He discarded any cheesy opening line, and went with the truth. "I've been thinking about what you said last night. About re-creating my youth."

"Yeah?" She continued to wipe and not meet his eyes.

"I'm game if you are."

She straightened, her gaze finally rising to meet his. "Are you serious?"

"I'm serious about everything. What would you like to do first? Wade the river? Paint the water tower?" He lowered his voice, hoping he sounded flirty. "Maybe you'd prefer skinny-dipping?"

She chuffed, but a flush pinked her cheeks. "Wading the river isn't risky. Didn't they have rivers in Scotland? What's so special about ours?"

"That's like asking what's special about the sunset over the pines. Or the smell after a storm rolls through. Our river belongs to us, right?"

Staring into his eyes, she took a step toward him. The bench caught her knees and her hand shot out for balance. It landed over one of his pecs. The muscle jumped.

"Sorry," she whispered, but her hand stayed where it was. He stood as still as possible, not wanting to spook her. Her green eyes swallowed him, made his stomach churn. Or maybe the gut-wrenching reaction was because of her hand.

She spread her fingers, rasping over his nipple. He hadn't considered that part of his body particularly sensitive—until now. Even the movement of his chest hair under her palm sent sparks through his body. He was dangerously close to embarrassing himself again. Obviously, he needed ironclad underwear or a codpiece like knights wore in the Middle Ages.

His breathing fractured. It could have been from the aftermath of his hard workout, but he had a feeling it had something to do with her light touch on his bare chest. He might require hospitalization if she touched him more intimately.

She sucked in a quick breath and jerked her hand away, tucking her fist under her chin as if she'd been burned. "You had a piece of dirt or lint or something."

The bands around his chest eased now she wasn't touching him and inciting lurid fantasies about her hand in his shorts and oxygen masks. A shot of something— satisfaction, happiness—coursed through him. If he wouldn't look like an idiot, he'd go find the first person he could and ask for a high-five. The confusing currents weren't one-sided.

She grabbed up the cleaner and the rag and moved to the next piece of equipment, presenting her back to him. He followed her even though it was obvious she was doing her best to ignore him. "When do you want to do this? Tonight?"

She wiped and sprayed and wiped again, not looking over at him. "You really are serious."

"All college professors are serious."

"Do all college professors have stacks of comic books in their bedrooms?" Her bland demeanor was in contrast to the tease in her voice.

"Good point."

She faced him, popped a hip, and checked around them. Her expression grew animated as the air seemed to vibrate around them. "All right, here's how it's going to go down if we're painting a water tower. I'll get the supplies. Uncle Delmar and his crew are playing Saturday night by the river for the Fourth of July. We'll make an appearance, but slip out early. Wayne and his boys should be mostly occupied with the crowd and teenagers being stupid with fireworks. Less chance of getting busted."

For a second, he wondered what getting arrested would do to his chances of tenure. He was a rule-follower by nature. The smile on her face banished the worries. "You seem awfully excited about our walk on the wild side."

A smile that held secrets flashed. "I'll admit it's been awhile since I've done something that's gotten my blood racing."

"Anything you want me to bring?"

"Something to toast the moon by?"

"I can do that." He hesitated. "Are you working tomorrow?"

No," she drew the word out. "Not at the gym at any rate. I have some bookkeeping to catch up on."

"Come onto the river with me. I want to see our old stomping grounds."

Something akin to fear crossed her face and drew her gaze away from his. She clutched the bottle of cleaner close to her chest. "I don't know."

He considered his play, the abrupt shift in her attitude surprising him. She seemed more afraid of a law-abiding wade up the river than an illegal defacement of public property. Why?

"We won't be gone all day. I'll pick you up early before the bugs and heat get too bad." He dropped his voice and skimmed a finger down the back of her hand. "Come on, Tally, I don't know if I remember the way without you."

Still she didn't look at him. "I'm not into catching frogs anymore."

The harder she pushed back the more imperative the trip became to him. He couldn't explain why, but the only way he could revisit the river was with her. He played his trump. "I dare you to come wade the river with me."

Her green gaze eviscerated him. A wealth of emotions

flickered in a split second before they shuttered once more. "I'm not fifteen anymore. You can't goad me into doing something."

He *bocked* like a chicken.

She huffed and rolled her eyes to the ceiling, but a small smile played at her lips. "Fine. A quick wade up river."

He retreated before she had a chance to come up with some other excuse.

Chapter Six

Tally woke at dawn, did some intensive dusting to expend nervous energy, but mostly looked out the front window. She had a good view of the parking lot. If he'd been picking her up to go toilet paper someone's house or deface the side of a water tower, she would have been dusting out of adrenaline-fueled excitement. Wading the river cut too close to old pains she rarely took out for examination.

Her mind worked around the problem of Nash, trying to determine his intent. Was she only a walk down memory lane? Was he lonely and looking for a friend? Or did he want something else? His brown, soulful eyes had cut through her bullcrap and asked for more than she was willing to give anyone. Her wildly inappropriate dreams hadn't helped clarify her feelings.

But his smile exuded trustworthiness, if she believed such a thing existed in a man. The toast she'd choked down tumbled in her unruly stomach. Was it the imminent step into her past or the thought of present-day Nash ratcheting her nerves higher?

His Jeep-like truck pulled into her lot. White. Like a good knight from his medieval histories. Was that an omen? She locked her door and met him halfway on the steps. He looked around, his eyebrows up.

The exterior of the 1980s-era apartment building was in need of an extensive power washing. Ivy grew out of unkempt bushes around the perimeter and up the sides of the brick. A brown Dumpster took up several parking spots at one end of the lot, adding to the impression of shabbiness. The building housed eight one-bedroom apartments on two floors, bisected by a staircase.

She'd moved into an apartment on the second floor right out of high school. Sharing the small trailer with Cade had been torturous after she'd dropped the bombshell she wasn't going to college like Sawyer. He'd been upset, but it was the disappointment and weariness in his eyes she couldn't handle, like she'd failed him somehow. She'd gotten a job in retail on the Mississippi side of Cottonbloom and moved out.

Six months later, certified as a personal trainer and working all over both sides of Cottonbloom, she began to save and scrimp every penny for the next few years. Still, without Cade, she would have had to work for another decade before she could have saved enough money to start her own gym. At this point, she could afford a bigger, better place, but she was comfortable in her apartment. It was familiar and safe.

"What?" she asked, feeling the need to defend her choice.

"Nothing." His voice was even and gave no hint to his thoughts.

"It's not much to look at, but I like it."

He held up both hands. "I didn't say anything."

"You're thinking it. You're thinking, why don't I move?" She strode toward his truck, knowing nerves were driving her pissy attitude.

He followed close behind her to the passenger side of

his truck and snaked his hand around her to grab her forearm. "Other side, I'm afraid, unless you're driving."

"What are you talking about?" She opened the door and was confronted by a steering wheel. She turned and found herself blocked in by his arms, one hand on the opened door and one on the roof. Her heart tapped roughly against her breastbone. "It's on the wrong side."

"For America, yes." His smile was slow and drew crinkles around his twinkling eyes. His unruffable attitude calmed her. Even as children, he'd had the power to cut down her fears with his logic. With a hand on her lower back, he guided her around the bumper.

"I can—"

"I know you can, but I'm trying to be nice. Let me." His amused exasperation made her smile in spite of herself.

He opened the opposite door and gestured her inside with a flourish. She slipped onto the leather seat and glanced around her. It wasn't the most luxurious of vehicles, but the mere foreignness lent it a sophistication her plain sedan would never match.

It started with a rumble. "I brought it home with me. Something to remember my time in Scotland by." He backed them up with a jerk of gears and got them headed down the road. "Instead of crating and shipping all my books, I loaded most of them into the back."

At the mention of his extensive library, a measure of tension returned. "You have a ridiculous number of books."

"I actually pared down some when I moved but selling them felt like getting rid of old friends, you know?"

She hummed. She didn't know at all. Books were her enemy.

Once they were on the road, he glanced over at her. "So . . . why don't you move?"

She chuffed and turned toward the passenger window, the pine trees a blur of brown and green. "It was the first place that felt like home after my parents died."

The caress of his fingers on her clenched hand drew her attention to her lap. A callus on his middle finger where a pen would rest was pronounced and expected, but the calluses along his palm were not. She'd forgotten he was a lefty.

Without conscious thought, her fingers relaxed under his touch, and he wrapped his hand around hers, squeezing slightly. No more questions came.

They drew closer to their old neighborhood. "If you want to wade behind our old houses, we're going to have to park on that old dead-end street off McComb. You remember?" She pointed to the right.

"Vaguely." His voice was far away, and his hand left hers for the wheel.

He turned down the correct street and parked in a graveled area where the pavement was fighting the encroachment of grass and losing. He hopped out. She didn't give him a chance to open her door, but was at the bumper by the time he walked around.

He wore shorts made of thin, water-resistant fabric and a pair of water shoes with black-soled bottoms and blue straps. All she could find were too-short khaki shorts and a pair of old, beat-up tennis shoes that would be waterlogged in ten seconds.

The river had been a constant in her life, but she'd avoided it for years, coming up with one lame excuse after another when Sawyer invited her out on his boat, until he'd quit asking. The thought of climbing the long narrow ladder to the top of a water tower filled her with excitement, while wading the knee-high river filled her with a nervous reluctance. The irony wasn't lost on her, but some things didn't need revisiting.

Nash collected a net, slipped a backpack over his shoulders, and grinned. "You ready?"

His enthusiasm was like an inoculation against the aching sadness, and she found a brief half smile for him. "Looks like the path is overgrown."

She led the way through sparse new-growth trees toward the river. At one time, there had been plans to develop houses along this stretch, but the draw to newer, more stylish neighborhoods had killed the project.

The closer she drew to the water, the faster her pace. The feeling of being weighed down faded with each step, leaving an anxious need to reconnect with the river with Nash by her side. The air crackled with memories. She stopped and put her hand on Nash's arm, halting him as well. Their gazes met and held.

The white noise of the river was cut by trilling birdsong. A woodpecker's rapping crescendoed, then died away only to start again a few seconds later. She pulled off a handful of pine needles and rubbed them between her fingers. Closing her eyes, she breathed them in, the sharp tang firing synapses in her brain that had been lying dormant.

He wrapped a hand around her wrist and leaned in close to sniff them. "You think it's lost forever, yet it all comes back in an instant."

"What do you remember?" she whispered, feeling as if they were under a spell.

"Building the lean-to of branches and crawling inside. Lying under the trees on the pine needles."

"We told each other stories about the squirrels, remember?"

"How could I forget Jubal Grayskull?"

Her laughter peeled through the trees, frightening a pair of mockingbirds into flight and breaking the spell. She'd loved making up stories with him. Stories she wasn't required to read or write down. It had been fun. "I can't believe you remember."

"I can't believe you'd think I'd forget."

Did he keep their shared experiences as close to his heart as she did? She couldn't quite believe it. He had travelled the world, seen more than she could imagine. She walked on and he kept pace beside her, occasionally stepping ahead to push brambles down with his foot so she could step over unscathed. The river grew louder.

They came out of the trees and onto the bank. The river here was only a few feet at its deepest point, but the sides of the bank rose at least ten feet on either side. The gurgling echoed and sounded ferocious. In reality, it was a stream that aspired to great things.

Tally went first, lowering herself over the edge. She found slippery footholds in the muddy bank and jumped the last few feet into the shallows. Her feet sank ankle deep into river mud.

Nash knelt and propelled himself over with a hand on the bank, landing in a crouch a couple of feet farther in. Water splashed her legs and dotted her tank top. She might have teasingly complained, but with the heat already rising, the water felt refreshing. His entry had sent water halfway up his shorts, the thin material clinging to his muscular thighs. Thighs she needed to stop staring at.

"Alrighty, let's go." Her voice pitched high as she started upriver.

They walked in silence for a few minutes in single file. The river widened by another ten feet and slowed. He came up beside her, but she kept her focus on where she put her feet.

"You still fish?" he asked.

"Nope. It was never my favorite thing."

"You did it with me all the time, and I never heard you complain once."

"That's because it was *your* favorite thing." She glanced over to find him staring at her with a soft look in his eyes. A look she wanted to wrap herself in like an old security blanket. Forcing her gaze away, she looked upriver toward a sharp right bend. "Do *you* still fish?"

"Whenever I can. I took up fly-fishing in Scotland. It's amazing there. Wilder even than our marshes in some ways. Like the waters are veins full of ancient magic."

When they were kids, he had a way of talking that made her believe in his comic books or the outrageous stories he would spin. After reality ripped their lives apart, she'd lost any feeling of enchantment. No superhero had swooped in to save her, no fairy godmother had appeared, but it seemed he hadn't lost the ability to weave his spells.

"I've hardly ever been out of Mississippi or Louisiana. Cade flew me to Seattle a couple of times. Took me to Mount Rainier. It was cool." The truth was she'd been homesick the entire trip. Admitting that aloud would make her sound at best provincial but most likely pathetic.

"I'll bet. I've never been that far west. Does Cade miss it?"

"Doesn't seem to. Do you miss Scotland?"

"I miss the architecture and being able to touch and smell the parchment in the university's research library. I get the facts, but not the feelings, by reading them online. On the whole, though, I don't miss it."

"No Scottish lass pining away for you?" She bit the inside of her lip.

He huffed, but it was filled with more regret than humor. "No. I couldn't seem to maintain a relationship for long."

"Why not? You're—" She bit off her incredulous words.

"I'm what?"

"I'm not going to detail all your good points. Your head might explode. Why didn't they last?"

"The work was more interesting than the women." He shrugged and waved the net in front of them. No-see-ums darted in all directions. "Plus, I always knew Scotland was temporary. It never felt like home."

She was afraid to ask the question that burned to escape. Did Cottonbloom feel like home or was this a temporary stop on his world tour?

They reached the bend that signaled the start of their street. The houses were set well back from the river, leaving no landmarks as to where they were, but she knew.

It would take another hundred years or more for the river to carve a new path over the land. The river would flow the same route as long as she lived. Instead of depressing her, the thought helped wash away a familiar melancholy. Some things couldn't be destroyed in an instant.

In silence, they trekked upriver and for the first time, Nash took the lead, wading faster against the current. He stopped exactly where she knew he would. The bank was lower here, and they could see over it. Beyond the swaying reeds was the browning summer grass of his old backyard. A playset rose in the distance, the chains of two swings and the start of the slide visible. The house was too far back to see.

"I guess a family moved in. Do you know them?" he asked.

"It's changed hands a couple of times. Last I heard a family that moved up from New Orleans after Katrina was living here." Silence settled over them. She wanted to tell him more, but as much as Nash wanted to remember, she'd worked hard to forget.

"Hi there!" A little voice peeped from the bank.

Nash stood his ground, but his heart pounded from a surge of adrenaline. Tally yelped and stumbled backward. A little girl crawled out of the reeds and plopped on her stomach at the edge of the bank, her chin resting on her hands. Her skin was a dark walnut, and her hair was pulled up into two lopsided braids above her ears, different-colored ribbons on each one. If he had to guess, she looked seven or eight.

He sidled a step closer, afraid she might balk and run, but she only watched him curiously, no fear in her face. He tried on a smile, his heart slowing. "Hello there. We didn't even hear you."

"I know." Pride wove the girl's words, her gap-toothed grin huge. "I snuck up on you. What're you doing in my river?"

"Well, now this might surprise you, but this used to be my river." Nash gestured toward Tally, and she moved up beside him. "Our river, actually. And that"—he pointed behind the little girl—"used to be my house."

The girl shifted to sit on the bank and let her legs dangle over the side, her bare feet dirty, grass and mud smudging her yellow sundress. Her nearly black eyes were fathomless and seemingly wise beyond her meager years. Two hundred years ago, he might claim she had the makings of a wise woman.

"Are you Nash?" Her question sent him reeling backward a step.

"How did you know that?"

"Found your name on my closet wall where your mama ticked off your height every year. My mama does me right beside you." She thumbed at herself before pointing at him.

A wave of heat that had nothing to do with the Louisiana summer came over him. He'd forgotten his mother had stood him up against the wall and drawn careful lines each year on his birthday. Except for the last year when she'd been too sick to even remember. Everyone had forgotten his birthday that year. Everyone except Tally who'd given him two new comic books she'd bought with her allowance.

Tally's hand slipped into his. "I like your pretty hair ribbons."

The girl made a face, sticking out her tongue. "My daddy did my hair so we could go see Mama in the hospital."

Nash swallowed past a lump, his voice coming out craggy. "Is she . . . okay?"

"I guess. That *thing* came out of her stomach. It bawls all the time, but her and Daddy seem awful happy about it."

"She had a baby." Relief corkscrewed through him and unwound the bands around his chest.

"Yep. I have a brother. Asked if we could trade him for a sister, but Daddy said no can do."

"Are you out here hiding?" Tally asked with a smile in her voice.

The little girl looked over her shoulder, her grin gone. "They didn't even notice."

"They will," Nash said.

"Not for a while yet. I can walk with you if you want. Show you where I lost my two front teeth."

Before he could answer, she jumped down, splashing in the water in front of them. The water was up to her knees, licking the hem of her dress.

"Your parents might not like you walking with us," he said.

"They told me to never, ever go off with strangers, but you're not a stranger, you're Nash." It was impossible to argue with the no-nonsense logic in the girl's voice. She turned to face them by hopping, splashing and giggling, the bottom few inches of her yellow dress now soaked. She looked him up and down. "Thought you'd be shorter though. The tick marks stopped when you weren't much taller than me."

"Yeah, I moved when I was ten. I kept growing even though my mama couldn't measure me anymore." Sadness for an alternate future rocked him. He didn't let himself dwell on 'what-ifs' often. What if his mother had lived? What if he and Tally had stayed friends?

"Did she not move with you?"

He squeezed Tally's hand too tight, yet couldn't seem to loosen his fingers. She squeezed him right back. "She passed away."

The girl nodded sagely, her giggles gone. "Preacher says the best are taken too soon from the earth."

"What's your name?" he asked.

"Margaret." She made another face, able to stick her tongue through the gap in her missing two front teeth. "But everybody calls me Birdie."

As if sadness could be shed as easily as a heavy coat, Birdie splashed and jumped her way ahead, keeping to the shallower part, close to the bank. He looked to Tally, but she just shrugged, a half smile on her face. They followed her, still hand in hand.

"Over here is where I lost my teeth." Birdie patted the branch of a cottonwood that extended so low over the river, they had to duck underneath it. "My cousin Derek was out here with me, and we rigged up a tree branch with string. He pulled it back and then let it go and both teeth came out like a catapult. It was pretty awesome."

"Sounds like it." He fought a spurt of laughter and lost. Her good humor was infectious and drove away any lingering sorrow like the sun to fog.

Bubbles gurgled to the surface of the water at her feet. She poked at the mud with a three-foot-long stick she had acquired from the cottonwood tree. She dropped the stick to dig at the mud, coming up with a bullfrog the size of a small salad plate. It croaked and wiggled in her hands.

Nash offered up his net, and she plopped the frog inside. "I haven't seen one this big in years."

"My uncle brings me gigging with him. Says I'm the best frog spotter this side of the Mississippi."

"What do you want to do with this one?"

"Let's let him go," Tally said softly.

Nash turned the net inside out and the frog swam back to the mud to burrow down. He would emerge when darkness fell to hunt and find a mate. They walked on, Birdie leading the way.

The river was the same yet different. Some landmarks were achingly familiar while others had been wiped away by time and nature. The trek to Tally's old house seemed both longer and shorter.

Tally turned to the bank, the narrow trail up to her old backyard overtaken by vegetation. High grasses dominated the view. She pulled herself up the bank by grabbing handfuls of grass. The girl scrambled up to stand next to Tally, and Nash followed.

"Who lives here, Birdie?" Tally stared into the ocean of tall grass. The willow tree they had lain under so many afternoons had most certainly grown, yet seemed smaller to his adult eyes.

"No one now. Mama says it's a cursed house. Like the ones in Naw'leans after Katrina came."

"I used to live here. Years ago."

Birdie slipped her hand into Tally's. "It's a good thing you left before something bad happened to you too."

Tally's face reflected an old wound uncovered and exposed to salt. She was the strong one, the one who had held him together when his mother was sick. Maybe that strength was a façade. No, not a façade. She *was* strong, but more complicated than he'd imagined. The night they'd spent together had peeled back layers, and today was exposing more of her to him. All of it was a surprise.

A whistle pierced the sounds of the river and the rustling of leaves in the trees. "Uh-oh. That's Daddy. I'd best skedaddle. Bye, y'all."

Birdie jumped off the bank and landed on her knees in the river. Popping up, she took off at a run, her pretty sundress wet and muddy.

"Bye, Birdie!" Nash hollered before she cleared the first bend and disappeared out of sight. Somehow he wouldn't be surprised to discover Birdie was a ghost. Old Southern gothics had left their indelible mark on him.

"You okay?" he whispered into the silence that crashed around them.

"Yes. No. I don't know. I've avoided coming back here. It's been years since I've had cause to drive down our old street."

She walked through the thigh-high grass and weeds toward the house. He stayed on her heels. The grass absorbed their footsteps as if they were the ghosts. Once the back of the house came into view, she stopped. One shutter hung askew while its mate was absent. This time, he slipped his hand around hers.

"Do you remember Mama's flowers? They were so wild and pretty. And Daddy was proud of his grass."

"I remember. Looks like Sawyer inherited your mama's way with a garden." The wildflowers Sawyer had planted along the bank on the Louisiana side of Cottonbloom were amazing. They had drawn him over the bridge to join Cade's welcome-home party a few weeks earlier. He'd kept a lookout for Tally that evening but left disappointed.

"Sometimes I dream about my parents. Like they're still here. Waiting for me. Then I wake up." Her words came out choppy and cold, but a mishmash of emotions were vying for dominance over her face.

Nash understood every one. "When I look at old pictures of my mother, it's like seeing someone I vaguely recognize but can't recall from where. I can't remember her smile or laugh or touch."

They stood in silence until a blue jay squawked overhead. He tugged her back toward their tree. The ground around the trunk was shadowed and mossy. "Are you hungry?"

"I guess."

He shrugged off the backpack and unloaded sandwiches, oranges, and two Cokes from an icepack. Sitting cross-legged on the ground, she tossed an orange between her hands. He leaned against the trunk, stretched his legs out, and popped the top of the Coke, the can already sweating.

She dug a thumb into the orange and pulled off the skin piece by piece. The tangy scent drifted to him on the breeze, and he closed his eyes.

"Have you ever seen a ghost through all your crypt wanderings?"

"Like in *The Mummy* or something?" He smiled.

"You don't believe in them?"

He opened his eyes, and her intense stare seared his smile away. She was serious. "I've never seen one. Or felt the presence of one for that matter, and I've been in some creepy places. Do you believe in ghosts?"

"No." She popped an orange section in her mouth. "But it's almost as if this place is haunted by *us*. The old us. As if time stopped before both our families were destroyed, and we both left something of ourselves here. Does that sound crazy?"

It did a little, but the feeling also rang true somewhere deep inside of him. Maybe that was the source of his melancholy. Maybe he'd come out here to find the part of himself he'd left behind. His heart hitched, and he closed his eyes again to get a hold on his breathing. It was rarely the physical, but the emotional that triggered an asthma attack these days.

Her heat radiated into him as she scooted next to him. His arm came up automatically to circle her shoulders and hug her close. She notched her head under his chin and snaked an arm across his chest to lay on his shoulder.

The careening between past and present was giving him emotional whiplash. The past grew distant, and he became aware of the woman in his arms, her breasts pressed into his side, her long, bare legs beside his, the scent of her surrounding him. Her hand snuck over to his neck, her fingers playing in the hair at his nape.

He was usually careful and methodical with his decisions, yet he stood at the edge of the cliff, contemplating jumping. A kiss would change everything. Or would a kiss change nothing? He wasn't sure which outcome scared him the most.

He set his Coke down. Whispering her name, he cupped her cheek and tilted her face to his. Her green eyes blinked languorously as if she were caught in a spell.

He'd always known her eyes were pretty, but with her face dappled in sunlight, he could see the shades of brown and blue that hid in the green. Beautiful eyes. Complicated eyes.

She was why none of his relationships had ever lasted. He hadn't left part of himself on the river, he'd left part of himself with her.

Chapter Seven

Dear Lord, Nash was going to kiss her. The intent in his eyes was clear. His lips parted, and it was all she could do not to jerk him closer, faster. The pure animal in her wanted him to take control and drive her crazy—if she didn't already qualify—but the part of her that this jaunt down the river had uncovered cowed in fear, already overwhelmed by a flurry of emotions.

Nash was her anchor—solid and logical and dependable . . . and sexy as all get out. She'd always thought of herself as a daredevil. She'd done things without thought to the consequences her whole life—jumped off bridges, climbed water towers, smoked pot. Even once she was grown, she wasn't afraid to take chances. Starting her gym business had been a huge risk, but she'd approached it with total determination and no fear.

His lips were a whisper away. She could almost taste the tangy orange on his tongue. Her blood fired and sped through her veins like a rain-swollen river.

Kissing Nash was too scary to contemplate.

A noise came from her throat as she pulled away and wrapped her arms around her knees. Her body's protest. It longed to stay pressed against his hard, hot body. She rocked on the mossy ground for a moment before standing. Facing the river, she brushed her hands down her shorts, blowing out a long, slow breath. "We should head back."

"Tally—"

"It's been a strange morning, hasn't it? We should head back."

"If that's what you really want."

The rustling of him packing everything up came from behind her. She didn't look over her shoulder, but felt his eyes on her nonetheless. If she stared into those deep, brown eyes again, she'd be a goner. She might do something totally insane like throw herself on top of him.

She didn't want to be just a way for him to connect with his past. She wanted to be something more. The realization was like jumping out of an airplane without a parachute. Too risky, even for her.

Their trek downriver was made in silence. Birdie's backyard was deserted. Tally hoped the girl didn't get in too much trouble for messing up her pretty dress or walking off with two strangers.

She led the way to his Defender, but his hand hit the passenger door handle the instant before hers, leaving their fingers tangled.

"Tallulah." The way he whispered her name added to her confusion. Exasperation, amusement, worry, but she couldn't discern anger or the hint of a shattered ego. "I don't want things to be weird between us."

"They're not weird."

Things *were* weird. Even her voice sounded weird, all high-pitched and squeaky. The fact she hadn't taken her hand off his was weird. The wish he'd turn her around and press her up against the cab launched things beyond weird. Thank goodness he wasn't telepathic.

"Sure, not weird at all." His hand flexed under hers as the door unlatched.

She hopped into the cab and pulled the heavy door shut. In the five seconds it took him to circle around and join her, she cast around for something normal to say. Before he even got the truck started, the words poured out. "Saturday should be fun. Delmar's band is surprisingly good, and Old Rufus will pull his smoker out. His barbeque is still the best in the parish. Sawyer even said something about the church ladies selling pies."

The engine rumbled to life. "I got used to hot tea, but never stopped craving a good pulled pork sandwich. What time?"

"People start gathering around five, but the sun goes behind the trees around six and cools things down. That's when I'll close up and head down."

"Sounds like fun. I'll meet you at the gym, and we can walk down together." Nash backed out, and she almost asked him to drive down their old street, but it would only make her sad. They turned onto the parish road that led toward her apartment.

Once there, she didn't immediately hop out, but took a careful look around the parking lot. It was instinctive now. Seeing nothing, she heaved a sigh and opened the door. He caught her arm.

"Let me see your phone." He dropped her arm and held his hand out.

"Why?"

"So I can put my number in it." She handed it over. His thumbs worked with dexterity, considering how big his hands were. "If you won't call the police, I want you to call me if you see Heath lurking or if you get scared. You can even give me a call if you get bored or lonely. Promise me."

He held her phone between two fingers, but when she went to grab it, he jerked it out of her reach. "Promise me."

"Fine. I promise." It was a promise she didn't intend on keeping. She would handle Heath on her own.

His eyes narrowed as if he were actually telepathic, but he let her pull the phone from his fingers. She slid out of the truck and kept her head down on the jog up the stairs to her apartment. He had backed up but idled at the curb. He wouldn't leave until she was safely inside. Her annoyance disappeared under the flooding warmth.

She unlocked her door and went straight to her front window, peeling the curtains back and waving. After waiting for a few more heartbeats, he drove off and she watched until his taillights disappeared. She stepped back out her front door, walked the few paces across the breezeway, and knocked on the opposite door. A woman in old-school Jane Fonda workout gear answered.

"I didn't mean to interrupt your workout, Ms. Effie."

"I was finishing up my stretching. Come on in, young lady. I'll fix us some refreshment."

Before she could protest, Ms. Effie was off to the kitchen. The woman was a marvel. Seventy-seven and a whirlwind of energy. She was diligent about keeping in shape and taking care of herself. She knew that as soon as she was unable to climb the steps to her apartment, her son would insist she move into a nursing home. He worried about her and wanted her somewhere she would be taken care of. A burden taken off his plate.

She came out of the kitchen balancing a tray with two tall glasses and a plateful of cookies. Nudging her chin toward a flowered couch, she set the tray down on a low-slung coffee table polished to a shine.

Tally sank down onto the springy cushion and took a bite of a cookie. Peanut butter. Her father's favorite, which meant her mother had made lots of batches of peanut-butter cookies.

"Tell me what's going on between you and Nash. I didn't realize the two of you were acquainted." Waggling her eyebrows, Ms. Effie leaned into the corner of the couch and crossed her legs at the knee, a striped leg warmer bunched around her calf. Tally prayed her legs looked half as good as Ms. Effie's when she hit seventy.

"He's an old friend, is all. We grew up on the river together. How do you know Nash?"

"Goodness, I've known Nash for ages. His aunt would bring him to quilting circle on occasion. Nose always in a book as a young man as I recall, but so polite. Not like some of the young'uns today."

Tally hadn't considered Ms. Effie's friendship with Nash's aunt through the Quilting Bee. "His aunt . . ." She took a bite of cookie.

"Leora's a character, that's for certain, but a good woman. Loves Nash like he was her own." Ms. Effie took a sip of tea and tilted her head as if waiting for something.

"Maybe so, but she doesn't hold much stock in me. In fact, I think she hates me."

Ms. Effie made a humming sound. "You can blame your family name for that."

"What do you mean?"

"Not my story to tell."

"But what—"

"I want to hear about Nash. What's he like now? He dropped Leora off at the Quilting Bee the other morning and had half the ladies reaching for their blood-pressure medicine. The other half needs new glasses."

A laugh welled up and out, like the top of a pressure

cooker releasing steam. The hours of the morning had been packed with a gamut of emotions—all intense.

"Nash is—" How to describe him? One word wouldn't suffice. She shrugged. "Nice. And funny. And sweet. And smart. And, really, really, really good-looking."

"Thank you, Jesus," Ms. Effie held her hands up to the heavens revival-style. A grin drew her face into a myriad of crinkles. While she had the body of a fifty-year-old, her face bore the damage of too many years spent sun worshipping. "You're finally pursuing a man who sounds worthy of you."

"I'm not pursuing Nash. We're childhood friends."

"So this really, really, *really* good-looking guy is just an old friend."

"Exactly." Tally pulled at a loose thread at a seam of the couch. "Except he tried to kiss me. Or maybe I tried to kiss him. Either way, it would have been a huge mistake."

"Now we're getting somewhere. So you wanted him to kiss you?"

Tally rolled her eyes and shoved a cookie into her mouth.

"I'm taking your deflection as a yes. Do you have plans to meet up again as friends?" Ms. Effie air-quoted the last two words.

"We're going to the Fourth of July block party on River Street. But it's not a date or anything." Best not to mention the illicit plans they had for the water tower. Although knowing Ms. Effie, she'd probably want to ride along.

"It's a start. What about Heath?"

"What about him?"

"He was here."

Her stomach fell to her knees. "When?"

"Two nights ago. He was banging on your door and

hollering loud enough to wake the dead. One of his buddies dragged him back down to a car. I hadn't seen him in weeks. Thought he'd finally given up on you."

"He showed up at the Rivershack Tavern that night looking to start trouble. I ended up staying with a friend." Wanting to downplay her worries, she forced a nonchalance she didn't feel into her voice. "He was drunk and it was a one-time thing, I'm sure."

"You need to go to the police. I know you're independent—believe me, I sympathize—but some things are too big for any one person to handle. Asking for help doesn't make you look weak."

"How about stupid for letting him into my life to begin with?" She looked away before Ms. Effie could see too much of the truth in her eyes.

A soft, cool hand took hers and squeezed. "Not stupid either. In fact, you're probably the first woman to toss him to the curb. He couldn't keep you under his thumb, and your rejection is stuck in his craw." Ms. Effie took a sip of tea. "My ex-husband was not a nice man—God rest his soul—and I stayed. I think my son blames me for that. And rightly so."

Tally sandwiched the woman's hand between hers, now the one offering comfort. "I'm so sorry, Ms. Effie."

"I got married out of high school, had a baby nine months later, and pretended to be the happy homemaker. Not only did he make my life miserable, he helped tear this town apart with his pig-headedness. I forgave him for what he did to me, but not to my son and not to this town."

"I always heard the separation was about fishing rights on the river." The breaking of the town over the river boundary happened well before she was born. By the time she was old enough to remember the stories, they had grown into outrageous tall tales.

"Aaron was a blustering loudmouth who attracted followers. He got a group of prominent Louisiana men riled up about men from the Mississippi side trolling for crayfish on this side. We always had the better spot for spawning. He made a big hoopla about it, offended the 'Sips and before anyone could make peace, the town split. A bunch of men playing little boys with their toys is what happened."

"No one could talk sense?"

"We tried. The women would gather at the Quilting Bee and make plans to bring everyone together, but you have to remember the times . . . the leaders were all men and no one listened to a bunch of biddies who quilted." Decades-old anger singed Ms. Effie's words. "We decided to keep meeting in spite of our husbands telling us we shouldn't. In spite of our differences and in spite of the town splitting, we stayed united."

"That's amazing." A new respect grew for the gathering of women at the Quilting Bee. They were rebels.

"We are pretty darn amazing. Those ladies have gotten me through some hard times. Aaron died not two years after the havoc he caused. Can't say that I missed him even though I worked my tush off to keep us afloat."

In all the years she'd known Ms. Effie, Tally had never seen a glimpse of the woman's past struggles. She seemed the picture of optimism and light. Did everyone have tragedies shoved away in their dark closets?

Ms. Effie pushed a strand of hair behind Tally's ear in a gesture so motherly that tears rushed to her eyes. "You've already been through so much, sweets, seeing you with a peckerhead like Heath broke my heart."

Tally's heart stuttered, and she was torn between laughter and crying. "Ms. Effie, what if I'm wrong about Nash? What if he's not everything I remember him being?"

Ms. Effie's gleaming eyes flared and a smile tipped her lips. "So you *are* interested in being more than friends?"

Tally poked at the ice in her glass and shrugged.

"Are you worried he'll hurt you?"

"Not in the same way Heath might have."

Ms. Effie hummed. "Nash might very well break your heart if you take a chance."

She waited for more wisdom to pour forth, but Ms. Effie scooted back into the corner of the chair, crossed her legs, and took up her tea glass once more. Tally waved a hand around. "That's it?"

"I can't tell you everything will work out, sweets. Part of life is throwing yourself in the fray while praying you find a safe place to land."

"That sounds terrifying."

She nodded and pursed her lips. "Oh, it is. It most certainly is."

Chapter Eight

Tally smoothed a hand over her simple tank top and black shorts, the slap of her flip-flops echoing in the empty gym. Maybe she should have packed a sundress to change into for the Fourth of July block party. No. This wasn't a date. In fact, a sundress would have been silly, considering what they had planned for later. Even so, she'd left her hair down.

She checked the clock. After six, and still no Nash. What if he'd had second thoughts? She wouldn't blame him. Painting the water tower was not something adult, upstanding members of society should be doing. Disappointment lurked behind her nervous excitement ready for its cue if he bailed.

Her phone rang, and she answered without looking at the display. "You're chickening out, aren't you?"

A moment of silence. "What the hell are you talking about?"

A chill passed through her. Heath's growly voice used to be a turn-on, but now she recognized his natural intimidation tactic. She hated that it worked. Her hand grew clammy around the phone.

"Quit calling me." Her lips barely moved, weakening the command.

"I want to know what the hell is up with you and that wimp Nash."

Anger sizzled like a frayed electric wire helping to unfreeze her tongue. "He more than held his own with you. For your information, he happens to be my"—the word "friend" hung in her head, but something else came out of her mouth—"boyfriend. I've moved on and so should you."

"Quit fuckin' with me. No way are you dating Nerdy Nash. I asked around. He's some wonderboy professor up at the college. He's smart. You two have nothing in common."

His words were as painful as a physical blow. A familiar ache blossomed in her gut. The same ache she'd battled every day on her way to school, where she was met with condescension and ridicule. Coming after Sawyer, who'd been valedictorian of his class and the captain of the baseball team, had only highlighted her struggles, both academically and socially.

The end of her sophomore year a keen, enthusiastic student teacher had urged the administration to test her for a learning disability. The diagnosis of dyslexia had been both devastating and a relief. She wasn't technically an idiot, but even with the extra help, school had been a struggle. Her college entrance test scores had been cringeworthy.

"Nash and I have plenty in common." Deep down she knew she wasn't dumb. Her voice wavered with uncertainty anyway. Did she and Nash have anything in common except for a finite number of childhood memories? She shook her head, concentrating on Heath. "And even better, he's not a jerk."

"You'll come crawling back to me, sweetheart." The hint of a threat lurked in his statement.

"If you do not leave me alone, I'm going to the police to get a restraining order. Do you understand me?"

A double beep sounded. He'd disconnected. She stared at the screen, her hand shaking. The emptiness of the gym normally wouldn't bother her, but she needed to be surrounded by people. She stepped out, locked the front door, and tested it with a strong pull. Someone tapped her shoulder, and she flinched aside, getting her arms up, her hands in fists.

"Whoa there. No hits below the belt, thank you kindly." With a slight smile and serious eyes, Nash stepped back, his hands up in a picture of surrender.

"Sorry. You caught me off guard."

"Didn't think you were ever off guard," he murmured.

It felt like a dig, but before she could question him, he fingered a piece of hair that had fallen forward. His hand was mere inches from touching her breast. Her body swayed forward before she forced herself back on her heels.

"I forgot how pretty your hair was."

Teenagelike awkwardness overtook her, and she tucked her hair behind an ear, pulling it out of his hand. "I about gave up on you."

"I stopped by the Quilting Bee. Aunt Leora and her cronies decided to finish their patriotic quilt-in-progress."

"That's serious dedication."

His hand settled at the small of her back, the heat like a flint to her body. He got them walking side by side toward the river. Discordant notes of several instruments tuning echoed against the bricks. "I wouldn't be surprised if they don't prop the door open to enjoy the breeze and the music."

"Why don't they come on over? It might be good if everyone could put their differences aside and forget about the festivals for one night. A truce."

"Some of the other ladies would be game, but Aunt Leora considers herself above such frivolities." The cadence of his speech took on a foreign lilt that made her wonder if she knew him at all.

A cool front had settled over them in recent days bringing a break from heat and humidity. The night was comfortable and dry, and a northerly breeze lifted her hair. The music kicked off, guiding them to River Street. Sawyer had towed out a parish-owned set of generator-run towered lights usually reserved for roadwork.

Her uncle stood at the front of the raised platform, tapping his foot, his fingers a blur on the mandolin strings. After they'd moved to the trailer, she'd hear him playing and sometimes singing, the sound amplified by the river. Although, she'd hadn't been able to decipher the words, the way he sang them had settled in her heart and made her cry into her pillow when she was young. Behind his unruffled, easygoing smiles, her uncle understood heartache.

"He's good." Nash nudged his chin toward Delmar. "Actually, the whole band is good."

"Most of them have been playing together for a decade at least. Uncle Delmar used to be the youngest one up there. Their old bass player broke his hip and got put in the nursing home last fall. I wasn't sure if they'd find anyone, but looks like they roped someone into joining them." A middle-aged black man with a slight potbelly played an upright bass, his eyes closed, bouncing on the balls of his feet to the rhythms he plucked. "Not a lot of interest in learning bluegrass these days."

"I used to play the guitar a little." His face was impassive, his hands stuck deep in his pockets.

"I didn't know that."

"I was alone a lot." The simple statement seemed to hold a wealth of pain, but a slow smile materialized. "Aunt Leora wanted me to learn the piano. I insisted on guitar. I was under the impression guitar players got all the chicks in college."

Her lips had curled to match his. "Did they?"

"It's a little-known fact that even 'Stairway to Heaven' can't overcome being an acne-covered sixteen-year-old freshman who has yet to hit his growth spurt."

Even though he smiled, loneliness still lurked around the edges. She lay her cheek against his shoulder, slipped her hand around his elbow, and squeezed. "It must have been scary to go off like that."

He shrugged under her cheek. "Freedom is risky and the unknown is scary. It all worked out."

Considering he'd come full circle and was marking time in Cottonbloom, she tended to disagree. Someone hip-bumped her, and she yanked her hand from Nash's arm, knitting her fingers in front of her.

"What's up, girl? How's it going, Nash?" Monroe poked her head around Tally to grin at Nash.

He looked around in mock surprise. "Can't believe you ventured on this side of the river. What would Regan say?"

"Probably that I'm sleeping with the enemy." She winked.

Cade joined them. He handed a lemonade to Monroe before sliding his arm around her shoulders and pulling her tight to his side.

"How're you doing, Sis?" Cade reached over to squeeze her nape. Their father used to do the same, and Tally wondered if it was an unconscious gesture on Cade's part.

"Hey, Nash. Does your aunt know you're consorting with a bunch of swamp rats? Surprised she didn't try to lock you in your room."

"She never had to lock me in my room growing up. I never got invited anywhere." His chuckle did little to mask to the awkward silence that blanketed them.

As the song came to an end, Cade said, "I'm surprised you never snuck down to see Tally."

Nash made a noise somewhere between a laugh and a sigh. "Oh, I did."

"What? When?" Tally shifted to stare at his profile.

Nash rocked on his feet and pulled at the collar of his shirt. "It wasn't a big deal."

Tally sensed it had been as pivotal as her trip to see him. "Tell me anyway."

"Biked by your old house a couple of times before I realized you'd moved." His jaw muscle twitched. "Then, one day after lunch, I skipped out of school. I was fourteen, I guess. A junior. It had been a . . . bad day." Again, she sensed the understatement. "I waited outside of the school for you. Thought I could catch you before you got on the bus."

It would have been her freshman year. Her test scores had placed her in honors level math, but remedial classes for everything else. Most of her day was spent with kids who had learned not to care. She still cared, but it had been easier to pretend not to.

"Did you find me?"

"I saw you. Barely recognized you. You had grown up. Changed. You were dressed all in black. Dark eye makeup and pale skin. A nose ring. Even your hair looked darker. I was still short and skinny and wore glasses. You got into a car with a couple of older-looking guys. I rode off on my Huffy." The shot of sarcastic humor tempered the sad bitterness of his recollection.

"Nose ring?" She could feel Cade's gaze on the back of her neck.

"The nose ring was fake. And, I had put a temporary dye in my hair. Goth was the style for most of the kids in my classes. . . . Let's just say, I was doing my best to fit in." Tally ran both of her hands up his arm and lowered her voice so her brother and Monroe couldn't hear. "If you would have come up to me, I would have ridden off on your Huffy handlebars, I swear."

"The Fates conspired against us back then."

Tally wasn't so sure the same forces weren't at work in the here and now, but she stayed quiet.

Red flashed in the corner of her eye. "Hello again!"

Birdie stood in front of them with her hands fisted on her waist and her feet planted wide. Tonight her braids were perfectly aligned and smooth, bows to match her black-and-red polka-dot dress drooped over the tops, the ribbons trailing to her neck.

Monroe smiled. "And who might you be?"

Birdie thumbed her chest. "I'm Margaret Thatcher."

All four of them burst out laughing. Birdie popped a hip and crossed her arms. "Why do grown-ups always laugh at me when I say my name?"

"We're not laughing at you, Birdie. You share a name with a very strong, smart woman from England who had a nickname too. She was called the Iron Lady." Nash still smiled but Birdie nodded, her face thoughtful.

"I wonder if I could be an Iron Lady too?"

"I think you could be anything you want," Nash said with such confidence that Birdie's chin ticked up.

"Birdie lives in Nash's old house." Tally shot a look toward Cade, who didn't react. "Are you enjoying the music, Birdie?"

"Not really, but Daddy loves it. He's up there." She

stuck her tongue out between her lost teeth and chucked
her head backward toward the stage.

"So is my uncle. He's plays the mandolin."

"I know Mr. Del. He's nice. He always has a candy for
me even if it's all warm and squishy from his pocket."
Birdie grabbed Nash's hand again and tugged. "Oh, you
have to come meet Mama. She thinks I made you up, and
I got in trouble. I can't wait to see her face when I introduce the boy from my closet."

"Well that doesn't make me sound at all creepy, does
it?" Nash tossed a smile in Tally's direction, but let Birdie
lead him away.

Tally waggled her fingers. He and Birdie stopped in
the middle of the crowd and looked around. In a flurry
of red and black polka dots, he lifted the little girl onto
his shoulders so she could scan the crowd for her mother.
Nash walked in the direction she pointed with her still
perched high. The girl's giggles floated above the music
and the crowd.

"Well, well, well." Cade's voice was a whisper in
Tally's ear.

She flinched and wiped the ridiculous-feeling smile
off her face with a clearing of her throat. Monroe had
been drawn into a conversation with a sixtysomething
woman who worked her elbow in Monroe's face.

"What?"

"Are you and Nash messing around?"

"How is that any of your business?" Old resentments
bit at her words.

Cade's eyebrows rose along with a sly smile. "It's not.
But I think you just answered my question."

Tally grabbed her brother's arm. "We're not messing around, so don't you dare go spreading that gossip
around. We're hanging out, that's all. Old friends." She
dropped her hand and turned toward the band so Cade

wouldn't guess she wasn't being completely truthful, yet she wasn't lying either. She didn't know what they were to each other yet.

"You two were inseparable when you were kids. I heard Mama and Daddy talk about it more than once."

She stiffened. "What did they say?"

"Mama thought you should have at least one other friend, preferably another girl. But, Daddy laughed and told Mama to simmer down since you were too young to run off and get married."

She could almost hear their daddy's big belly laugh. Sometimes when Sawyer got really tickled about something, he would laugh like that. The memories rushing through her scraped her hollow. "It's been really good to reconnect with Nash, you know? He was my best friend. When I think about how things were before they were killed, how happy we were, I get sad. My memories of Nash aren't . . . tainted with grief. Does that make any sense?"

Cade wrapped an arm around her shoulders. "I wish I could have made things easier, better. I tried." His voice was thick.

Tally turned and gave him a hug. Because he was older and had assumed responsibility for her and Sawyer after their parents' death, he'd turned from playful big brother into a grim, serious man seemingly overnight. She'd never seen him cry. Now that she was older and a little wiser, she understood that he'd suffered as much, if not more, than her and Sawyer. Not only had he been dealing with the grief of the past, but the responsibilities of the future.

"You did great, Cade."

"What? Did I miss the invite to the family hug fest?" Sawyer's arms came around them. Tally was grateful for the intervention, otherwise she might be tempted to burden Cade with all her troubles, and he'd had enough of that to last a lifetime.

"Nice turnout, right?" Sawyer looked around with a critical eye and a frown.

"Sure is," Tally said.

"Everyone seems to be having a good time."

"Everyone always has a good time, Sawyer. What's the problem?" she asked.

"My former boss reneged on his donation since I quit—can't say I totally blame him there—and Regan stole the Cottonbloom, Mississippi, marching band back with the promise of a new tuba. What if the festival is a disaster?"

"Your effort to spruce up the storefronts has done wonders. Getting the graffiti off the bridge made a huge difference. The flowers are lovely. All you need is music and food to make it a success. The point is to bring everyone together," she said.

"The point is to blow those journalists' socks off and win that grant money." He pulled at his bottom lip before adding, "And bring everybody together."

Nash walked back, having lost Birdie but gained two pecan pies.

"If you're planning on eating both those," Tally pointed back and forth, "then you'd better pony up for a gym membership."

"I could kill at least one, but I thought I'd see if the Quilting Bee ladies would like some."

"Yes," Sawyer hissed and tapped his steepled fingers together like a cartoonish evil mastermind. "You're turning into my secret weapon, Nash. Those old ladies probably think you poop cotton candy, don't they? While Regan might be mayor, those ladies rule the town, and they haven't thrown their social weight behind Regan yet, have they?"

Nash's eyebrows rose over the rim of his glasses, but he only nudged his head toward the footbridge and held out a pie. "Want to help me, Tally?"

She took it, but Sawyer grabbed her arm. "Bad idea. Tally would ruin your plan."

Nash shook his head. "I have no evil plan. I'm simply offering pie to a lovely group of ladies. In fact, consider me Switzerland. I hope both festivals are a rousing success."

Sawyer took a step forward and poked Nash in the chest. "But you demonstrated your Louisiana loyalty during the rabbit hoopla."

Nash patted him on the shoulder. "Sawyer, my man, you're going to end up committed by Labor Day. You coming, Tally?"

He didn't wait but ambled toward the footbridge. Tally gave her brother a squeeze around the waist. "He's right, you know. You are slowly losing it."

Sawyer gave her a playful shove, and she ran to catch up with Nash. The Mississippi side seemed unnaturally quiet and still. She looked over her shoulder at her friends and neighbors laughing and drinking, some even attempting to clog to the music. The scene took on an unreal quality, like looking at a movie. As if in agreement, they stopped in the middle of the footbridge to look down on the water.

"It's funny that the river doesn't care," she said.

"Doesn't care about what?"

"The strife it's caused this town. It flows along, cutting the divide a little deeper every year." She picked at a fleck of sun-faded brown paint.

He shifted toward her, resting an elbow on the rail. "You don't think once Aunt Leora's generation is gone, things will get better?"

She envied Nash's optimism. Even more, she envied

his resilience. They'd both had more than their fair share of tragedy, but he didn't need to search for a laugh or a smile. "I hope it does, but the rivalries have been bred into the children on both sides. We're still swamp rats and they're still 'Sips."

"I guess I'm the rare breed who's both."

They walked up the slope to the common area, the grass already wetting with dew and itching her feet. The skeleton of the new gazebo rose like a phoenix on the burnt grass.

Light from the Quilting Bee sliced from a narrow parting of the curtains, but Nash had been right, a chair was lodged in the door. Uncle Delmar's voice, singing a timeless bluegrass ballad in a haunting minor key, drifted across.

"It might be better if I stayed out here while you deliver the pies." She shoved the pie at his chest, but he refused to take it. Ms. Effie was probably inside, but then again, so was Ms. Leora.

"Nope. You're my friend. Anyway, I'm Switzerland, remember?"

He bumped the front door open with his hip, a smile on his face. Voices rose around him like a chorus. She sidled in after him, hoping to blend into the quilts that hung along the way, but her foot caught the leg of the metal folding chair that had been propping the door open. It clattered to the floor and the door shut, blocking out the music. Silence descended. Everyone looked in her direction.

"We brought pie." She hoped she hadn't sounded as stupid as she felt, but judging by the look on Ms. Leora's face, she'd crossed into village-idiot territory. Heat prickled her face.

The few seconds since her spectacular entry felt like an eternity. Nash's lips twitched, and unbelievably her lips tilted into an answering smile. He took over, leading the ladies to the counter like the Pied Piper.

Ms. Martha, the owner, emerged from the back with paper plates, plastic forks, and a silver pie cutter. She had inherited the Quilting Bee when her mother died and was a decade younger than most of the women. She bustled with a no-nonsense urgency that Tally found abrupt and off-putting.

Ms. Effie sidled over with a sliver of pie. "Isn't this a surprise. Having fun?"

"I was until Nash dragged me over here," she murmured.

"Come on, now. We're harmless." Ms. Effie grinned as Nash called for the pie Tally was holding.

She approached as if the ladies were a pack of wild dogs ready to chomp her hand off. She placed the pie on the end of the counter, and one of the ladies slid it down to Nash who was surrounded on both sides by stooped, chattering women of a certain age.

He doled out slices. As each lady received one, they drifted away to stand in conversational circles she wouldn't attempt to penetrate. Even Ms. Effie had been assimilated. She backed toward the wall, keeping her eyes on her feet.

Tally bumped into a warm body. "Terribly sorry."

A petite woman with gray curls and bottle-thick glasses graced her with a smile. "No worries, my dear. You're Tallulah Fournette, aren't you? I've heard about you." Her voice was upscale 'Sip from a different era.

"Yes, I am." She forced a smile back, wondering what sort of rumors were floating around. Ms. Leora wasn't more than three feet away and leaning in their direction.

"I'm Vera Carson."

"Nice to meet you, Mrs. Carson." The name was one of the oldest in Cottonbloom. Her husband had been mayor of Cottonbloom when the town broke apart, but she'd been a widow for more than two decades now.

"I've been meaning to talk to you, so this is fortuitous."

Tally fought the urge to look over her shoulder. "To me?"

"Effie has been raving about you and your gym. I was thinking—well, we all were actually—that you should offer a class for seniors."

"A class?" Tally said dumbly.

"Aerobics. Or yoga maybe. Just last month, the AARP magazine was saying how good yoga is for old bones." Mrs. Carson's smile gave the impression of sincerity.

"Several of the quilting ladies are interested?" Tally gestured around at the gathering, but her gaze fell on Ms. Leora, who had sidled a few inches closer even though she didn't seem to be paying them any attention.

Mrs. Carson's eyebrows rose over her glasses, her smile turning impish. "Not all the members of our quilting circle are game to try new things, but many are. If we spread the word through the ladies' circles at church, you might have more old women than you can handle."

A zing of excitement drew a grin to Tally's face. Her specialty wasn't seniors, but she could learn. "I'm working on expansion plans now. A yoga studio was on my short list. In the meantime, I can work up some low-impact aerobics classes for you ladies to try."

"You let me know the details, and I'll get the word out. The businesses on either side of the river need to watch out for one another, don't you think?" Mrs. Carson's eyes flashed with a message Tally couldn't decipher.

"We should." She would have pumped Mrs. Carson's hand in an overzealous shake of good faith if the other woman hadn't been holding a piece of pie. Mrs. Carson glided away with a grace that reminded Tally of actresses in old black-and-white movies. A group of chatting ladies expanded to receive her.

Nash propped a shoulder on the wall next to her and held a narrow sliver of pie on a plate. "Last slice. We can share."

She opened her mouth to share her news, but before she could speak, he slipped a bite into it. She hummed as the sweetness exploded.

He licked his bottom lip as if he too tasted something sweet. The moment felt oddly intimate even though more than a dozen chaperones buzzed around them.

"You try some." She picked up his abandoned fork and speared a portion, raising it to his mouth. He opened and took the bite.

His aunt joined them, looking as if she wished she had a crowbar.

Nash shot a half smile at her, but didn't step away from Tally. "Were you enjoying the music? Would you like me to prop the door open again?"

"It had gotten stuffy." Ms. Leora sniffed.

"Delmar Fournette's voice is something special, if you ask me."

"Well, I didn't," she shot back. Under the biting words were other emotions. Emotions Tally couldn't classify, but none of it boded well for anyone claiming the Fournette name.

"Aunt Leora," Nash said with a hint of warning.

"How nice of you to help Nash carry the pies, Miss Tallulah."

"You can call me Tally." As soon as it came out of her mouth, she knew she'd taken yet another misstep.

Ms. Leora pursed her lips. In spite of the years gone by, Tally's heart rate picked up and her tongue wanted to make tripping excuses. Ms. Leora's condescension was Tally's kryptonite. She felt powerless to stand up against it.

"I'm planning on leaving before the fireworks start. Will you be home shortly, Nash?"

"Actually, we're going to stay awhile. Not sure when I'll make it home. I'll come check on you in the morning."

The penetrating stare that was obviously an attempt at ESP didn't faze Nash. Ms. Leora gave in first and huffed. "Fine. Be careful." Her warning seemed to insinuate Tally was dangerous. And, considering their plans for the evening, maybe his aunt really did have ESP.

"Finish this off, won't you, Tally?" Nash took up the last bite of pie on his fork. She stared at the incoming bite until her vision blurred. The sweet, thickened corn syrup hit her closed lips, prompting her to open for him. His face seemed to move closer and no one else in the room existed.

"Let's go." He handed the empty plate to his aunt and guided Tally out the door with a light touch at her back. Once outside, he said, "I'm sorry about my aunt. She can be a bit of a character, but she means well."

It was almost exactly what Ms. Effie had said about her. Tally saw only a bitter old woman. "Not exactly the word I would have chosen. It's fine, though, I'm used to it. She's never liked me. Isn't it strange that she tolerates Ms. Effie fine, but mention the name Fournette and she looks tortured?"

"I'm not sure what her problem is. I know the family was against my mother moving across the river and marrying my dad. Not sure if it was a swamp rat–'Sip thing or if they thought my mom could do better. Or both."

"Your dad worked hard to give her a good life. Nothing to be ashamed about there." She didn't remember much about Jack Hawthorne, but he'd always been nice to her.

"Worked hard and was never home." A bitterness she'd never heard from him flavored his tone. Instead of offering a platitude, she slipped her hand in his. She wasn't normally a hand-holder, but with Nash the gesture felt natural.

The night grew quiet. Her uncle Delmar and his band were packing their instruments away. A few people milled around the back of the platform while the crowd out front had grown throughout the evening.

"Looks like they're getting the fireworks ready. We'd better hurry."

They skirted the edge of the crowd, nodding or exchanging waves with a few people. No sign of either of her brothers, thank goodness, and the side street where they'd parked was deserted. The less questions they had to answer, the better. She grabbed the bag with the spray paint out of her car and joined him in the Defender.

Anticipation had buzzed in the background all night. She'd forgotten what a rush doing something a little crazy could be. Being with Nash added a different element of adventure. "Is your favorite color still red?"

"I can't believe you remember my favorite color." He gave a little laugh.

"Superman's color. Do you remember mine?" She tensed.

"Let's see, blue when you were about six, but by age eight, that was too boring, so you decided on periwinkle."

She relaxed and looked out the passenger window so he wouldn't see her smile or the gleam of sudden tears. His answer had been more important than the simple question. "I still have a soft spot for periwinkle, but black is kind of my signature color now."

"Dark and dangerous. It suits you." His voice rumbled with humor.

"Do you normally go out with dark and dangerous women?" She didn't need to fake the flirty tease in her voice.

"Are we going out?" His head swiveled in her direction.

Embarrassment burned her from the inside out "I didn't mean . . . of course, I don't think this is a date. I was just saying, you know," she finished weakly.

He hummed and reached toward her. She breathed in sharply and held it, but instead of touching her, he pulled something from behind the seatback. "I did some research this afternoon, and it seems Cottonbloom boasts more than one water tower. Do you have a preference?"

Half a dozen yellow highlights glowed over the map he spread out. Laughter bubbled out of her. Mr. Organized. "Let's go with secluded and short. That would be the one in Cottonbloom Parish close to Silas's old market. You remember where it is?"

"I think so, but don't let me miss the turn." He maneuvered them through the crush of parked cars and onto the parish road.

She cracked the window, leaned her head back against the seat, and closed her eyes. Night air rushed over her, whipping her hair around her face. The earthy smell of pine and water and mud entered her bloodstream and pumped through her heart.

"I should tell you something." She didn't open her eyes.

"What's that?" The two words tread cautiously between them.

"I kind of, sort of, told Heath that you were my boyfriend. To get him off my back and hopefully stop the incessant calls."

"When was this?"

"Right before I saw you tonight. He called—again—wanting to know what the deal was with us." She opened her eyes and glanced over at him. His hands were tight on the wheel, and his mouth was drawn into a frown. Apparently, his good humor had a line and she'd jackknifed over it. "You're mad. I shouldn't have—"

"Yes, I'm mad. But not at you. What do you want to do?" His voice had roughened, giving him the dark and dangerous edge.

She knew what he was asking—did she want to go to the police or to her brothers? Right now, she wanted to crawl into his lap and try to reproduce the same feelings of comfort and warmth that had wrapped around her like a security blanket when she'd awakened in his bed.

"I want to climb a water tower and deface some public property. What do you say?"

He didn't say anything. The old market came into view around the curve. It was a shell of concrete blocks, grass growing inside higher than the walls. The roof had long ago fallen in. A faded sign advertising live worms and cold Cokes lay propped against the front door.

Nash cut the Defender over the broken pavement of the abandoned parking lot. Darkness was overtaking dusk under the trees, and his headlights cut across the overgrown road. Knee-high grass outlined two ruts.

The truck lurched back and forth, bugs swarming in the high beams. The gray support struts of the tower emerged from the shadows, and he pulled up next to a short fence surrounding the base.

He cut the engine. Now not even the instrument panel lit them. The relative silence and darkness wrapped her in a cocoon, and she could have sat in the cab with him all night. He leaned over the middle console and tilted her face to his with a single finger on her chin.

"Are you sure you're okay?" His voice was low with a hint of his sizzling anger, his mouth so close, goose bumps rose along her arms at the soft touch of his breath. His heat radiated into her, arousing and comforting at the same time.

For the first time in a long time, she wanted to share her troubles, but ingrained habits had her saying too brightly, "Of course, everything's fine."

"I don't believe you."

How could he see the truth hidden behind her uncomfortable smile? She dropped the pretense. The pressure inside of her needed an outlet, but pouring her heart out to Nash wasn't an acceptable release.

She was the first to move, pulling away and hopping out. The night was anything but quiet. The call of cicadas crested and ebbed like ocean waves, bullfrogs called for mates, and the delicate sounds of crickets played above it all. A soft glow shone at the edge of the treetops where the moon was peeking over.

"What do you think? Are you excited?" Her gaze cast upward toward the top of the water tower. Even though this was one of the smallest towers, standing underneath and looking up invoked a wash of vertigo.

"I'm worried I might be insane."

"The one I climbed in high school was even higher."

"Was it fun or scary?"

"Both. Sometimes the best things are, you know."

"Is that why you did it? To have fun?" He sounded like he thought she was the insane one now.

Why had she done it? Someone had dared her to. A boy with stringy dyed-black hair and pierced ears. Once the idea had been planted, making the climb became more than fulfilling her end of a dare. It had been an act of defiance.

"I did it more out of anger than fun. A way to prove my existence." The night sounds seemed to swallow her voice.

With the cacophony of noise around them, she wasn't even sure he'd heard her. The meager light reflected off his glasses, leaving his expression a mystery. "Why are you climbing one tonight?"

To be with you. The answer was scarily simple or maybe plain scary. But she offered a different reason. "Because you dared me. Are you ready to have an adventure with me?"

His smile cast its own gravitational pull. Her problems and responsibilities faded in importance.

The ladder to the top was open for about fifteen feet, then a latticed metal half circle surrounded the back for safety purposes. She took a deep breath and put her foot on the first rung. Her hands slipped over rough, rust-pocked metal.

"Good Lord, we're actually doing this, aren't we?" he asked.

She tossed a smile over her shoulder. "Come on, this is for your list." The chicken sounds she made had him stepping forward.

"I'm overriding my strong sense of self-preservation, but lead on." He tapped her shoulder and handed her a small penlight.

She flicked it on, held it between her teeth and climbed, looking down every few rungs to make sure he was following. She breached the top onto a rectangular landing about six feet long and four feet wide. It seemed newer, the metal smooth and untarnished. She bounced a couple of times, and everything felt secure.

He climbed up beside her, the space forcing their bodies close. Her shoulder brushed his arm, their hands only inches apart on the rail. Minutes passed. While she gazed over the treetops toward Cottonbloom, her other senses were focused on him.

The slight movement of his body as he breathed in and out, the heat that passed between them, sparking a warmth deep inside of her, the scent of his woodsy cologne, subtle enough to make her want to bury her face in his neck.

She flashed back to watching a shirtless Nash jump rope, graceful and agile. Her attempt to hide her wide-eyed stares had resulted in pristinely clean equipment. The second time she was confronted with his bare chest had been as startling as the first. Her stumble had been innocent enough, but touching his damp, hard pec was her downfall. She couldn't stop thinking about running both hands up and down the muscles. And lower.

Colors burst over the trees, the bangs reverberating a few heartbeats later. She climbed onto the lowest rail and raised her arms, calling to the night sky, the sense of freedom exhilarating.

He wrapped an anchoring arm around her thighs and laughed. "You really are wild."

The show lasted less than fifteen minutes, the finale a short continuous burst of color and sound.

"From up here you can't tell where Louisiana ends and Mississippi begins, can you?" His voice rumbled in the still aftermath.

The trees spread as far as she could see, but the river was down there somewhere, twisting and flowing. A protectiveness surged through her. "Did you tell people about our little town and have a good laugh?"

"I didn't talk about home much."

"Why not?" She hopped off the rail and propped her hip against it.

"Once I left, it was like stepping out of a fairytale.

Talking about home, analyzing my childhood would have destroyed it somehow."

How could he look back at his mother dying, the loneliness he'd experienced, the bullying at school with nostalgia? "What fairytale were you living in? Because my life was closer to a tragedy or maybe a horror movie."

He faced her and tucked a piece of hair behind her ear, trailing his fingertips down her neck in the lightest of caresses. Tingles followed in their wake.

"Most of the fairytales passed through the ages were depressing and bloodthirsty. A way to warn against immorality. But the best had an element of magic. That's what Cottonbloom has as well. Can't you feel it?"

"A dark magic maybe." She wished she could take his glasses off and search his eyes for answers to questions she would leave unspoken. How could they resurrect a friendship that she'd thought had died years ago? Was the sparking attraction between them part of Cottonbloom's dark magic that would end in tragedy and tears?

He broke first, shrugging off the backpack, setting it on the platform, and unzipping it. A blanket emerged first, and he covered the metal-latticed floor. He sat, his legs dangling over, and patted the spot next to him. She joined him, a smile ghosting over her lips.

Next came a bottle of wine and two red Solo cups. It was when he pulled out a fancy corkscrew that humor gained the upper hand over the mishmash of emotions tumbling in her chest. She had smiled and laughed more with Nash over the course of two days than over the past year. Her cheeks were sore from it.

"You have got to be kidding me. If we were really in high school, you'd bring a flask of Jack you siphoned off your dad, not wine."

"We don't have to reproduce the experience with complete accuracy. Anyway, I'd pick a nice single-malt

Scotch if I were going that route. I thought you might prefer something milder." The cork came out with a pop, and he poured them each a glass.

She took the cup and swirled the red wine around. "I'm not much of a drinker period, and certainly not a wine aficionado. Is this something you picked up along with hot tea?"

"Yep. I started for the most pretentious of reasons. To impress a woman."

"What happened?"

"The woman didn't stick, but my appreciation of wine did."

She pulled at a loose string on the blanket to cover her discomfiture at the thought of Nash with another woman and took a too-large gulp. She choked off a cough. The wine was woodsy and rich, meant to be sipped and not guzzled like a bottle of Boone's Farm.

"Did she break your heart?" The question strangled out of her throat.

"Bruised it. She was older, more sophisticated. The relationship took on shades of *Pygmalion,* with me playing the part of Eliza Doolittle." He smothered a husky laugh. "I learned a lot from her though."

She wasn't sure if she was imagining the sexual undertones in his admission or not. Pygmalion sounded like pig latin, but the name Eliza triggered a memory. "You mean *My Fair Lady*?"

"That was the movie version of the book."

Why did it always come back to books with him? How could she expect to hold his interest when her favorite show was *The Bachelor* and his was probably Discovery Channel documentaries? She took another sip. "What's your favorite TV show? Be honest."

"Come on, seriously? That show about the Green Arrow, of course."

Laughter sputtered out of her. Maybe he hadn't changed so much after all.

"What's *your* favorite show?" His question cut her laughter off like closing a water spicket.

"Discovery Channel documentaries?"

His side-eye glance said more than words. She hid her smile in the rim of the cup, pretending to take a sip. "Fine. If you must know, it's *The Bachelor*."

The humiliated sting of her confession was worth it when his laughter rolled through her. "I've never seen it, but I've heard of it. Why do you like it?"

"I suppose it makes me feel better about my choice in boyfriends. Heath doesn't look so bad compared to some of those losers, and I don't look so pathetic." She was aiming for a joke, but his smile reversed itself and he stared at her for a moment.

"You deserve way better than him, Tally. Have you looked in the mirror lately?"

"My looks aren't the problem." She fiddled with the ends of her hair. While she might not be the male ideal splashed across swimsuit magazines, she was in good shape and never had a problem attracting a certain sort of man.

"Then what is?"

She shrugged. The childlike motion was foolish and evasive. Nash deserved more. More than her. "I squeaked through high school."

"So you keep saying, but lots of people aren't cut out for college. Seems to me you've done extremely well."

She had. She told herself that all the time. "You're right. I'm doing fine. Hey, can I have some more? What's so special about this wine?"

Her tactic was probably as transparent as Saran Wrap, yet he went along, detailing the wine's pedigree as if it were a prize pureblood hound. While she had initially been feigning interest, his enthusiasm poured into her, and she found herself asking questions.

"I'll bet kids line up to get into your classes."

He dangled his hands over the lowest rail, letting the cup swing in his fingers. "Sorry, I tend to ramble on when something interests me."

"No, I was being serious. Your passion is infectious, and you're incredibly eloquent. I guess that comes from all the reading you do."

His smile was as infectious as his enthusiasm for wines and just as intoxicating. Her heart picked up its pace, a mild buzz from the wine drowning out her nerves. She needed to loosen up. Have fun. Who knew how long this thing between them would last?

"We didn't make it down to grab some of Rufus's barbeque. Are you hungry?" he asked.

"You brought food too?"

"Simple crackers and cheese."

"Sounds perfect." And it did.

She faced him cross-legged while he arranged a circle of Brie and crackers on a paper plate. He scooped a chunk on a cracker and held it out to her. Her breath caught in her throat as she opened her mouth and took his offering. The rich soft cheese exploded in her senses. She took a sip of wine, the flavors mixing in perfect harmony. Everything seemed focused and sharper.

Once they'd polished off the cheese and wine, he pulled a can of spray paint out of the backpack, stood, and brushed crumbs off his lap. "It's time to get down to business. What should I write?"

She joined him, the volume of her low buzz increasing. "Nothing too high-falutin'."

"High-falutin'?" His laugh echoed around them. "You're funny."

"I love your laugh."

He froze midshake, his laughter withering. She covered her mouth, shocked into stillness. Why had she said that? It was true, but he didn't need to know how she felt. Darn Nash and his delicious wine.

"You always were sweet," he said softly.

"I'm not anymore. I'm bitter and sour."

"Why do you think that?"

"I never learned to make lemonade, I guess." A breeze swirled around them and moved him closer. Even though they weren't that high up, the air felt cooler, thinner.

"There's one thing on my list I haven't told you about." The tease in his voice had been roughened away.

"How am I going to help if you don't tell me?" She couldn't stop staring at his mouth, and dabbed her tongue along her lower lip.

"I wasn't sure if you'd be willing to help me cross it off."

"Is it dangerous?"

"Could be. Might start a fire even." He removed his glasses and tucked them into a pocket of his shorts.

The moon had risen and his brown eyes seemed to reflect back the meager light.

"I want to kiss you." The words fell between them like it was a done deal, yet he moved more like a predator, slowly, cautiously, giving her a fighting chance at escape. "Not a peck on the cheek like when we were eight, but an honest-to-goodness, grown-up, man-woman kiss. Does that freak you out?"

It totally did. Not because she was disgusted or creeped out. The opposite. The compulsion to kiss him at the river had almost overtaken her. But this was Nash. *Her* Nash. Her stomach spiraled in a slow arc of nerves and anticipation.

Whenever she was nervous about something, like the school spelling bee, Nash had made her list the worst,

most outrageous things that could go wrong. She reverted
to old habits, the questions popping out in a rush of words.
"What if you start thinking about Charlemagne to keep
from being bored? What if you're totally grossed out?
What if you can't look at me the same way? What if we
can never be friends again?"

She had backed into the tower, and he braced his
hands on either side of her head. "I can guarantee I won't
be disgusted or bored. I've been thinking about kissing
you since that first night at the Rivershack Tavern. Maybe
you'll hate me slobbering all over you."

"Maybe," she whispered, even knowing it was a lie.
Every part of her was drawn to him like filings to a mag-
net. Good sense kept her from confessing her biggest
fear.

What if she didn't want him to stop at a kiss?

"Listen, this is just an item on my list. One kiss. If the
kiss is weird and either one of us doesn't like it, let's agree
that it won't affect our friendship. We'll keep hanging
out."

"What if we do like it?" The possibility threw open
a door she wasn't sure she wanted to slam shut or run
through.

"Well, then. I might have a lengthy addendum to my
original list." He cocked his head. "What'd you say we
do something really crazy?"

Unlike at the river, the narrow platform offered no escape, and she was glad. She didn't want to escape, even
as the most vulnerable parts of her screamed at her to
run. While she was perfectly willing to risk life and limb
and trouble with the law, the risk Nash posed to her heart
was too great to contemplate. But this was only a kiss—
how dangerous could it really be?

"Okay." The word came out as soft as a breath.

He wrapped an arm around her waist and pulled her

into his body. She didn't fight the compulsion this time, but reached for him, one hand threading into the hair at the back of his head, the other grasping at the shifting muscles across his shoulder.

Maybe the wine had lowered her natural inhibitions, but the reality was she'd wanted this since the moment he'd walked into the bar too. The possible fallout didn't matter—nothing mattered—when his lips touched hers.

The passion that exploded caught her off guard. He tugged her bottom lip into his mouth, skimming his tongue along the sensitive flesh before nipping it lightly. Something thumped to the platform, followed by a clang and a thud. The entire platform could fall and she wouldn't have noticed until impact.

He cupped her face with both hands and forced her fully against the slight curve of the tower. The metal had retained a portion of the sun's heat and stoked the sparking fire inside of her body. He pressed into her, lifting and fitting them together until she was on her toes.

Her mouth parted in invitation, and he accepted, curling his tongue around hers. A whimpery moan escaped her throat. She didn't have a chance to be embarrassed. An answering rumbly growl vibrated his chest and ratcheted up their kiss to inferno levels.

His hair slipped through her fingers, soft and springy. She sought bare skin and snaked her other hand up the bottom of his shirt to caress back muscles she'd admired in the gym. He felt even better than she'd imagined—smooth and hard and strong.

She wanted his hands all over her. She wanted him to bend her over the rail and take her from behind. She wanted to re-create the scene from their morning together but this time stay to take him in her mouth. She wanted to lie back and stare into the treetops while he drove her wild. She wanted all the naughty, dirty things she'd dreamed about. And more.

His erection settled against her hipbone, and she squirmed. In contrast to the biting passion of his lips, he caressed her face and massaged her scalp and neck with gentle fingers. He slid his lips along her cheek to tug her earlobe between his teeth. Her head lolled, offering him her throat. He skimmed his lips down her skin, stopping to nip at her pulse, his stubble offering its own caress.

All she could see were stars. They seemed closer and denser than ever before. Too many cold, hungry nights had taught her a special kind of practicality, but in that moment, she believed in his magic.

"Nash, please." Her voice was unrecognizable.

"Please, what?" His lips moved against her throat, his chest vibrating against her breasts.

She knew exactly what she wanted. Screw checking a box on his list. "Kiss me again."

He did, this time grabbing her wrists and forcing her hands above her head. The position pressed his chest into hers and should have made her feel dominated, yet the gentleness of his mouth against hers was a revelation. The inferno had banked into a long-lasting blaze.

Sometimes a kiss felt like the obligatory prelude to sex. Not this kiss. This kiss went on and on, each second liquefying her body a little further. She wanted more, and at the same time, never wanted the kiss to end.

Finally, yet too soon, he pulled away. Like waking from a spell, she opened her eyes. He rubbed his nose against hers, the tenderness of the moment as potent as the passion had been.

"How was that?" His voice was light, and his lips curled up. She bobbed her head forward to kiss him once more, a simple brush of her mouth against his. He let go of her wrists, and she grabbed onto his biceps. They flexed under her touch.

"Not bad, Professor." Her voice trembled. Could he guess how affected she was by a simple kiss? It hadn't felt simple. She searched for a way to regain her footing. "Have you decided what you're going to paint?"

Peeling himself off her, he harrumphed. He pulled his glasses out of his side pocket, slipped them on, and looked over the rail. "You got me all distracted, and I dropped the can."

A wave of happiness coursed through her. He wasn't as unaffected as he sounded. She pushed off the steel tank and joined him at the rail, her knees shaky. Had a kiss ever made her knees weak? She had assumed that was reserved for fairytale heroines.

"We could climb down and back up."

"Nah." His smile lit him from the inside out as he shuffled a hand through his hair. "We got close enough. Anyway, after tonight, I need to draft that addendum. I have the feeling we won't make it back around to climbing water towers."

A half-moon had risen over the trees, and she stared into the distance. "Will our kiss change anything?"

Chapter Nine

Their kiss changed everything.

His new list would include kissing her lips along with a subset of every body part he could name and a few he couldn't. He'd have to pull out his *Gray's Anatomy* book for a complete breakdown. Once he got past kissing her, there were about a hundred other things he wanted to do to her—with her. The amount of self-control he'd exerted over his body had been worthy of a medal. Forget the Purple Heart. Was there one for blue balls?

He wouldn't even pretend he hadn't thought about her as a kissable woman since he'd moved back. It's why he'd gone to the Rivershack Tavern, after all. Not to have sex with her, but to get to know her, discover if the girl he remembered lurked in the woman. She was there, but he was finding the tough, capable woman she'd grown into to be even more fascinating.

In his arms though, she'd seemed vulnerable and a little uncertain. The combination had flashed warnings somewhere in the recess of his brain not focused between his legs. He would need to go slow. Woo her.

"It was a simple kiss." His white lie was for her benefit. What they'd shared hadn't been simple. Not for him, and not for her either. He'd felt her trembles, sensed the same desperation he'd wrestled, but he didn't want her avoiding him because she was uncomfortable or fearful at the intensity of his feelings. However, he wasn't above using the pretense of this list to spend more time with her.

They stood side by side. The silence was heavy and serious in contrast to their earlier teasing. A blanket of stars surrounded them, the moon providing slivers of soft light.

"I love Louisiana nights. It's been a long time since I've taken the time to be still and look up at the stars." Her voice treaded softly between them. "There's this clearing out by Uncle Del's. On clear nights, I would go lie in the middle. All I saw were tree-framed stars. So many stars, yet each one was a little different. They made me feel big and small, unimportant and unique. I guess that sounds silly."

"Not at all. For centuries people have looked to the stars for answers." He cleared his throat, cursing his distant, scholarly tone. Being a professor and getting lost in his books made him feel comfortable. It was the real world that intimidated him. "Some nights, when my mother couldn't sleep because of the pain, I'd sleep outside. I'd stare into the sky and wish I could fly to another planet where I'd be special—you know like Superman."

Her hand slipped over his. He loosened his clutch around the rail, not feeling the bite of metal into his palm until she'd touched him. "I understand."

From someone else, it might have sounded like a platitude, but from her, the two words resonated in his chest as truth. "I wish I had spent more time with her at the end. Listened more, asked more questions. I see pictures and remember her, but I didn't really know her. I should have tried harder."

"You were ten years old, Nash. Death should have been an abstract concept. You were confronted with it daily."

A confession he'd never spoken aloud, could hardly admit to himself clawed out of him. "Part of me was relieved when she died."

He dropped his face into his shoulder, away from her. The decades-old shame roiled to the surface as if it had been yesterday. His lungs squeezed, refused to process the air he sucked in through his mouth. From far away, he heard her voice, but couldn't distinguish the words through the buzz in his ears. He dropped to his knees and pulled the backpack toward him. He'd been through the routine enough not to panic. He wasn't in danger of dying. His attacks weren't that severe.

He fumbled in the side pocket and took a pump from his inhaler. The bands around his chest fell away, but his heart still knocked against his ribcage like he'd been jumping rope. She'd joined him on her knees, her hands held out as if she was scared to touch him but wanted to. Her eyes were huge and fathomless.

"I'm all right." He sounded bereft of air.

"You scared me." Now she did touch him. She grabbed onto his arms and pulled him into a hug, both of them on their knees. One of her hands dropped to his chest, covering his heart. "Could you have died if you hadn't had your inhaler? What if you'd dropped it?"

"I wouldn't have died. Maybe passed out. Probably would have been awkward to call 911 considering we're up here illegally." His voice was jokey, but she didn't respond in kind.

"We should go." Her voice was soft but firm and slightly chilled. "You need to rest."

Had his reprehensible confession repulsed her? What kind of person felt relief when someone died—especially a parent? Deciding some things were better dealt with alone and in his nightmares, he shoved any evidence they'd been there into the backpack.

After a brief argument about who would go first, he led the way down the ladder. If she fell, he would catch her. The attack had been relatively mild, and he was fully recovered. Her over-solicitous tone and manner rankled. It reminded him too much of Aunt Leora's coddling during his childhood.

Back in the Defender, they didn't talk, the rumble of the engine filling the silence. He swung the truck around in a U-turn and headed back to the main road. With the break in the trees signaling the road was ahead, a set of headlights cut into the cab, making him squint.

The track was only wide enough for one vehicle, so they were stuck playing chicken until the two vehicles closed the distance to six feet. The red and blue lights on top of the car flashed once, but no siren sounded. Nash cut his headlights off and rolled down his window, but kept the engine running. An officer got out of the car and adjusted his gun belt.

"You know him?" Nash asked Tally.

"Wayne Berry, the sheriff. Decent guy in normal circumstances."

The officer kept them pinned with his headlights and flipped on a Mag flashlight on his walk to Tally's side of the truck. He shined it into the cab, blinding Nash like the flash of a camera, before directing the circle of light to the ground. He knocked on the window and Tally lowered it.

"Well, now. If this isn't the darnedest truck I've ever seen. And, Tally Fournette. Who's your friend, here?" Wayne looked to be fortysomething and even though his voice was stern, Nash could tell the man was more used to smiling than not.

"Nash Hawthorne." Nash held out his hand, his arm brushing across Tally's breasts. Wayne transferred the flashlight to his left hand and reached in for a firm shake.

"You Ms. Leora's boy?" The man's gaze was curious but not suspicious.

"Her nephew, yes. I'm teaching up at the college come fall."

"I was expecting to find some teenagers out here setting off fireworks or defacing property. Don't tell me you've been up to no good."

"Depends on what you consider no good, Wayne."

"Painting the water tower? Don't you think you're a little old for that?"

She laid a hand on Nash's thigh. His muscle jerked, and she squeezed, her fingernails biting.

"Nash and I were . . . well, you know how it is." Tally's drawl was sugared.

"Yes, ma'am." Wayne cleared his throat, looking as if he wanted to teleport back to the station. "You'll need to find somewhere else to . . . This is parish land, you understand. Technically you're trespassing."

"We were headed home. You can drive on down to check that nothing was disturbed." She leaned against Nash, her hand inching up the inner seam of his shorts. "Can't you let us head on and pretend you never saw us? No one knows Nash and I are . . . you know."

Wayne bobbed his head, his Adam's apple bobbing. "Sure thing, Tally. But stay off parish land, you hear?"

"Will do. Thanks, Wayne." She called out as the officer retreated to his patrol car and backed up the track.

Nash swiveled toward her, putting their faces only a few inches apart over the narrow console. She'd only said all of that to get them out of a mess. One kiss—albeit a very long, seductive, mind-numbing one—did not mean they were actually dating. No matter what she'd told Heath and now Wayne.

The sight of her tongue darting along her lower lip made him want to make it two long kisses. He couldn't seem to tear his gaze away from her mouth. Her white teeth pulled at her upper lip, letting it go slowly as if she were tormenting him on purpose.

The mouth moved, her words knitting themselves together in his disheveled mind. "Wayne'll wait out at the main road. We'd better get on."

He cleared his throat, gathering himself before shifting into drive and flipping his headlights back on. She was right. A police car sat on the shoulder of the road and gave them a toot. He gave Wayne a wave out his window and got them headed back to town. The road was deserted. She didn't settle back into her seat. Her hand stayed on his leg, her head against his shoulder.

He snaked his arm around her, and she tucked herself under his chin as if it was the most natural thing in the world. Keeping his eyes on the road, he dropped his face enough to feel her hair against his lips and smell the wildflower scent of her shampoo.

The miles passed too fast even though he puttered along like his aunt. Both sides of town were deserted. A few pieces of litter and the flatbed truck remained as evidence of the festivities. He pulled up behind her car, not sure what his play should be. She didn't move from his side, but splayed a hand over his chest.

"Relief that someone is out of pain or even relief that your life doesn't revolve around someone else's sickness isn't anything to feel guilty about, Nash. It's natural. Especially for a ten-year-old kid. It's okay to let that go now." She rubbed circles over his heart.

His shame melted. It didn't disappear exactly, but

receiving Tally's absolution had changed its form into something more manageable, something that didn't dominate. He couldn't say whether it was her words or the warmth in her voice, or maybe just her. He closed his eyes and leaned his head back.

She brushed a kiss against his cheek, scooted to the door, and hopped down before he could move. He swung out, calling over the roof of the cab. "Tallulah—"

"I'll see you later, Professor. You come on by the gym soon, if you want, and we can talk about the rest of your list."

He prayed he wasn't imagining the flirty tease in her voice. She was in her car and out of sight before he could reply. He slid back in the truck and headed in the opposite direction to his little cottage. Unspent arousal, the disintegration of a decade-old guilt, and a letdown feeling at how abruptly the evening had ended made for an uncomfortable mix.

Tomorrow he'd promised Regan he'd work on the gazebo. She wanted it ready well ahead of the festival, which was under two months away. While he'd grumbled about Regan calling in an old debt, he didn't really mind helping out. It kept him from moldering away with his books. The gazebo would be simple compared to the architecture of medieval Europe.

He approached the gingerbread guesthouse and suppressed a shudder. Thank goodness this was a temporary stop. Whenever he'd pictured his future, the river was the only constant. He wanted to be able to see it, hear it, touch it.

His long-term plans included a cabin on the river, preferably the Louisiana side. His aunt didn't understand his fascination with the river, but every morning, she handed over the paper already opened to the real estate listings.

He went through his usual routine before slipping between the sheets naked and grabbing a book. Words had always brought him comfort. The characters seemed more real to him than the people around him sometimes, and growing up, they'd been his only friends. But, tonight, he couldn't concentrate.

What was Tally doing? Was she in bed thinking about him? Damn, he hoped so. He slapped the book shut and turned out the light. What should they tackle next on the list? Skinny-dipping? He imagined water sliding over her bare skin and his hand following in its path. Getting her naked seemed presumptuous and not part of his slow-woo plan. He should take her to dinner first. Dinner and dancing and *then* skinny-dipping.

The truth was he would be happy sitting on the end of a dock with their feet in the water doing nothing as long as he was with her. The acknowledgment of how far gone he was settled his restlessness. It wasn't that the knowledge didn't scare him. It did. But it also felt inevitable. The feeling was something he'd carried with him since before he could remember. He was meant to love Tallulah Fournette.

The next morning he backed his truck up to the blackened ground surrounding the charred remains of the last gazebo and the frame of the new one. His truck bed was full of two-by-fours and assorted tools. Studying a copy of the design, he figured he could finish the bottom and the bench seats on his own, but would need an extra set of hands with the roof.

The humidity made it difficult to take deep breaths. A solid two hours of work yielded a half-complete octagonal floor. He took a glance around. A Sunday morning meant the shops were closed and most people were at church. Grabbing the hem of his T-shirt, he pulled it over his head and tossed it aside. Sweat dried in the slight breeze, cooling him. He got back to work, kneeling on the flooring with a nail gun.

A knocking sound had him looking up. Tally leaned against one of the support posts, holding two cans of Coke. She was in workout gear, a tank top, shorts, and tennis shoes, her hair in a sweeping, high ponytail.

"Need a break?"

He put down the nail gun, pushed safety glasses to the top of his head, and stood, his back popping. "You must be psychic."

He took a sweating can and held it to his forehead before popping the tab. Half was gone before he came up for air, the cold burn like heaven.

"Here, take this one too. You need it more than I do." She held out the second can. He took it and sat on part of the finished flooring in the shadow cast by his truck, his feet over the edge. She joined him, drawing circles in the dirt with the toe of her shoe.

"I thought the gym didn't open until this afternoon?" He squinted up at the sky where the sun was almost directly overhead.

"It's almost noon, and I needed to work up costs for this thing Sawyer wants me to do for the festival." She sounded strange, and he tried to catch her expression, but all her concentration seemed focused on the movement of her foot in the dirt. Maybe their kiss had changed things—and not for the better.

"Are you okay?" He touched her arm.

"I'm totally and completely fine. Seriously. No problem." She drew out the word 'no,' popped up, and backed away from him. "I saw you and you looked . . . hot." Her gaze dropped to his chest and stuck there.

She was checking him out—again. Relief and a stab

of arousal quickened his heart. Maybe he *should* move straight to skinny-dipping. "Listen, how about we—"

"Nash! Oh, Nash, where are you?" His aunt Leora's singsong voice wavered over the clearing. Could he hide and pretend he hadn't heard her? He wasn't a kid anymore.

He stepped from behind the shadow of his truck. "Over here."

His aunt approached in the same low-heeled pumps she always wore. He wondered if she'd bought them in bulk in the 1980s. Her flowery cotton dress was also a leftover from a bygone era, but nothing beyond burning all her clothes to cinders would get her to shop at one of the trendy boutiques springing up in Cottonbloom. She was holding onto a woman with blonde hair and a red dress, pulling her along by the arm. "Nash, you remember Bailey, don't you? She was in your class at school."

His stomach tightened and performed a series of backflips. It was the same feeling he'd battled every morning before school. He pulled his glasses out of a side pocket of his cargo pants and slipped them on, the two women coming into sharp focus.

Bailey was still pretty in a Miss Mississippi–pageant kind of way, although her excessive makeup seemed to be sliding south in the heat and her skin had an unnatural orangey glow. How could he forget her when she'd haunted his nightmares for months?

"Of course. How have you been, Bailey?" He forced an unaffected smile.

"Just wonderful. Miss Leora has been talking up a storm about you. A professor at the college she said, and working on a book." Her smile never broke form, making her look like a ventriloquist's dummy.

"The church is having their annual summer picnic

Saturday." His aunt stared at him. He knew exactly what she was up to. In addition to waving the real estate section in his face, she had taken to introducing him to eligible women from her church at every opportunity.

"That sounds hot, but fun, I'm sure."

"Bailey is known for her potato salad," his aunt said.

Everyone stood in silent anticipation while another cryptic look was aimed at him from his aunt as if "potato salad" was code for something else entirely. Nash wasn't interested in her potato salad or anything else she had to offer.

He turned toward Tally hoping her inclusion might divert the direction of the conversation when his aunt said, "I thought you and Bailey could go to the picnic together."

He turned back, his mouth opening but nothing coming out. As soon as he got his aunt alone, they were having a serious talk. Bailey's smile gained a few more watts.

He sidled backward, put his arm around Tally, and hauled her into his side. "Sorry, Aunt Leora, but Tally and I were just now making plans for Saturday. Bailey, are you and Tally acquainted?"

The woman's smile faded slightly, but stayed in place as if it was something she practiced on a regular basis. Smiling in the face of disappointment. A burst of satisfaction at turning her down in front of witnesses shocked him.

Tally put on a strained smile. "I'm not sure our paths have ever crossed."

"You teach aerobics at a gym?" Bailey gestured toward her outfit.

"Tally *owns* the gym across the river," Nash said before Tally could answer.

Bailey made a small sound of acknowledgment, as if she were suitably impressed but surprised. Nash had the feeling Bailey knew all about Tally and was playing dumb to gain the advantage.

"You asked me to the prom. Do you recall?" Bailey took a step closer and tilted her head, her manner openly flirtatious.

The humiliating incident had replayed in his head close to a thousand times. He'd obviously been delusional.

"Did I? Times change, don't they?" His dig didn't go unnoticed. The look that flashed over her face made him wonder if this was how the male praying mantis felt right before being devoured.

"You could bring Miss Tallulah to the picnic since you've already made plans together," his aunt said with obvious reluctance.

"Actually, we're doing something else."

"What?" his aunt asked.

"Yes, what?" Tally turned toward him, still under his arm.

"I'm taking Tally dancing up in Jackson."

"You are?" His aunt and Tally spoke on top of each other in almost identical shock.

His aunt patted Bailey's hand. "Well, perhaps you could take Bailey out tomorrow night. She's already said how much she'd like to get to know you now that you're both grown."

In reality, Bailey looked like she wanted to retreat to lick her wounds. He'd torched that bridge. Malicious laughter threatened to erupt. "Sorry, but Tally and I are getting a drink together after she finishes up at the gym tomorrow."

Tally's fingernails dug with a little too much fervor into his skin. Nash and his aunt stared into each other's eyes for a long moment. His aunt surrendered, transferring her attention to Bailey. "Well, perhaps another time then. Could you walk me back up to the Quilting Bee, darling?"

"Of course, Ms. Leora."

His aunt wrapped a hand around Bailey's elbow, and they walked away together, their heads close. His aunt would continue to plant eligible women from her church in his path like landmines. She wasn't one to give up so easily, especially as they had both drawn battle lines.

As soon as the women were out of earshot, Tally moved away from him, running her hands over the back of her shorts.

"Sorry I got you all sweaty," he said. "And sorry I pulled you into that."

"I didn't mind. Turnaround is fair play, considering I told Heath and Wayne we were dating." The corner of her mouth lifted. "I can't believe you asked Bailey out in high school. I used to see her picture in the paper. Homecoming queen, Miss Cottonbloom. You really aimed for the stars there, stud."

"You don't even know. I pumped myself up for weeks. The result of reading too many comics where the nerdy kid ends up getting the girl at the end. And hormones. And maybe simple stupidity." He ran a hand through his hair, his chuckle rueful. "I did more than crash and burn. I exploded. Definitely a top-five most humiliating moment for me."

"Ugh. Why did high school have to be so hard?" Tally leaned against one of the columns in the shade.

He joined her, propping a hand above her head and moving in close to share the shade. "Was it hard because of your grades or the crowd you ran with?"

"Both." She kicked at the dirt, her eyes downcast. "Everyone expected a female version of Sawyer and were highly disappointed when they got me."

"I doubt that's true."

"It's hard to misinterpret things like 'Your brother's so smart, what happened to you?' or 'Why can't you be more like your brother?' Sawyer was good at everything, straight A's, captain of the baseball team. I might have seriously hated him if he wasn't the coolest brother ever." A smile snuck through the childhood pain.

"High school for me was purgatory."

"Yeah, but you got out. Away. You've seen the world." An odd thread of jealousy strung her words together.

"If you hated Cottonbloom so much, why didn't you leave?"

A shiver passed through her in spite of the glaring sun. An excellent question. One she'd asked herself time and again. Sometimes she did resent Cottonbloom. She felt trapped and stuck. Yet, Cottonbloom made her feel safe. It wasn't a feeling she took lightly, not when devastating things could happen in an instant.

"I don't hate Cottonbloom." Her words were defensive but true.

She loved her job, her family, her friends. She loved walking down to Rufus's place and not even having to order because he knew what she wanted. As much as it sometimes hurt, she loved hearing stories about her mama or daddy and how they were good people. If she left, who would she be?

She checked her watch and took a step to the side, thankful she had an excuse to escape. "My class starts in fifteen. I'll see you around, I guess."

"Hold up. I wasn't blowing smoke back there. Let's grab a drink tomorrow night."

"You think your aunt is going to check up on you?"

The sound of his laugh grounded her, eased the

unwelcome self-examination he'd instigated. "I wouldn't put it past her, but that's not why. I want to hang out with you. Is that a problem?"

He grabbed his shirt, but instead of pulling it on, he rubbed it all over his torso. She followed the motion with her eyes wishing she could take it away from him and finish the job herself.

The problem was the man was turning her brain into a mash of inappropriate sexual desires. She'd already had to refrain herself from licking him when he hauled her into his bare side. What would Bailey and his aunt have thought about that?

"Nope. No problem."

"Good. And, Saturday, let's drive up to Jackson. What do you say to that?"

Hanging out during happy hour was one thing. Driving to Jackson for dinner smacked of a real, live date. "Is this about the list? Because I can assure you skipping prom has not kept me up at night filled with regrets."

"I'll have you know, I haven't gotten a good night's sleep since Bailey rejected me." He winked.

A shot of excitement had her shifting on her feet, even though he hadn't answered her question about the list. "You'll take me somewhere nice? Not Church's Chicken?"

He tossed his head back with a full-bellied laugh, and she couldn't take her eyes off the tendons of his throat. Still wearing a grin, he said, "I think I can spring for something a little nicer. Although as I recall, their chicken rocks."

Her lips curled up in a Pavlovian response to his smile. She scuffed the toe of her shoe against the beginnings of a dandelion that had sprung up from the charred grass and glanced up at him through her lashes. "So you're using me to avoid any more matchmaking from your aunt?"

"You wouldn't condemn me to standing around in ninety-degree-plus heat, eating rancid potato salad, and making small talk with every eligible woman in Cottonbloom, would you?" His voice dropped to a husky tease. "Come on now, I thought we were friends."

Were they friends? Certainly, they used to be friends, but the aggression that flooded her at the thought of a bevy of desperate women stalking Nash at the church social was decidedly *unfriendly*. Nash was the Bachelor of Cottonbloom, and she wasn't letting one of those other women win. Not after their kiss.

She nodded, and he rubbed his hands together. "Excellent. We'll have fun."

Fun. If he wanted to take things slow and just have a good time, she could go along with that. In fact, maybe it was better that way. If things never got serious between them, there would be no reason to tell him about her dyslexia.

She attempted a light, flirty tone to match his. "You think it will take the rest of the summer to finish your list?"

"Longer, I hope." The sudden switch from laid-back humor to smoldering intensity made her wonder what he'd added after their kiss. Her stomach squirmed in a not unpleasant way.

"What time are you closing up tomorrow?" he asked.

"Actually, Reed closes up on Mondays. I can be ready by six." She checked her watch. "Good grief, I need to get back. My class starts in five minutes."

"I'll pick you up around six tomorrow night." He lifted her hand and brushed a kiss over the back.

Who did that sort of thing anymore? It should be ridiculous. Somehow Nash pulled it off with charm. Perhaps it was because he was a world traveller while she had barely left the parish limits. When he let go of her hand, she touched the spot still cool from the touch of his lips as if his kiss was a tangible thing.

She backed away, and he propped a shoulder on the column, crossing his arms over his chest. The movement made his biceps pop and emphasized the planes of his chest. She swallowed, knowing she should turn around before she tripped on something and totally humiliated herself.

He had acted the perfect gentleman, and all she could think about was playing hooky and exploring every inch of him on the gazebo floor. That would give the Cotton-bloom Church of Christ congregation something to talk about. Before she backed herself into the river, she turned and jogged to the gym.

What kind of game was he playing with his list? Did she care if it meant they got to spend time together? She didn't. The admission popped into her head in flashing neon. Whether it was two weeks, a month, or until the end of summer, she would go along with his list. It would eventually end and the fun and games would be over. Everything good always came to end.

Chapter Ten

The next evening, Nash knocked, then pushed open the back door of the big house. "Aunt Leora?"

No answer. The occasional hiss of water hitting the hot eye filled the silence. Tea bags sat on the counter next to a pot half full of water boiling on the stove. He turned the heat off and dropped the tea bags in the water to steep.

No sign of his aunt on the ground floor. His heart quickened and he took the steps two at a time calling her name again, this time more forcefully, "Aunt Leora, where are you?"

"In here." Her reedy voice penetrated the closed door to her bedroom.

Treading closer, he rapped twice before trying the handle. The door opened with a squeak. His aunt was sitting on the edge of her bed, tears trickling down her face. Her hair hadn't been shellacked into its usual helmet with hairspray. A red shoebox familiar from his childhood sat on her lap. It was usually stashed high in his aunt's closet. He'd imagined many times what she might be hiding inside but had never had the courage to sneak it down.

"What's wrong? Are you hurt? Do you need a doctor?" Nash squatted down in front of her. A picture slipped from her fingers to lay facedown in the box.

"What? No, I'm fine. Why are you asking?" Her mouth tightened even as her voice still wavered.

"Because you're crying?"

"Am I?" She patted her cheek, startled. "I didn't realize . . ."

Slowly, so as not to spook her, he took the shoebox off of her lap. "Why don't you lie down for a few minutes? I'll finish up the tea and bring you a glass."

"That sounds lovely, Nash. I am feeling a bit peaked."

She lay back and swung her feet onto the bed. Without her pantyhose as camouflage, varicose veins and dark bruises riddled the pale skin of her legs. He backed out of the room, still holding the shoebox, and closed the door.

He stood in the hallway for a long moment, listening but not hearing anything from her room. The contents of the box appeared to be mostly letters and pictures. He would return it to her after her rest. Unsettled, he retreated to the kitchen and laid the box on the table while he finished sugaring and icing the tea.

He poured himself a glass and pulled the shoebox closer. He really shouldn't. It was obviously private. Remnants of his childhood curiosity had him fingering the picture she'd been holding.

On the back, in a masculine hand, was written *Promise to wait for me—D.*

Nash flipped the picture over. Dense jungle framed a man in marine fatigues. His stance was casual, and the way he held his machine gun spoke of familiarity. A cigarette hung from his smiling bottom lip. The picture was black-and-white, but Nash could imagine that the bandanna tied around his forehead was blood red and the drooping vines dark green. The man was handsome and rough-hewn and squinting as if the sun was shining in his eyes. Nash didn't recognize him.

He set the picture aside and pulled out a letter. Creases made some lines illegible as if the letter had been read many times. A glance at the top put the letter writer in Vietnam in late 1965. He didn't read farther, folding the letter and setting it on top of the picture. Had his aunt kept something special from his mother?

He bit his lip. His stomach swirled with the knowledge he was snooping. He couldn't stop himself. Flipping through the remainder of the box revealed more letters from the mysterious D, but no more pictures and nothing about his mother. The letters stopped in 1968 during the middle of the Tet Offensive. Had the man in the picture been killed? Was that why his aunt had remained un-married?

He cast his eyes toward the ceiling. His aunt was crying over a man who'd been gone close to five decades. He swallowed past a lump. He didn't want to be crying over a picture of Tally when he was in his golden years, full of what-ifs. He wanted to hold tight to the real thing.

He put everything back as close as he could to how he found it, fixed his aunt a glass of tea, and trekked back upstairs. Rustling sounded on the other side of her door and his rap was answered immediately.

A fog of hairspray hung in the air, not a hair on her head out of place, and she had put on her hose and shoes. Her eyes flared at the sight of the red shoebox. She snatched it out of his arms and retreated, holding the box close and folding her arms over it.

"Thank you for the tea. You can set it on my night-stand."

He did as she asked. Her eyes followed his every movement as if he were a threat.

"Are you feeling better?"

"I was fine. I *am* fine."

He debated a moment. "I glanced through the box. I'm sorry."

Her arms tightened and crumpled the sides slightly. "Did you read the letters?"

"Of course not. I looked at the picture though. Was that your boyfriend?"

Her jaw worked. "My fiancé."

The truth bounced around his stomach like a rubber ball. "Was he killed?"

"He didn't come back." A wealth of pain was etched across his aunt's face even though her voice stayed even.

"I'm sorry." The trite words seemed inadequate. His aunt had suffered too many losses. How many secrets hid under the layers of the past? It was the question that drove him to major in history, but he'd never thought to uncover secrets so close to home.

"Thank you for the tea, Nash."

He heard the dismissal in her voice, and at one time he would have heeded the silent command. With heavy feet, he approached her and folded her into his arms for a quick squeeze. She smelled of bottled roses and hairspray. Pulling back, he patted her boney shoulder before stuffing his hands into his pockets. The awkward silence that followed made him regret his impulsiveness.

Her hand, cool and soft, brushed his forearm. The touch translated into a wealth of thanks and love. Two things they never discussed.

"Are you still planning on going out with that Fournette girl?" Aunt Leora turned to check her appearance in the mirror, her fingers probing into hair that barely moved.

Nash closed his mouth tight. The walls had been mortared up again in an instant. "If you mean Tally. Then, yes."

Their eyes met in the mirror. "I assume you're only sowing your wild oats on that side of the river."

"You assume incorrectly. I like Tally. If it's up to me, you'll be seeing a lot more of her. And, for Christ's sake, don't push any more women like Bailey in my direction. She is the last woman I would ever date."

"Nash, the Lord's name." His aunt's face scrunched like she'd smelled a fart at communion.

Stifling a sudden spurt of laughter, he said, "Sorry, ma'am. I'm headed now to pick Tally up. What're your plans?"

"Bridge night. A new lady is joining us." She shuffled toward the door and Nash followed.

"I was sorry to hear about Ms. Aster."

"Goodness, she's not dead, just shuffled off to Shady Acres. Why don't they rename that terrible nursing home Out to Pasture?"

This time Nash let his laughter loose. They descended the stairs side by side, his aunt keeping careful hold of the banister and taking the steps one by one. Decisions loomed on the edges of his mind, but for now he waved his aunt off in her minitank before he climbed into the Defender for the drive across the river.

Tally must have been watching for him, because he spied her skipping down the steps in his rearview mirror, his hand still on the door handle. Her outfit was similar to the she'd been wearing when he'd approached her in the Rivershack Tavern. Black T-shirt, dark jeans, and motorcycle boots. Her hair was in a loose braid hanging over her shoulder. She looked tough and sexy as hell.

She hopped into the Defender and clicked the seat belt home. Dark liner smudged her eyes, emphasizing the green. She wore very little other makeup that he could discern, her lips a natural pink. The light flowery scent she stirred through the truck was in contrast to the visual package. Complicated and intense and sweet all wrapped up together.

He wanted to take her back to his place and unwrap her.

"Are we going to sit here all night?" Her brows rose.

"You look nice." The words came out like Tarzan. He cleared his throat. "I mean, I like your . . . shirt."

The only outstanding quality of her shirt was the way the cotton stretched across her breasts and the V-neck hinted at her cleavage.

"Thanks. I like your shirt too." The corners of her mouth twitched and he had the feeling she was making fun of him, but he didn't even care. He smoothed a hand down his green-and-gold plaid button-down shirt that reminded him of Scotland, even as he was grateful to be in Louisiana.

"You smell nice too. Like flowers." How old did he sound? About twelve? He might as well pass her a note asking, *Do you like me? Check Yes or No.*

She moved closer. He stilled, afraid the slightest movement would scare her backward. Her nose brushed his cheek, and she hummed. "You don't smell so bad yourself."

He slipped his hand around her neck, tilted her face to his, and took her mouth. His awkwardness turned into a distant memory as he deepened the kiss, his tongue touching hers. She curled her hand around his wrist, but not to push him away. Instead, it felt like a manacle, binding him to her. He sucked her full bottom lip between his.

A whimpery moan came from her throat. The sexy noise was like striking a match and throwing it into dry tinder. His body's desperation to get closer colored the kiss. Her hand left his wrist to pull at his collar.

He was seconds away from hauling her into his lap

and leaning his seat back. She broke away, laying her forehead against his chin.

"Usually the kiss comes at the end of the date." She sounded breathless and her hand still clutched the collar of his shirt.

Date. Satisfaction spurred his heart even faster. His lungs tightened, and it took two deep breaths to bring them under control. "I guess I'll have to consult my list and pick something to top that kiss later."

She cleared her throat and sat back in the seat. His collar was wrinkled where she'd gripped his shirt like a drowning woman. She'd felt like she was drowning under the sensations. His gentle domination was like nothing she'd ever experienced. It made her feel both cared for and wanting to beg for more.

"Where do you want to go? The Rivershack Tavern?" Her voice sounded too high in her ears.

"How about we head to the Mississippi side? The bar smoke fires up my asthma, and as much as you don't like Regan, she did get a smoking ban passed."

"I never said I didn't like her." Tally picked at her fingernails. He'd see the lie in her eyes.

He grunted what might have been laughter. "You didn't have to say it. What did she do to you?"

"Nothing to me. But she broke Sawyer's heart."

"I always got the impression Sawyer is the one who broke Regan's heart." He pulled into the parking lot of the Corner Pocket and found a spot in the middle of a row of cars and trucks.

"Maybe that's the story she tells, but I saw my brother after it all went down. We were worried he might drop out of college. The woman is a selfish snake." Her brother's golden-boy confidence had not just been shaken, but smashed into tiny pieces. He'd worked hard to reconstruct a carefree, good-old-boy persona, but sadness lurked where it never had before. Even more telling was the fact her brother hadn't gotten serious with another woman since to her knowledge. He was likely to end up a grizzled bachelor like their uncle Del.

Nash turned the truck off, his expression unusually solemn. "When I got skipped up to her grade in high school, Regan was one of the only girls who talked to me. Her and Monroe. I don't know whether they felt sorry for me, or if Regan felt some compulsion to be nice because her boyfriend was a swamp rat too, but she stuck up for me. Not many did."

The cab grew stifling, and she pushed the door open and swung out. Tally didn't want to think about Regan Lovell as more than the snobby, rich 'Sip who'd destroyed her brother out of spite. The reality of her being nice to Nash ripped at the fabric of her assumptions.

Nash joined her at the corner of the truck bed and took her hand. "You okay?"

"I don't know. It's like in *Star Wars* when Darth Vader is dying and takes off his helmet. You can't help but not hate him as much, right?" Tally shot him a half smile as they walked toward the entrance.

Nash laughed, put his arm around her shoulders, and pulled her into his side. "God, I love a woman who can work *Star Wars* into a serious conversation."

Her footsteps faltered the same time blood rushed to her face. Love? Nash didn't notice her sudden hesitation, stepping ahead to open the door for her. His easy smile stayed in place. Unlike at the Rivershack Tavern, no bouncer sat out front.

Of course, he hadn't meant it like *that*. Like she loved oranges, but she had never felt the urge to kiss one. Suck on one, maybe. Her mind blazed down an inappropriate path. The picture that had been emblazoned on her memory of Nash standing at full attention in his underwear flashed for the billionth time.

She dabbed the back of her hand against her forehead, trying in vain to dissipate the heat coursing through her. Until he'd kissed her, he'd been off-limits. Now, her body had called open season on history professors.

He didn't help matters, being all gentlemanly, smelling so intoxicating, and looking downright sexy. Guiding her with a hand on her lower back, he called out greetings to a few people along the way, some college-age kids and some older adults. Instead of country music, the hum of alternative rock provided background noise.

Nash dropped his lips close to her ear. "What'll it be to drink?"

"A beer is fine."

"You mind what kind?" His brows raised.

"Whatever you're having." Somehow she doubted this place had her go-to Coors Light on tap. While Nash talked to the bartender, she studied the room. The crowd was an eclectic mix of ages, and although she didn't notice the factory blues that dominated the Rivershack Tavern at happy hour, her requisite uniform of T-shirt, jeans, and motorcycle boots didn't seem out of place.

"You play?" He held up a set of darts.

She scoffed and held out her hand for her set. "Do I play? Are you prepared to get spanked?"

"Are you?" His voice dropped an octave.

Instead of handing her the darts, he caught her hand in his free one and pulled it up to lay a kiss in her palm. She was the one who was having trouble catching her breath. Apparently, the new dynamic of their relationship included sexual teasing and innuendo. Under her nerves, excitement crackled. She liked the blaze in his eyes and the rumble in his voice.

He transferred three darts to her. She hoped he didn't notice the way her hand trembled. She tightened her grip around the warm metal. They took a bar-height table in front of an open dartboard. A waitress delivered their drinks. Dark beer the color of sassafras lipped the edges, topped with a caramel-colored foam.

He took three big swallows. He closed his eyes, hummed, and licked the foam off his top lip. Tally swallowed air and chuffed.

"Nothing like a fresh pint of Guinness."

"I've never tried it." He motioned toward her glass, and she took a tentative sip. It was rich and thick and foreign-tasting, but good. She took another pull, this one bigger. "It's interesting. I like it."

He smiled and gestured her forward. "Ladies first."

She took her mark at the line and aimed her dart, moving her hand in preparation for release.

"Time to see who's going to get spanked tonight," he added in his let's-get-it-on voice.

The dart wobbled off its mark and embedded into the wall. She whirled, grabbed the front of his shirt, and yanked him close. "You've got to stop doing that." The threat she tried to force past her smile sounded less than intimidating.

"Doing what?"

"Talking like you actually want to spank me."

"You're right." Disappointment loosened her hand on his shirt. A slow smile crinkled his eyes behind his glasses. "Because spanking you is one of the last items on my addendum. There's about a hundred things I'd rather do to you first."

She flattened her hand on his chest. "Nash, be serious."

He covered her hand with his, the thump of his heart providing accompaniment to the music around them. His smile dropped, and his gaze held hers. "I am totally and completely serious. I know you feel it too."

She did feel it. There was no question she wanted to have sex with Nash, even if admitting the fact was completely surreal. But what frightened her was that the draw to him wasn't merely sexual. It wasn't even *mostly* sexual. She enjoyed everything about him. She had fun with him. It didn't matter where they went—the river, a water tower, a bar.

"Nash, I—"

A hand clapped him on the shoulder. They both startled. He turned to greet a man around their age wearing black suit pants, a white button-down, and a loosened tie. They gripped hands and exchanged shoulder bumps.

"Tally, this is Boone. He's over in the math department and my usual adversary at darts."

Tally shot Nash a look. "Didn't realize you were a regular here too." She stuck her hand out and shook Boone's hand. "Nice to meet you."

"Likewise. I hope you're having better luck beating his butt than I do." Boone's drawl was slow and honeyed.

"Considering my first dart went into the wall . . ." She grinned and shrugged.

"I was unfairly distracting you. Go on and try again. This is a warm-up round." Nash settled a hand against the top curve of her backside and nudged her forward.

She shuffled back to the line, but kept her ear attuned to the conversation behind her. College politics. Aiming the darts, she let the last two fly in rapid succession, not hitting the bull's-eye but landing in the inner circle.

Nash clapped, and she gave a fake curtsy. "Not bad, but let me show you how it's done."

He stood at the line, stretched his neck, and rolled his shoulders. Tally stayed close behind him and slid a hand over his butt the instant before the dart left his hand. Its trajectory was short, and it hit the floor a good three feet in front of the board.

His eyes narrowed on her, but he couldn't keep the corners of his lips from twitching. "Glad I didn't bury that dart in a bystander."

"Go on and try again, Professor." She patted his butt and retreated to the table.

While Nash lined up his next shots, Boone's twinkling blue eyes and grin caught her attention. "You and Nash, huh?"

She wasn't sure what Nash wanted to tell his Mississippi friends, so she stayed with a partial truth. "We've known each other since kindergarten. We're old friends."

Boone's grin only widened. "Old friends rarely grab my butt."

Nash turned and gestured toward the board. His last two darts were side by side in the bull's-eye circle. "Warm-up's done. Prepare to lose, Tallulah Fournette."

She threw her darts, concentrating hard, and marked her score on the adjacent chalkboard. Boone picked up the thread of their conversation as soon as she came back to the table.

"You're going to break the hearts of a bunch of ladies at the college."

She stopped with her beer glass half-raised. "What are you talking about?"

"The highlight of my day is watching Nash navigate campus, completely and totally oblivious to the stares of admiring women. My favorite is when one actually works up the courage to approach him."

Nash was preparing to throw his final dart, and she leaned closer. "What does he do?"

"Treats them with the upmost respect and leaves them mightily disappointed." Boone took a long drag on his beer, but his piercing gaze never left her face.

She broke eye contact and took a sip of her beer to cover her discomfiture. Nash rejoined them, and she retreated to take her turn. Nash's booming laughter raised the hairs on her neck. She missed her targets and the rest of the game continued in that vein, leaving her spanked by him—at least figuratively.

Nash dragged over a bar stool for her to perch on as she watched Boone and Nash play a round. Between his turns, Nash returned to her and stood close. She found herself reaching out to touch him at any excuse. A brush of her hands down his arm or adjusting his collar or at his waist. He put his hands on her arms or hips or legs just as often.

A leggy blonde in a dark gray skirt and pink silky shirt walked over. "How's it going, Nash. Boone." When she transferred her attention to Tally, a cool blast of animosity remained, putting Tally on alert. The woman's gaze coasted up and down her body as if assessing an opponent. "Hi, I'm Emma."

"Tally." She raised her chin, but the woman was already heading around the bar table to where Nash stood at the line, preparing to throw. Tally felt dismissed.

Emma stood close to Nash, her breasts pressed into his biceps as she whispered something close to his ear. He laughed and shook his head. Tally enjoyed kickboxing and sparring in her gym, but this was the first time she'd felt the compulsion to actually start a fight by yanking Emma away from Nash by a hank of her perfectly blown-out hair.

Boone muttered something that would have had Nash's aunt Leora clutching her pearls, before draining the rest of his beer. "Tell Nash I'll catch him later."

He stalked off. As soon as he was gone, Emma peeled herself off Nash and stood on the other side of the table from Tally.

"Goodness, I hope I didn't run Boone off?" A hint of an unidentifiable accent sharpened her words, her smile belying the statement.

"He didn't say." Tally shot a look toward Emma.

"Did you two already make introductions?" At Tally's curt nod, Nash continued. "Emma and I work in the history department together. Her area of expertise is twentieth-century America."

"Sounds interesting." It didn't sound at all interesting to her, but no doubt, Nash found the woman endlessly fascinating.

The woman's tight-lipped smile seemed strained. "And what do you do?"

"I own a gym over the river in Louisiana."

"That's nice." Emma shot a side-eye look toward Nash who was as oblivious as Boone described.

"Tally and I grew up together. She's my best friend." He smiled into Tally's eyes.

The words were like a punch in the chest. Happiness and disappointment vied for her attention. They were best friends, even after all the years gone by. Monroe came in a distant second. It had been a long time since someone really got her. He stood there, looking at her with the warmest, kindest eyes she'd ever seen.

That's what they were. Best friends. A frisson of awareness zinged through her. All right, best friends with potentially major benefits. If their kisses hadn't changed things, it had at least modified them. Part of her wanted him to claim her as more than a friend, even a best one. She wanted him to tell this ridiculously leggy blonde professor that she was his girlfriend.

Emma cleared her throat. "I'm going to take off. I've got advisor meetings set up all day tomorrow."

Nash only chucked his chin, never taking his gaze off Tally. "Have a good evening."

"She seems . . . nice." It took a lot for her to squeeze out the lukewarm compliment.

"She's a great lecturer. Whip-smart, if slightly intimidating."

She rolled her eyes and harrumphed. "Are you really that blind?"

"What do you mean?" He adjusted his glasses and shifted a little closer.

"I mean, the woman was on you like white on rice, and poor Boone looked ready to puke. She wants in your pants, and he wants up her skirt. Probably the smartest love triangle in Mississippi." She swiveled back around and drained the last of the beer without taking a breath.

"I think you're misreading the situation."

"O-kay," she drew the word out, suddenly perturbed at him. "You want to give me a lift home?"

She didn't wait for an answer, but led them out of the bar and into the muggy night. He grabbed her upper arm. "Why are you mad?"

"I'm not."

"O-kay," he drew the word out in an exact mimicry of her.

She stomped her foot and jabbed a finger into his chest. "How can you not realize that woman was into you? Her boobs were all over you."

He blinked and his mouth opened and closed. "Are you jealous?"

"Is that where men's egos always lead them?" She threw up her hands and stalked toward the Defender, her boots scuffing the blacktop. The truth was she *was* jealous. Not of that woman's blonde hair or sophistication, but of the common ground she shared so easily with Nash. A ground Tally would never claw herself up to.

He wrapped an arm around her waist from behind as

she reached the passenger door of his truck. "You *are* jealous." His breath whispered over her ear.

"I'm not." She tried to twist out of his grasp, but only managed to turn around, trapping herself between him and the door. Sure the truth was in her eyes, she pressed her face into her shoulder, her gaze on a clump of milk-weed valiantly pushing through a crack in the pavement.

"Emma isn't interested in me. She's only flirting with me to get Boone's attention." His laugh rumbled through her. "I think it backfired on her."

Tally didn't buy what he was selling. What woman in her right mind would overlook what Nash had to offer?

His voice dropped. "Anyway, why are you jealous? You're the one I'm on a date with."

"Is that what it is? I thought we were best friends? Or checking things off your list or something."

He was quiet for a long moment, and she could feel his eyes willing her to meet him halfway. "You really are my best friend, Tally."

She raised her face to find his so close their cheeks brushed. His slight stubble rasped an erotic caress along her lips, and her thighs clenched. "You're my best friend too, Nash." She said it so softly she wasn't even sure he could hear her.

"But there's no reason we can't be even more to each other. The fact we're already friends makes it even easier, doesn't it?"

Did it? She wasn't so sure, but with him so close, she didn't care about the complications. Her lips moved within an inch of his, close enough to feel his breath. This time, *she* instigated the kiss. A whimpering moan escaped when their mouths made contact. Later maybe she'd be embarrassed by the desperate nature of her need, but in the moment, all she could think of was surrounding herself with him.

At her back was the smooth, cool metal of his truck. At her front was the hard heat of his body. His tongue pressed into her mouth. His kiss at the water tower had been gentle and sensual and exploring. His dominating kiss in the truck had been confined to the few square inches of their lips. This kiss was a combination of both, the intensity startling and scary. If it wasn't Nash, she might have pulled away. But she trusted him, and in that trust was her surrender.

She pushed his glasses to the top of his head as his mouth slanted against hers in hot, openmouthed kisses that stole her breath. He circled his hands around her ribcage, an inch shy of her breasts. Her nipples pebbled, and she arched her back, begging for his touch with her soft moans and squirms. He complied and squeezed her breast, hard enough to course shivers between her legs, gentle enough to weaken her knees.

His erection pressed into her hip. She raised on her toes and fit him closer to help alleviate the ache. Her movements only made it worse. She let her head loll back on the truck, stars filling her vision. He trailed his lips down her neck, this teeth nipping at her pulse, the pad of his thumb glancing across her peaked nipple.

A wolf whistle pierced her haze of lust, and embarrassment and fear poured into the rift.

She pushed at his shoulders. He lifted his face, but didn't let her go. "You're freaking out again, aren't you?"

"No." *Yes*, her inner self screamed.

"Look, you knew me as a weak, wimpy kid, but you need to accept me as a grown man. I know it's hard—"

A borderline hysterical giggle shot out of her. She could still feel his very prominent erection against her hip.

"Trust me, I'm not having any problem accepting you

as a very, very grown man. Anyway, you were never a weak or wimpy kid."

"You were never in the boy's bathroom where I was on the receiving end of countless wedgies. My asthma—"

"Stop." She took his face in both her hands. In the dim parking-lot lights, she couldn't see his eyes. "You were the strongest person I ever knew. The way you handled your mama's cancer and afterward. And then instead of turning into a bitter, resentful man, you're funny and optimistic and still the strongest person I know." She wrapped her arms around his shoulders and pressed a kiss against his cheek.

"You always knew exactly what to say," he murmured close to her ear. He drew away, dropped a light kiss on her nose, and reached for the door handle. She slid onto the seat and rubbed her hands down her jeans, off-balance from the evening.

By the time he climbed behind the wheel, she'd located a fake smile. "Where to now?"

Silent, he started the truck before turning in her direction. "I'm going to take you back to your place"—arousal sped through her body like a shot of liquor—"and I'm going to head back to mine, and I'll see you on Saturday." His words were a fire extinguisher, leaving uncertainty to fall like ash.

"I thought maybe . . ." No way could she put her wishes into words.

"I don't want to rush in to anything."

She looked out the side window so he couldn't see the spike of tears. Was he trying to tell her he had doubts?

He pulled into her parking lot, and she had the door open before he even brought the Defender to a stop. "I'll see you on Saturday, I guess."

"Tally—"

She closed the door and ran for the steps to her door. She peeked through her front window. He sat for a long moment, but eventually, he backed up and disappeared. She sighed, not sure if she was relieved or disappointed.

Chapter Eleven

The days until their Saturday night date crept like spilled molasses in January even though it was hot enough to fry eggs on the asphalt. A combination of nerves and anticipation had her watching the clock all day. His sporadic texts during the week checking on her hadn't helped matters.

She left Reed to close up the gym so she could shower. In lace panties and bra, she flipped through the clothes in her closet close to panic. The dress that had seemed perfectly fine the day she had picked it out now screamed "church social" not "fancy dinner." The rest of her wardrobe consisted of jeans and T-shirts.

She grabbed her phone. Monroe answered on the first ring. "What's up? I was going call you later and see if you wanted to watch a movie or something. Your brothers are having a powwow about a gasket."

"I've got a date." Tally hoped her panic didn't transmit over the cell network.

"That's great! At least I think it is. Please tell me you haven't taken Heath back."

"No. Someone else." She was surprised, and not a little grateful, her brother hadn't relayed his suspicions to Monroe. Maybe she'd done a better job than she'd thought at denying her interest.

"Thank God, because if you'd said yes, I would have locked you in a closet until morning. Is it someone I know?"

She hesitated. Actually saying it aloud made her nearly sick from nerves. "Nash."

Monroe's gasp was audible. Tally waited for her to spout something about her shock and how they had nothing in common. "You two are perfect together."

Tally sank down on the corner of her bed, needing both hands to hold the phone steady. "What are you talking about? We couldn't be less alike. He's brilliant and charming and nice. And, I'm . . . well, I'm . . . none of those things."

"For goodness sake, for such a strong, smart woman, your self-confidence is crap. Do you need me to come over there for a pep talk?"

"Maybe so. I also need something to wear. Like a dress or a skirt or maybe a pantsuit. He's taking me to Jackson for dinner. Can I borrow something? Anything?"

"A pantsuit? Unless you want to repel him, I'd go with something he can get his hands under."

"Monroe!" Tally squeaked out her name. "It's a date, not a booty call."

Giggles bubbled across the phone. "I've got something that will look fabulous on you. I'll be over in ten." Monroe disconnected. Tally lay back on the bed and stared at the ceiling fan making lazy, off-kilter circles.

The knock on the door pulled her out of her trance, and she grabbed a T-shirt to pull over her underwear. Out of habit now, she checked the peephole. Blonde hair filled her line of vision. She unlocked the door, and Monroe walked in with a dry-cleaning bag draped over her shoulder and silver strappy heels dangling from her other hand.

She jiggled the shoes on the way to Tally's bedroom. "I hope you're somewhere around a size seven and half. Figured your motorcycle boots would ruin the lines of the dress."

"Close enough. What does the dress look like?"

"I've only worn it once." Monroe stripped off the bag, revealing a beautiful midnight blue dress that appeared to be missing a swath of fabric down the front and back. She waggled her eyebrows. "Your brother certainly liked it."

"Gross. In that case, I'm glad you had it dry-cleaned."

Monroe pushed the dress into her arms. "Go try it on."

Tally retreated to the small bathroom, stripped off the oversized T-shirt, and slipped on the dress. She walked back into the bedroom to examine herself in the mirrored closet doors.

Monroe huffed a laugh. "Lose the bra, girlfriend."

The open V of the dress extended at least three inches past the bottom edge of her bra. "Can't we pin it together?"

"No, we can't. You are in fabulous shape and can totally pull this dress off." Before Tally had a chance to object, Monroe unfastened the clasp, slipped the straps down her arms, and pulled the bra out through an arm-hole, old-school. "There. Gorgeous. I assume you want to leave your hair down."

"Unless you have a better idea." Tally moved her shoulders around and leaned forward, but the cut of the dress ensured a nip-slip wasn't likely.

Monroe tilted her head. "Down is good. I can do your makeup if you want."

"Sure." Tally wasn't sure if her hands were steady enough to apply eyeliner anyway. She sat on the edge of her bed, feeling like a doll. "Don't go overboard. I'm not entering a beauty pageant or anything."

"Close your eyes." Tally followed Monroe's commands automatically. "Maybe not a pageant, but it sure sounded like this date was a big deal when you called. I knew you were friends as kids, but didn't realize you two had a romantic thing going on."

"We don't. I mean, we sort of do, I guess."

Monroe choked off giggles. "Don't make me laugh or I'll mess up your liner. Could you be any more vague? Have you kissed him?"

A few "wells" and "ums" came out of Tally's mouth.

Monroe sniggered again. "I'm taking that for a yes. How was it?"

"The first time—"

"The *first* time?"

This time an answering giggle snuck out of Tally. While she had never been one to pour her heart out to anyone, Monroe had become a good friend the past few years. If things progressed like she thought they might, Monroe would be her sister-in-law before too long.

"Let's just say history isn't the only thing he's studied up on since he left Cottonbloom."

Monroe hummed like she'd eaten something delicious. "Tell me about it. When I saw him walk into church with his aunt at the beginning of the summer I about *died*." She swiped blush over Tally's cheeks and stepped back. "Is that subtle enough for you? I'll let you do your lips."

Tally checked herself in the mirror. At the gym she didn't wear makeup, and when she went out she favored the smudgy, goth look she'd carried with her from high school. Between the dress and the makeup, and with her hair out of its braid, she looked more sophisticated and curvier.

Instead of feeling like Cinderella, though, she felt like Quasimodo outside of his bell tower. Not that she felt ugly exactly, but . . . exposed and vulnerable. As if her motorcycle boots, jeans, and T-shirts were her armor, now stripped away. If she couldn't hide behind her tough exterior, then Nash might see every lurking insecurity.

"You really think Nash and I could work? I mean, he's got a PhD."

"You're putting too much stock in schooling and degrees. Cade didn't even finish high school, but it's never mattered to me. He's brilliant in his own way. And so are you. Why are you so worried?"

Besides her brothers, no one was privy to her struggles with dyslexia. Sawyer had known for years. She used him to proofread her advertisements and flyers, but she'd only told Cade a few weeks ago. Had he told Monroe?

"I don't like to read."

Monroe appeared unfazed by the announcement. She picked a piece of lint off the skirt and adjusted the shoulder straps of the borrowed dress. "So what?"

"You haven't seen his place. Books everywhere. And, he's writing a paper about Charlemagne. A paper I probably won't even be able to make heads or tails of."

"Pretty sure an interest in Charlemagne isn't a requirement to be with him. That would greatly decrease his dating pool. Especially in Cottonbloom." Monroe tilted her head, her blue eyes dancing.

Monroe didn't get it, and she never would. She was smart and possessed a strength belied by her petite frame and Southern belle looks. She was an open book. An internal dark chuckle nearly broke free. Tally broke eye contact, slipped on the strappy heels, and applied lipstick. "He'll be here in fifteen minutes."

Monroe stood behind her, smiling like a proud mama. "I suppose that's my cue to skedaddle like your fairy godmother, although don't be surprised if I'm out hiding in your bushes to get a look at Nash's face when he sees you. You look fabulous."

After Monroe let herself out, Tally stared into her mirror for a few more minutes. If she had anything to change into, anything at all, she would have done it. Instead, she paced in front of her couch, checking the clock every thirty seconds or so.

Promptly at five, someone rapped on her door. She glanced through the peephole, her already skipping heart picking up to a sprint. Of course, he was on time. She rubbed her lips together, took a deep breath, and opened the door.

In a charcoal slacks, a gray button-down with the sleeves rolled up his forearms, and a vest, he looked like he'd stepped from the pages of a European *Vogue*. From behind his back, he produced a bouquet of periwinkle-colored violets. She stared at them in shock. No man had ever bought her flowers. Much less blooms of her favorite color.

"You look amazing." He held out the flowers with a small bow.

You are amazing. She barely stopped the thought from shooting out of her mouth. She took the bundle and dropped her face into the blooms to sniff, covering her sudden burst of emotion.

"Let me put these in water and we can head out." She walked into her kitchen, thankful to be out of the energy field he generated for a moment. Did she even own a vase? She couldn't recall. All of her mama's things were stored at Sawyer's farmhouse. She hadn't had much use for china or linens. A Mason jar was as close as she came.

When she walked out of the kitchen, her step stuttered. The skirt of the dress floated around her, brushing her legs a couple of inches above her knees. His gaze was blatantly sexual and hungry. She felt like a husk of bread thrown to a starving man.

Her legs were shaky, and she had to concentrate on not rolling an ankle in the heels. Or maybe she could fake a fall to get out of the date, but now that he was here in front her, staring at her like that, she wondered what it would feel like to be devoured by him. Would he be gentle or rough or the perfect combination?

She turned her back, set the flowers in the middle of the table and smoothed her skirt down, hoping he couldn't see every lecherous thought that flitted through her head. "Thank you. They're pretty."

"Not as pretty as you are, Tallulah."

Normally, she hated when anyone used her given name, but the way Nash said it imparted an exotic sophistication she could never claim.

"Are you ready?" He crooked his arm, and she hesitated. The gallant action was usually reserved for movies or *Gone with the Wind*–era books. Feeling slightly foolish, she tucked her hand in his elbow, and he covered it with his own.

On their walk to his truck, he kept her from stumbling twice and kept a firm hand on her elbow when she climbed into the passenger seat. As he was walking to the driver's side, she checked the state of her breasts, tugging at the material even though they were both decently covered. If she ever borrowed a dress from Monroe again, she would ask about percentage body coverage.

"Everything okay?" He slid into his seat and started the truck.

"Fine. Great. Looking forward to dinner." Her voice came out too bright and sparkly. Not like her at all. "I'm not used to wearing a dress, if you must know, and this one . . ." She tugged on the top.

His hand covered hers, the very tip of one of his

fingers brushed the fabric over her breast. He probably didn't even feel it, but nerve endings sparked, her nipple hardened, and her back arched. Her lack of control over her body was embarrassing.

"The dress is lovely, and you look sexy as hell in it."

She swallowed and allowed him to take her hand in his as he drove out of her parking lot. "But I—"

"Learn to take a compliment, woman." Any bite in the words was mitigated by the humor in his voice. Silence reined until they were on the north road out of Cotton-bloom.

"Did you ever drive to Jackson for parties?" he asked.

"Went a couple of times."

He side-eyed her. "Didn't enjoy it?"

"I hung out with a partying crowd, but it was mostly all show for me. What about you?"

"I visited with a bunch of history majors. We were more interested in touring the old houses than keggers." He sighed but there was a smile behind it. "Ah . . . the life of a nerd."

"You aren't a nerd anymore," she said.

"And you aren't the poor Louisiana girl who made bad grades." Although he said the words lightly, they hit her with the force of a punch.

"That's not . . . Why do you think that bothers me?"

"You might as well be wearing a sandwich board sign instead of that sinful dress."

She extricated her hand from his and tugged at the fabric once more. Pines flashed by her window. She didn't say anything, didn't know what to say, because he'd hit a bull's-eye.

"Tell me how you started the gym."

As she told him, her awkwardness faded. This, at least, she was comfortable talking about. Enthusiasm crept into her voice and she turned in the seat to face him as she described her journey from high school to the present. "The next phase is an expansion, so I can offer yoga and Pilates. The night of the street party, Mrs. Carson asked me if I had thought about offering classes for seniors. I'm working up some options now. That would open an entirely new demographic. None of the other gyms are focusing on the elderly."

The *Welcome to Jackson* sign flashed, and she realized she'd talked about herself almost the entire way.

"What about staff? You already work insane hours. You'll need another full-time manager. What about Reed?"

"I offered him more hours and a bump in pay a while back. He's got some family issues going on. Plus, he's restless. Now that his knee is better, I get the feeling he wants to fight competitively again before his window of opportunity closes." She chewed the inside of her mouth. Heath had hated Reed. Not because Reed was a jerk, but because he was a good-looking guy who worked closely with her. Heath's jealousy had incited a strange thrill for her at one time, until she realized it was another way of controlling her. "You like Reed?"

"Sure. He's smart and seems responsible." He made a turn onto a busy downtown street. "We've been playing online chess."

"Chess?" The unexpectedness incited a spate of giggles.

"He's good. Beat me several times which—not to toot my own horn—doesn't happen often." Not a hint of jealousy or animosity colored his expression, and she relaxed into the seat.

He pulled up to the curb in front of a restaurant with a French name she couldn't pronounce, much less translate. A valet opened her door and offered his hand, his eyes on her cleavage. She automatically splayed a hand over her chest while Nash handed his keys over.

Nash chuckled, took her hand in his, and guided her inside the dim, cozy restaurant. A parquet dance floor took up a good amount of space, with a grand piano in the corner. Booths lined the walls and white tablecloth–covered tables dotted the rest of the floor. It was what she imagined a bistro in Paris might look like.

"This is really nice." She leaned closer to whisper to him. The faint sound of music overlaid murmured conversations. The atmosphere was hushed like a library or a museum.

The maître-d' led them to a booth with a horseshoe-shaped bench. She scooted inside and he joined her from the other side, their knees touching. A menu made of rich, thick paper lay on top of their salad plates.

Fancy script danced across the page. She didn't recognize a single word. Panic loomed. Heat whooshed through her body, the skin of her forehead prickling. This was worse than any of her high school tests. She squinted at the words, willing them to make sense. Didn't help.

Nash tugged at the menu. She was clamping the sides so tight, the thick paper had wrinkled. "The translation is on the back."

"Translation?" She forced her fingers to loosen. He flipped the menu over.

"Yeah, French into English. Unless you know French?"

Relief poured over her like a cold shower. "I don't." Her relief was short-lived. The translation was written in tiny script as if punishing anyone who dared not know French. She glanced over at Nash. He was running a finger down the French side of the menu. Of course, he could read French.

She sank back into the buttery leather of the booth and pushed the menu away. "Why don't you order for me?"

The candlelight reflected off his lenses, so she couldn't determine the emotion behind the look he shot her. "You sure?"

It was either that or eeny, meeny, miny, mo. "Why not?"

A waiter wearing a stiff-looking tuxedo shirt and black pants returned. He and Nash conversed in French, with Nash pointing at various things on the menu. The waiter nodded, but didn't write anything down before retreating.

"You're fluent in French?" She toyed with the largest of the forks at the side of her plate.

"Had to learn. Most recorded history in the time I'm interested in was done in French. I'm better at reading it than speaking it though."

Of course, he was. Tally bobbled one of the forks, and it landed against the plate with a jarring clank that drew nearby eyes. The same prickling panic heated her body. She slipped her hands under the table and fisted them in her lap.

The waiter returned with a bottle of wine and sloshed a little in Nash's glass. Nash tried it and nodded his approval. Once her glass was full, she grabbed it like a lifeline and took two big swallows. It was smooth and delicious and probably expensive.

"Have you ever sent a bottle back?"

Nash huffed a laugh while he settled back into the booth and slipped an arm over the back, tickling the hair against her neck. "No. But I've seen it happen. When you're paying a hundred dollars for a bottle—"

She choked on a sip, performing a classic spit-take. This time the gazes she drew seemed more disapproving than curious. She shouldn't be allowed to eat anywhere but Rufus's Meat and Three. They served sweet tea and used plastic plates.

"You okay?"

"Fine, fine," she managed to sputter out between coughs. She pointed at the bottle with a castle on the label. "Was that a hundred dollars?"

"Enjoy it."

That was as good as a yes. "Nash. Seriously. You shouldn't."

"Shouldn't what? Try to make tonight special? Try to make you feel special?"

She stared at the wine label not sure how to respond. Part of her wanted to throw herself into his arms while the other part wanted to walk out the door and keep on going. Her compromise was to stay exactly where she was.

The waiter delivered their salads. She picked up the smallest fork—she'd seen enough movies to know which one to go for—and moved the six or so curly lettuce leaves around.

Their talk after that was small, seemingly unimportant, yet nuances of his character emerged with his funny stories of travelling through Europe or dealing with the politics of universities. Her tension cooled from a boil to a simmer.

Their entrées arrived and the waiter slid her plate in front of her with a dramatic flourish. She startled and let out a gasp. A fish eyed her—literally. Her stomach turned. She hated fish.

"I ordered trout for you. If you don't want it, we can switch."

She pressed her lips together. He had a tiny round steak and stack of au gratin potatoes on his plate. Rufus's Meat and Three was looking better and better.

A mature, functioning adult would have sent the plate

back and asked for something different. No telling what Nash was being forced to pay for the food. Apparently, she didn't qualify as mature or functioning.

Fish had been a staple of her diet growing up. Even if his traps stayed empty, Cade always managed to catch a fish to supplement the cans of pork and beans and boxes of mac and cheese from the food bank. Hunger wasn't an abstract concept for her, and she'd been conditioned to eat whatever was put in front of her. But as soon as she'd left the trailer and had money of her own, she stopped eating fish.

She flaked off chunks and forced them down with swallows of wine. Halfway through, her head got swimmy from the alcohol. On the plus side, her buzz made the fish more palatable. She managed to eat everything except its head. She spread the napkin over the carcass like she'd seen policemen do to dead people on TV shows. A giggle snuck out.

"Do you want to try my steak? It's really good." He held out a speared piece on his fork. She covered his hand with hers and guided the fork to her mouth. The meat was so tender and delicious she gave a little moan.

His naughty half smile rearranged her insides and made her feel even more lightheaded. Movement in one corner drew her attention away from him. One man shuffled sheet music on the piano while another settled behind a stand-up bass.

"Are you ready to get your groove on?" Nash's smile widened.

The men launched into the first piece of music. It took a moment to recognize the jazzy version of a Frank Sinatra song.

"Pretty sure Old Blue Eyes wasn't on the DJ's set list for either of our proms."

"True. While I'd love to see you shake it, this will be better." He stood and held out a hand.

Her gaze darted from his hand to the empty dance floor. "No one else is dancing."

"Thought you were wild and reckless. Come on, I dare you."

She rolled her eyes, slapped one hand into his, and scooted out of the booth, adjusting her skirt with the other. It felt like every eyeball in the restaurant was focused on them. Her overindulgence of wine was amplified once she was up and walking. Her ankle rolled over once in the heels, but she corrected herself, only feeling a slight twinge.

Once on the wooden parquet floor, he pulled her close, his chin and cheek smooth against her temple. He skimmed fingertips down the exposed line of her spine leaving a trail of sensation. She closed her eyes to block out the room and tried to relax in his arms, but couldn't. She didn't belong in a world of hundred-dollar bottles of wine and fish served unfried and dancing to live music in a pretentious French restaurant.

Nash was wrong. She wasn't wild. She wasn't brave. She was a coward.

Tally swayed like they were at a middle school dance, her hands on his shoulders, her body stiff. The evening should have been amazing. Special. He'd planned on wooing her back to his bed. As soon as he'd seen her dress, he'd imagined peeling it off her. Instead, an off-key note marred the vibe, but he couldn't quite pinpoint the source to muffle it. Was it his choice of restaurants or the cost of the wine? Was something wrong with him?

After two songs, she pulled back. "I'm getting kind

of tired. It was a long day at the gym. You mind if we head back."

"If that's what you want."

She nodded, slipped out of his arms, and headed toward their booth. She sat on the edge of the seat while he settled the bill.

An awkward silence descended while they waited at the curb for the valet to bring his Defender around. He helped her inside and politely put off the young valet who wanted to ask him questions about the truck.

The town lights faded, leaving the cab lit only by the dim instrument panel. A half-moon rose above the pines and wispy clouds dashed across the sky.

"What's wrong?" He glanced over at her, but she was angled toward the side window, physically and emotionally disengaged from him.

"Nothing."

He might not be a world champion at interpreting women, but when a woman said "nothing" in that vague, distant way, she meant "something is wrong, and I don't want to talk about it" or maybe "you have royally screwed up, and I never want to see you again." Either way, he was in trouble.

He debated. He needed to ease them back into a comfortable, harmonious zone. "So . . . I stumbled on a box of Aunt Leora's letters and pictures the other day from fifty plus years ago."

"Did you read them?" Her head turned toward him, and she shifted her knees over. A start.

"Not exactly. She was crying—"

"Your aunt was crying?" She said it as if he'd informed her he'd seen a pig sprout wings.

He could almost feel the oddness of the last few hours leak out onto the road as they drew closer to Cottonbloom. Even if he didn't understand it, he was thankful their old ease was returning. "She's not a robot. I know she has her prejudices, but deep down she's a good person."

"You're talking *really* deep, right? Like dig-a-hole-to-China deep?"

A hint of tease was back in her voice, and he gave a gusty laugh-sigh. "I didn't pry too far, but there was a picture of a U.S. serviceman on top. Good-looking guy. Vietnam era. I checked one letter, and it seems my aunt and that man were engaged to be married. He signed the letter D. Aunt Leora said he didn't make it back."

"That's terrible." Sadness replaced her earlier tease. "Uncle Delmar served in Vietnam, but he never talks about it."

His hands twitched. Delmar. . . . D. The man in the photograph had awakened a ghost of a memory. His aunt had said the man didn't return. He assumed that meant he'd died, but maybe not. Truth resonated from the bomb Tally had unintentionally dropped.

"What if the D in the letter was your uncle? What if Delmar and Aunt Leora were engaged?"

Her laughter petered out into the silence of the cab. "Are you for real?" She leaned forward. "No freaking way."

"I saw a picture, Tally, and now you've said it . . . I think it might be him. Do you remember your parents saying anything about them being together?"

Her hands were pressed flat on the seat, sending her shoulders to her ears. "Not that I can recall. Mama used to get frustrated with his rambling and lack of stability. I think Daddy was always giving him money, which is the only thing I ever remember them arguing about. Do you think you can get your hands on that picture again?"

"It would involve me violating my aunt's privacy, but probably. Or I could come out and ask her."

"Will she tell you the truth?"

At one time he'd assumed his aunt would never lie to him, but now that he was an adult, he could see his aunt was as fraught with human frailty as the rest of them. It's what drove him to dig past the recorded exploits of historical figures. He'd never failed to uncover events that could be extrapolated to explain their actions years later. It was how history came alive for him.

"I've learned that the more painful the past, the deeper people try to bury it. But there's always a trail. If my aunt denies it, we can look elsewhere."

Silence settled over them for several miles, but it was a different sort of silence this time. Less uncomfortable, more pensive.

"If they were engaged, and my uncle broke it off . . . It would explain a lot, don't you think?" She propped her elbow on the console and looked up at him with her chin on her fist. Her hair swung forward, and he dropped a hand from the steering wheel to play in the loose strands.

"What do you mean?"

"Her animosity toward me. The Fournettes in general, actually."

He muttered a curse. "Makes a strange sort of sense."

She hummed and sat back in the seat. He wanted to wrap his hand in her hair and pull her toward him. He didn't, not sure where he stood with her after the weirdness of the date. She didn't speak again. They hit the Cottonbloom, Mississippi, limits. Street lights flashed by, illuminating her face. Her eyes were closed.

With not a small amount of regret, he drove past the street to his aunt's house and pulled into Tally's lot. He parked and turned toward her, laying his arm over the back of the seat.

She was so beautiful, her pale skin and pink lips pronounced. He twirled a piece of her hair around his finger and stroked across her cheekbone with his thumb. She startled awake, her eyes wide and fixed on him.

"We're home."

She glanced out the window. "This is *my* place."

Confusion had him hesitating. Had he made the wrong call? "You seemed tired."

"I am. And a little buzzed to be honest. Too much expensive wine, I guess." She sent him a tight smile and opened the door.

"Wait a second—"

She hopped out. He followed suit and met her at the bumper.

"Thanks, Nash. This was . . . fun." No mistaking the lukewarm compliment.

He'd screwed up and didn't even know how to fix it. "What are you doing tomorrow?"

"Working tomorrow afternoon."

"Aunt Leora will probably drag me to church, but I'll be out working on the gazebo in the afternoon. Monday too probably."

She backed up toward the steps to her apartment. "Maybe I'll see you."

"Yeah, maybe."

She turned, climbed the stairs, and disappeared. If he was more confident where she was concerned, he would tramp up the stairs and demand that she talk to him, but he wasn't sure he wanted to hear the truth.

Chapter Twelve

Tally pressed her cheek against the sun-warmed bricks of the wall and peeked around. The thwack of the nail gun echoed across the river. Nash was over there, probably shirtless and sweaty and delicious-looking.

"Whatcha doing?"

She yelped and spun around. Monroe's grin and sing-song voice was a mixture of joy and tease. Since Cade had returned, Monroe had shed her too-serious earnestness revealing a more playful woman. Not that she wasn't just as dedicated to her girls at risk program, but optimism had replaced the desperation that she'd carried around for as long as Tally had known her.

"Taking a break."

"In the refreshing ninety-degree-plus afternoon? Or do you mean a beefcake break?"

Tally chuffed. "What are you talking about?"

"*Tally and Nash, sitting in a tree. K-i-s-s-i-n-g.*"

Tally covered Monroe's mouth with her hand as Mrs. Carson approached them wearing a T-shirt, jogging pants, and white orthopedic tennis shoes. "That was wonderful, Miss Tallulah. I can't wait to tell everyone about the new class. You'd best prepare yourself for a full house next time."

Tally dropped her hand from Monroe's mouth but gave her a warning glare before pasting on a smile for Mrs. Carson. "Please, call me Tally. I'm so glad you enjoyed it. I'm looking forward to next week."

Mrs. Carson patted her hand on the way by and made her way to the footbridge across the river.

Monroe leaned against the brick wall in the sliver of shade it offered. "How was last night? Did the dress work its magic?"

"It was fine. The dress was fine." Tally stubbed the toe of her tennis shoe against a break in the cement, sending pebbling skittering.

Tally couldn't stop herself from leaning out to look across the river. Nash had emerged from the gazebo to chat with Mrs. Carson. He was shirtless. Did he not worry about giving Mrs. Carson a stroke? She was old, but not dead.

Monroe let out a low whistle. "Was it disappointing? Did he not know how to work that bod?"

Tally bit the inside of her mouth. "We didn't *do* anything."

"Why not?"

"It didn't seem like the right time."

"Not the right time? The man took you to the nicest restaurant in a hundred-mile radius. You are obviously into him, and he's into you. You're both single. What's the problem?" Tally shrugged, and Monroe rolled her eyes. "Methinks you need to join the girls for a session in self-confidence."

Monroe pushed off the wall, and Tally fell into step beside her. "I'm confident."

"You *appear* to be confident, but I have the feeling

you're a mass of gooey insecurities underneath your shell."

"Please." Tally tried to blow off the assessment.

Monroe pulled an about-face before they got to the door and put her hands on Tally's shoulders. "I'm not saying I'd take the crown for Miss Confident, but I've worked with these young girls for long enough to recognize you're stuck in the past. You're judging yourself on high school standards of pass and fail. Life isn't about being graded, and it's okay to fail."

"But, Nash—"

"Nash isn't going home and scoring you. He's not assigning you a grade. Be yourself and he's sure to fall head over heels in love with you. Because you're awesome, dangit."

Tears stung the back of Tally's eyes. Instead of ducking away like she might have a few months ago, she stared at Monroe's slightly blurry face and blinked. "I'm dyslexic."

Monroe's eyes flared before narrowing in an eviscerating stare. "I'm surprised, but not shocked. Does Cade know?"

"Told him a few weeks ago."

"Have you told Nash?"

"Of course, I haven't. I'm not sure why I even told *you*." She chuffed and rubbed her nose, forcing the tears away. "It's no one's business. Anyway, this is really about the fact that Nash and I are better as friends. If we take things further and things go south like they tend to do, then I'll lose everything."

Monroe pulled her in for a hug, patted her shoulder, and whispered, "But if things go well, think of what you have to gain."

"He won't understand."

Monroe gave her a little shake. "You don't give the people who care about you enough credit."

Reed stuck his head out the door. "Yo, Tally, there's a dude here looking for work. You want to talk to him?"

"Sure, why not." She was grateful for the interruption and stepped past Monroe. The air conditioning wafted over her, chilly on her sweat dampened skin. A young man with light blond hair was studying the bulletin board with class schedules and announcements a dozen feet away. His hands were clasped behind his back, and he rocked on his feet, giving the impression of nerves.

Monroe was the first to react. "Oh my goodness, it's you!"

The man turned, his initial surprise fading into suspicion. "You're the lady from the bar."

Tally exchanged a look with Reed, but didn't interfere.

"I've been trying to find you to make sure you're okay and to thank you for your help that night."

"It was nothing." The man rubbed across his jaw and turned his head to the side, *Webster's* definition of uncomfortable.

"It most certainly was something. You put yourself in harm's way to protect me and Kayla," Monroe said.

Tally inhaled and pointed. She'd heard the story. "He's the one? And you're looking for work?"

"I thought you had a job lined up working crayfish traps?" Monroe stepped closer to him, and he backed into the bulletin board, sending a paper and its tack to the floor.

"Turns out that ass—pardon, me—that jerk from the bar was friends with my new boss's son. I only worked a couple of days before I was fired."

"That's terrible." Monroe turned. "Give him a job, Tally."

Tally held up both hands. "Now hang on. First of all, I don't have anything but part-time work to offer. And, secondly, your friend here might not even be interested in grunt work."

"I'll take anything, ma'am."

His earnestness was apparent, but there was more. An acceptance of defeat. An understanding that life wasn't fair. She had a feeling he had gotten the short end of luck more times than not. She could certainly commiserate.

The bells over the door tinkled. Cade only had eyes for Monroe, and immediately put his arm around her. Only once he had her anchored to him did he acknowledge the rest of them.

Monroe poked him in the side. "Cade, this is the young man I was telling you about. From that night at the Rivershack Tavern."

"Monroe's knight in shining armor." Cade stuck out his hand. "I'm Cade Fournette." The young man hesitated before returning the shake.

"Jeremy Whitehurst." He dropped Cade's hand and rubbed both of his down the front of his jeans. "Look, I'm not some hero or anything. Got my butt handed to me as a matter of fact."

"It was at least three on one." Monroe turned a sugared smile on Cade. "Jeremy got fired because he stood up for me and Kayla and needs a job. Tally has a part-time thing open here, but weren't you talking about taking on some help?"

"You know anything about engines? Mechanics?" Cade asked.

"A little. Learned how to keep my motorcycle running." Jeremy shifted again and stuck his hands into his back pockets.

Cade hummed, but a faint smile turned the corners of his lips. "That's how we country boys get our start, it seems. How about you come out for a two-week trial? We're still getting things set up in the new shop, but if you stick, you'll learn a trade and maybe more. Fournette Brothers Designs is on the cutting edge of engine technology."

"Here in Cottonbloom?" Jeremy's incredulity was clear.

Cade's laugh reverberated around the entry. An old memory surfaced, one Tally couldn't put a place or time stamp on, but it featured a laughing Cade tossing her in the air. If everyone wouldn't think she was touched in the head, she would have hugged Monroe for helping Cade find his laugh.

"Yes, here in Cottonbloom. You can start at fifteen dollars an hour. What do you say?"

"You don't even know me."

"I know enough, and I'll learn more, since you'll be in my back pocket all day, every day while you're training. If things don't work out, then we part ways after two weeks, no harm, no foul. Deal?"

This time Jeremy didn't hesitate to take Cade's hand. "Deal."

Cade and Jeremy stepped to the side to continue their discussion. Reed propped his elbows on the desk. "That still leaves us short. I'm sick of taking out the trash and sweeping on top of opening and closing."

Tally couldn't afford to lose Reed. "I know. Me too."

A gaggle of girls entered the gym. Monroe propped her hip on the side of the desk, greeting each one by name. "Hey, Kayla, come here a sec."

The girl peeled off from the group. "What's up, Monroe?"

"Weren't you talking about wanting some part-time work?"

"I was. All the sales jobs I've applied for interfere with

school hours." Kayla cast a glance over her shoulder. "Isn't that . . ."

"Yep. I wasn't sure you'd recognize him."

"I remember his eyes. A weird blue. Unless I was imagining it."

"He's going to start working with Cade in the shop. Tally might have something you can do around here." Monroe side-eyed Tally.

Tally assessed Kayla for a moment. It wasn't a bad idea. Kayla was familiar with the gym and despite some recent bumps, she was a good kid.

"That would be so awesome, but I understand if . . ." The girl shrugged, her big brown eyes shining with an expectancy that mirrored Jeremy's. An expectation of failure.

"It's not very exciting work. Cleaning equipment, the bathrooms, sweeping, taking out the garbage, but I'm flexible about when you work and could use you some on weekends too."

"Yes, yes, yes. I'm up for whatever you need me to do. I promise I'll be the best employee ever." Kayla clasped her hands and held them under her chin.

"Hey now, I don't need anyone making me look bad." Reed winked from behind the desk. Tally held his gaze and tilted her head in an unspoken question. He gave an almost imperceptible nod.

"Do you want to start tomorrow? I've got to get the signs for the festival designed and the senior aerobics class nailed down. Help with the all the routine stuff would be a big help." They stood a couple of minutes talking about pay and times before Kayla skipped-ran toward the locker room to change before Monroe's class. Jeremy's head turned to follow her progress.

"That was more excitement than I'm used to." Reed settled back on the stool and crossed his arms.

A minimized window in the right corner of the computer had her cocking her head. "I heard you and Nash have been going at it."

Reed tensed. "Who told you that?"

"Nash did. He said you've actually beat him a couple of times." She gestured toward the computer. "It's okay if you want to play while you're on desk duty. Just no chess porn."

Reed's laugh was a little too loud for her joke. "'Course not. Chess is my strange addiction."

"It's not strange."

Reed raised an eyebrow.

"It's unexpected. How about that? But very cool."

"Chess is not cool. It's nerdy and not sexy."

"Nerdy and sexy aren't mutually exclusive." Her voice had taken on a strident militancy, and she attempted to backtrack. "I mean, you know, some women are into that sort of thing. I've heard."

This time both Reed's eyebrows went up along with the corners of his mouth.

"Oh, hush up," she muttered even though he hadn't verbalized what was written all over his face. "Don't you have something work related to do?" She spun away and headed to her office in the back.

She sat in the swivel chair and stared at nothing, her mind circling the problem of Nash. She needed to get her relationship with him under control. Sure, they were having fun and were attracted to each other, but their date in Jackson had magnified their differences. Long term, a relationship wouldn't work, and taking things further with him physically would only complicate everything. Their friendship was the most important thing.

It would be simpler and smarter to put the brakes on whatever was developing before she did something foolish like fall in love with him.

* * *

She was nervous and sad and felt like something was clawing at her heart. Her stomach cramped. If they took things further and it ended badly, she might end up hospitalized. She couldn't, wouldn't risk their friendship. It was too important.

She rubbed her hands down her jeans, blew out a long breath, and knocked on the cottage door. No footsteps sounded on the other side. She tried again and waited. Nothing. She walked around to the front of the main house and hesitated. His Defender was in the driveway.

The last time she walked up the front steps of the main house, she'd been twelve and scared and desperate for a friend. She'd left feeling dirty and unworthy and unwanted. It seemed a blink of time, each step casting her back a few more years to the girl she'd been.

She rang the doorbell, multiple tones echoing. The clack of heels on a wood floor had her smoothing a hand over her ponytail and pushing her shoulders back. Ms. Leora opened the door, her mouth pinching as soon as she identified Tally.

Tally tried to smile, not sure if she was actually succeeding. "Hello, Ms. Leora. Is Nash here?"

The old woman's gaze was sharp, piercing Tally's false bravado. "He's at the college working. His battery died, and one of the other professors picked him up. A woman. A very attractive woman."

Ms. Leora had a glint in her eye. Satisfaction? Malice? Either way, her barb had found its mark. It sounded like Emma from the bar. She was perfect for Nash. Tally knew it, Ms. Leora knew it, and it was a matter of time before Nash realized it too.

"I guess you've given up on fixing Nash up with Bailey now someone even better has come along." Tally half-turned toward the stairs.

"It's difficult, you know." Ms. Leora's gaze had scooted off to the side.

Tally pivoted back to face the old lady. "What's difficult?"

"You can't stop people from changing. As much as I wanted to." Ms. Leora's voice took on a faraway quality.

"Are you talking about Nash? Or someone else?" Had Nash been right about his aunt and her uncle?

Ms. Leora's focus was back on Tally. "Love destroys. Look at your parents, my sister, me and . . . I don't want to see Nash follow down that road."

An echoing sadness resonated between them. An understanding that seemed impossible, yet was unmistakable. She wasn't sure if love equaled destruction, but love certainly hadn't saved her parents or Nash's mother. At best, love was a bystander to tragedy. "I don't want to see Nash hurt either, Ms. Leora. He's important to me. Always has been."

"He's all I have." Ms. Leora's voice warbled, and Tally's hand rose to offer comfort before she pulled it back, unsure.

"I'm not trying to take him away from you."

"He'll drift away, back over the river." Her voice held a hint of desolation.

"It's never too late, you know." Tally couldn't believe the words came out of her mouth. She was a realist. She didn't believe love could conquer all. It's why she was getting ready to tell Nash they were better off remaining friends.

The wispiest of smiles crinkled Ms. Leora's cheeks for a moment. "It's too late for me. Nash didn't tell me when he's getting home. Do you need his number?"

"I have it, thanks." Tally backed toward the steps, keeping Ms. Leora in her sights until she closed the door.

Tally drove toward the college, needing to settle things face-to-face. A phone call, while alluring, was the cowardly way out. The student lot was sparse, and she got a spot close to a stately redbrick building. Huge magnolia trees and an assortment of hardwoods dotted a green space criss-crossed by concrete walkways. Students sat on scattered benches, some reading, some scribbling notes, some talking. Buildings circled the common area, some tall, some squat, but they all looked part of an extended family.

The area vibrated with energy and youth. The last time she'd been on the Cottonbloom College campus was as a junior in high school on a field trip. She felt exactly as she had then—an unwelcome alien stepping foot on a different planet.

Fliers advertising for tutoring or roommates framed a plastic-covered map under an overhang. The arts and humanities building was at the near end, a five-story brick building with a metal modern sculpture in front. She had no idea what the artist intended, but the swooping curves were a perfect representation of the state of her stomach.

The directory inside led her to the third floor. Everything was quiet. Offices lined the corridor. The black-and-white linoleum floor shined, and the concrete walls were painted a stark white. The scent of institutional cleaners was overlaid by the smell of books and paper and lead. All things that cast her back to high school and grew the knot of dread lodged in her chest.

She was doing the right thing. Counting down to the number next to Nash's name on the directory led her to the last office on the right. The door was open a few inches and voices snaked out. Nash's deep laughter was cut through by feminine giggles.

Tally leaned against the cool concrete wall for a

moment, pressing her fingertips under her eyes to beat back the sting of approaching tears. She could cry later, once she was alone. A deep breath fortified her courage, and she knocked on the door.

"Come in," Nash called.

She toed the door fully open. Nash was kicked back in a swivel chair, his feet propped on the desk between two stacks of books, his glasses sitting on the tallest tower. Emma sat on the near corner, her black pencil skirt riding to mid-thigh and her leg swinging. The woman was even more attractive than Tally remembered. She had a foreign sophistication that was out of place in Cottonbloom.

"Tally." Nash dropped his feet to the floor and stood. He didn't appear happy or unhappy, just surprised.

Emma darted her gaze between them and rose. "I need to be going. My next class starts in a half hour. I'll catch you later, Nash."

"Sure thing, Emma."

The woman walked up to Tally, a smile on her face. None of the cold animosity from their last meeting colored her face or voice. "Nice to see you again."

"Likewise." She choked the word out and didn't even attempt an answering smile.

The woman tilted her head, her perfectly arched eyebrows quirking. "If you'll excuse me?"

Tally was smack dab in middle of the doorway, blocking the woman's exit. She side-stepped and gestured to the door. Emma walked down the long hallway, her heels tapping, before disappearing into an office halfway down.

Nash grabbed her hand, tugged her inside, and closed the door behind him. "What're you doing here?"

"Hope I wasn't interrupting." She lied. She was glad the woman was gone. Which made no sense if she and Nash were going to be just friends.

"Not a bit. Emma and I were talking shop. I like to give her a hard time about how she picked the easiest subject. Plus, she's a good sounding board for my paper, which is turning into something more."

Tally moved farther into the room and picked up a book, running her fingers over the fading gold words along the spine. "What do you mean?"

"I'm thinking of expanding my research into a book." Excitement thrummed the words, and his grin was lopsided and endearing.

"I can't read." The words blurted out and hung in the air like a comic-book bubble. Her entire body tensed, her lungs freezing.

His smile turned into a frown and he crinkled his forehead. "What are you talking about? I know you can read."

"I mean, I'm not illiterate, but I'm dyslexic."

His brow cleared, turning his face into a blank canvas. The silence seemed to stretch to infinity until she broke it, stumbling over her words. "It's why I asked you to order dinner for me in Jackson. I really hate trout, by the way. The typeset they used on that stupid menu was impossible."

She turned toward the window. Students walked from building to building, their laden backpacks making them look like migrating turtles.

"Wouldn't it have been easier to tell me?"

His voice came from right behind her, and her body leaned toward him instinctively. She corrected herself and put her back against the window. "I should have told you ages ago so you weren't wasting your time with me."

He pinched the bridge of his nose. "Wasting my time? What are you talking about?"

"I know we're messing around because of that list, but it feels like . . . I mean, I don't kiss my friends." She didn't add that she could count her friends of both sexes on one hand. "I think we should keep our friendship solid, don't you?"

"Are you saying you're not physically attracted to me?"

She'd never been more attracted to a man. His body, yes, but everything else about him was equally as attractive. It screwed with her sense of logic.

"Look at this place. And your house. Books are your life. It would take me a month to get through one of them. That woman—what's her name—" She gestured toward the door even though she totally remembered. "You two probably have a million things in common. You could laze in bed and read together. It would be perfect."

He dropped his chin to his chest with a huff that sounded suspiciously like laughter. Before she could react, he had his hands on the glass by her shoulders, trapping her. "When you and I end up in bed together, I promise reading will be the furthest thing from my mind. Anyway, I'm not remotely attracted to Emma."

Now it was her turn to huff. "Yeah, okay, whatever. She's gorgeous. I was attracted to her, and I don't even play on that team." More than a little jealousy snuck into her voice, and she could see a smile trying to curl his lips. Her let's-stay-friends strategy was not going to plan.

"You're gorgeous yourself."

"You're not wearing your glasses."

"I'm nearsighted. I can see you fine." Without his glasses, his eyes seemed even warmer, the gold flecks like the sparks of a fire. A small smile broke through, crinkling the corners of his eyes. "I dream about you every night and wake up in the morning in physical pain. I'm dying to get you into my bed, Tallulah Fournette, and not to discuss Charlemagne."

She dropped her gaze to the buttons of his navy blue

golf shirt. "What happens afterward? After all that fades. What do we really have in common? Nothing."

He wrapped a hand around her nape and tilted her face up, his thumb caressing her jawline. "You really believe that? You're the only person who understands where I came from, who I was, what I went through. Because you went through it too, didn't you? Our parents gone. We were both isolated in our own ways, weren't we?"

"I barely graduated high school."

He sighed and stepped back, crossing his arms over his chest. "Fuck that. You throw the same lame excuse out to avoid anything that scares you. You put on a good front of being this tough girl, but underneath you're terrified of so many things."

Her mouth had gone dry, her tongue turning clumsy. She had always been called the risk taker, the daredevil. Yet, his words had the resonance of truth, and uncertainty lilted her denial. "No, I'm not."

"Do I scare you?" His voice was gruff.

The answer was an unequivocal yes. He scared her worse than Heath ever had, because he didn't threaten her person but her heart. She turned her head to the side to avoid his eyes. A forgotten mug sat half full of old coffee. Words decorated the side, probably something irreverent and funny like Nash himself, but she lacked the concentration to decipher it.

A knock reverberated through the office. It took a second series of raps to get Nash to bark out. "What?"

The door squeaked on his hinges as it opened. A rotund, balding man stood in hallway. "Terribly sorry, Hawthorne. We did have an appointment, I believe."

Nash's outward calm seemed forced. "Of course, sir. Come in."

After the man crossed the threshold, she scooted out. Relief over the reprieve unknotted her stomach.

Nash took a step into the hallway and grabbed her upper arm before she had the chance to bolt. "We are not done discussing this. Tonight. Your place or mine?"

"Yours." She took a step away, and he let her go.

She was back over the river in record time, stepping into the gym and feeling as if she was back on her home planet. She would lay out her case, get his agreement to remain friends only, and hightail it home. The future she envisioned depressed her.

They would try to maintain their friendship, but it would fall apart. The gym kept her busy, and he had his life at the college. Two different worlds even if they were only a few miles apart. Exactly like when they were kids. His aunt would throw a party and invite every eligible woman in Mississippi, and she would watch from across the river like Cinderella.

She went for a run, caught up on some bookkeeping matters, and solidified plans for the gym's participation in the festival. She headed home and showered, her thoughts circling his accusations as the hot water poured over her.

Was she using her dyslexia as an excuse?

She hadn't gone to college because she was sure she wouldn't be able to keep up and would flunk out the first semester. She had worried about disappointing Sawyer and Cade. She'd refused dates with any of the young, single male professionals who used her gym because they intimidated her. As much as she sometimes felt confined by Cottonbloom, she also felt safe. Like a dog in its crate.

Nash was different. She felt safe with him, but he was more intimidating than any situation she'd ever faced. Because she was desperate for him. Desperate to feel his lips, his hands, his body moving over hers. She was as desperate to protect herself from being hurt. The conflicting agendas between her body and heart made for a confusing stew.

Thunder cracked. The storm suited her mood. Her customary T-shirt, jeans, and boots grounded her, and she headed to Nash's house. She parked at the curb in front of the old house. The glow of a lamp outlined a figure against the lacy drapes in the front window.

Dark clouds had tossed them into a premature night. Maybe she could get this done and be gone before the rains came. The closer she got to his cottage the slower her steps grew.

He opened the door with her hand up to knock. He was barefoot and in a pair of faded jeans and a T-shirt with a slogan across the front. Avoiding his eyes, she stared at the shirt, ticking off the words in her head. I'D FIND YOU MORE INTERESTING IF YOU WERE DEAD.

A nervous laugh snuck out. "Your shirt is cute."

"Yeah? You like geeky history humor? There's something we have in common." He ushered her inside. Everything looked exactly as it had last time she was there. Books everywhere. "It was a gift from one of my students."

"I'm surprised it wasn't a pair of panties."

"I don't wear women's underwear." His consternation was adorable. "Not that there's anything wrong with it, if that's what you're into. Which I'm not."

More nervous laughter spurted out of her. "Not for you to wear, silly. Like a rock-star groupie. You know, girls tossing their underwear at you while you're lecturing."

"Have you got the wrong idea. If a majority of the class is still awake at the end of my classes, I'm thrilled. Especially if it's at eight in the morning. You should come to one of my lectures this fall. If you feel the urge to throw your panties at me, I wouldn't complain."

"Hold up." She pressed the heels of her hands to her forehead wondering how the conversation had derailed so quickly into a flirtation. "I'm not here to talk about panties or sitting in on one of your lectures."

He hummed and propped himself against the kitchen doorjamb, his smile turning her inside out. "That's too bad. I wouldn't mind holding an in-depth discussion about your panties—including examples."

How was she supposed to put the brakes on their relationship when he was being so laid back and funny? "We're not discussing my panties. We're going to talk about why we"—she waggled her finger between them—"would never work."

"Because you can't read as fast as I can?" The sardonic way he said it made her feel foolish.

"Not just that."

"Then why?"

She cast around for another excuse. "Your aunt doesn't think I'm good enough for you."

He pushed off the doorjamb and stalked her. She backed away, prey to his predator. "We've already discussed the fact she is predisposed to dislike you based on her supposed past relationship with your uncle. Try again."

"You'll get bored with me." The backs of her knees hit the loveseat, and she plopped down.

He didn't stop his pursuit, leaning closer and forcing her to scoot back into the pillows. "You are the most exciting, infuriating woman I've ever met. What else do you have?"

She ended up half-reclined on the loveseat, his knee planted between her spread legs and his chest hovering over hers. She wrapped her hands around his tensed biceps, the strength inciting a spike of arousal, which wasn't doing her mental state any favors.

"I'm the bad girl from your past that you want to get out of your system. That's all this is, Nash."

"Bad girl?" His eyes sparked with emotion. "You are the purest, best thing from my memories."

"There. Right there. I'm not pure or perfect or some embodiment of your dream girl. I'm emotionally stunted. Why can't you see that?" She took his face between her hands with the intention of shaking sense into him, but ended up stroking her fingertips along his cheeks and jaw, committing him to her purest and best memories.

"See, that's what you're missing. I *do* see you. I see all your weird little idiosyncrasies and your perceived flaws, and they only make me want you more. I'm not trying to recapture my past, I'm trying to build my future. Why is it so wrong that I want you to be part of it?"

Her weird idiosyncrasies aside, his words turned her insides to a gooey, melty mess. Surrender hovered. She threw out her last excuse like a kamikaze pilot. "But Cottonbloom isn't your home."

He dropped closer, his elbows on the cushion by her head, his body pressing into hers. She wanted to wrap her arms around him and pull him even closer.

"Cottonbloom has always been my home, Tallulah." His whisper scraped away the rest of her defenses.

His sweet brown eyes were inciting foolish hopes, and she closed her eyes. "You're an expert in European history. We are about as far from that world as possible. You don't belong here anymore."

"I once asked you to run away with me." A yearning weaved his words.

What could she say? Maybe fear had kept her in Cottonbloom, but with Cade home for good, her roots had dug even deeper. Slowly, fearing what she would see, she opened her eyes. Instead of disappointment, she only saw understanding and need.

"I can't see into the future, but I have no plans to go anywhere anytime soon. Anyway, there's been a development called an airplane that can get you across the world in hours." His slow smile dissipated her worries like the sun over the foggy river.

"Our friendship is precious. I don't want to lose that."

"Sleeping together won't turn us into adversaries. Now, unless you come up with some other excuse, I'd like to take you to bed."

Although he still smiled, his voice had turned husky and seductive. A turning point loomed. Yes, they'd messed around, but once they slept together, no matter what he said, their friendship would be cast in different shades. Sex might destroy the ease that existed between them. A flicker of optimism beat back her doubts. Could something even more amazing take root, the past forming its foundation, solid and unshakable?

He waited, his gaze darting from her eyes to her mouth and back again. With a jolt, she realized he was waiting for an answer. Her past relationships had left the men with all the power, but Nash seemed more than willing to give her a voice. Confidence surged through her.

"All right, Professor. Let's go."

Chapter Thirteen

Nash felt like someone had just offered him a 1940s mint-condition Superman comic book. He tried to control his excitement. Tears gleamed in her eyes, and he could sense her trepidation. Maybe because the same fear loomed for him. Except he could see beyond it. She seemed paralyzed by it.

He needed to go slow with her, make her understand that he craved more than to be inside of her. Although now she'd given the green light, the urge to rip their clothes off and take her quick and hard kept inserting itself.

Reaching for a self-control he thought beyond him, he dropped his mouth to hers with the intention to woo her with gentle kisses. She annihilated his plans. At the first touch of his lips, she came alive. She clutched and pulled at his back and hooked her ankles around the back of his thighs, pulling him down on her.

He settled his hips between hers and rocked against her. A rather insistent and painfully large part of him wanted to take her on the loveseat. The rest of him balked. At least the first time, he wanted her naked and spread out for both their pleasure. The kiss stretched to forever, his tongue winding with hers, her teeth nipping at his bottom lip.

He raised his face and took deep breaths, his lungs squeezing in warning. He'd never had an asthma attack having sex. Sex had always been like working out, a physical release, not an emotional one.

He pushed off her, already missing her body against his. She lay sprawled on the loveseat, her legs spread and her expression dazed. He grabbed her hands and hauled her to standing, pulling her close into his body and laying a light kiss on her reddened lips.

"I want you naked," he whispered in her ear.

She jerked, but wrapped her arms around his shoulders, her lips moving against his cheek. "I can't believe we're doing this."

The years fell away to the terrible days after his mother died and he'd learned of his aunt's plans. The thought of losing Tally too had sent him into despair. For a while, he wasn't sure he'd survive, but he had, and now they'd come full circle. She was back in his arms, her lips against his cheek. He swept her into a cradle hold, her black motorcycle boots dangling.

"What're you doing? I can walk."

The breathless quality of her voice made him hope their connection was as unique to her as it was to him. "I know you can, but I want to carry you to bed like a gentleman."

"I'm not sure a gentleman would take an unmarried woman to his bed."

"Technicalities." He took the steps one at a time, savoring the way she notched her face in his neck, kissing his jumping pulse point. When he thought of how close he'd been to losing her, he hugged her tighter. She seemed desperate to convince him they wouldn't work, and with equal desperation, he would prove they would.

He laid her on the bed and resumed his earlier position, one knee between her legs, his elbows braced beside her head. This time she initiated the kiss, her hand tight around his nape. One night soon, he would spend hours making out with her, but not tonight.

He squatted back on his knees and shed his T-shirt. She propped herself on her elbows.

"I never imagined you'd grow up to be so sexy."

His surprise turned into satisfaction and fueled his desire. "I don't think of myself as sexy in the least."

"I know. It makes you even sexier, trust me." She shifted to sitting and grabbed the waistband of his jeans with both hands. "I haven't been able to stop thinking about the way you looked that morning. You don't know how many times I've dreamed of pulling your underwear down and . . ." She ran her tongue along her puffy lower lip.

"And, *what*?" He was damned either way. He had to hear her say it, even if he keeled over.

She tilted her head back, her green eyes huge, her face flushed. "I want you in my mouth so bad I can taste you."

The bands around his lungs tightened. He groped for his nightstand.

"You don't need a condom. I'm on the Pill. Unless you want to use a condom, which is fine." Uncertainty had replaced her sexy confidence. The woman was a mass of contradictions.

He rocked back on his knees, took a pump off his inhaler, and held up a finger. The attack had been mild. The second time he'd had to use his inhaler with her. When he found his voice, it was hoarse. "Glad you're on the Pill because I don't have any condoms. I haven't needed them since I moved back."

"Did me telling you I want to go down on you give

you an asthma attack?" Horror mixed with amusement in her voice.

"Yes, the thought of your mouth on me gave me an asthma attack. If you actually do it, I might have a heart attack."

Laughter snuck out, but worry crinkled her eyes. "What if you have an attack in the middle of sex?"

"I won't, but this is how things are going to have to happen. You're going to let me touch you. Everywhere. You will orgasm. I'd like to guarantee that I'll last long enough for you to come again, but I probably won't."

She collapsed to her back, giggling. "I appreciate your honesty."

When she went to the button of her jeans, he stopped her, dropped over her long enough to brush his lips over hers and whispered, "Let me take care of you."

"Nash." His name fell from her lips, begging and desperate.

He slipped his hands under her T-shirt to the soft skin of her waist. Skimming his hands higher, he brought the shirt with him, up and over her bra. She raised her arms and shimmied like they had practiced the move, and he tossed the T-shirt over his head.

Her ponytail spread like a spilled plume of ink over his comforter. Her bra was a simple white, a shade lighter than her skin. Not that he expected fancy lingerie. It wasn't her style. He snaked his hand under her back and fingered the clasp. "May I?"

Her throat worked, but no words came, instead she nodded, quick and jerky. As a teenager in college, he'd practiced undoing bras around a pillow until he was an expert. It had taken a few years until he got the chance to put his expertise into practice. Thankfully, it was like riding a bike.

Her bra loosened, and his breath caught as he drew the fabric away. Her hands fluttered to her stomach as if she were tempted to cover herself. Her breasts weren't large, but beautifully full, the nipples small and peaked.

He scooped his arms under her shoulders and lifted her. He took one nipple straight into his mouth and sucked. She arched, her head falling back. Her moan carried the echo of his name, and she threaded her fingers in his hair, holding him close.

The sounds that emerged from his throat were closer to growls. Her skin was soft, her scent intoxicating. He transferred his attention to her other breast, teasing her nipple with teeth and tongue. She squirmed, her knees clasping him at his waist.

He settled her back against the bed and rolled to her side. He pinched one nipple and then the other, gauging her reaction. Her body went taut, her bottom lip clamped between her teeth. Again, he could spend all night teasing her breasts, but there was so much more he wanted.

With one hand, he unbuttoned her jeans and pulled the zipper down, skimming his hand into the front until they found the soft cotton of her panties. When she made a move to shimmy them down, he rose and tutted. "I told you that I'd take care of you. A foot, if you please."

She raised her right one, and he worked her black leather kick-ass boot off to reveal a dark blue sock covered with Superman emblems. The sight was like a kick in the gut. He raised his gaze to meet hers.

"Comic books were easier to read. Less words, more pictures. I kept the stash you gave me as kids. I reread them so many times, I memorized them." She shrugged. "The socks reminded me of you."

He peeled the sock off and reached for her other boot, not trusting himself to speak. She'd held onto him in her own way. Time had tested but not severed their connection. He laid a kiss on the arch as he peeled her matching sock off.

He dropped her leg and grabbed the waistband of her jeans, pulling them off and tossing them aside. Her panties glowed white and very brief, hiding almost nothing from his greedy eyes. He reached for them as she raised her hips to help. She was naked, and he wished the storm away, wished the moon would light the curves and contours of her body.

"Now you," she said in a breathy voice.

He wasn't wearing shoes and made quick work of his jeans, kicking them aside. She inhaled sharply, her gaze on his boxer briefs. He was afraid to look down, but could feel his erection straining for release as if it had developed a brain. Or maybe his brain had migrated south.

He joined her on the bed, stretching out next to her and gaining a small amount of relief in pressing himself against her hip. He needed to be inside of her, but even more, he was desperate to please her.

She tried to turn toward him, but he pushed her flat, his hand splayed over her stomach. Letting his instincts guide him, he curled his hand around her hip and squeezed before slipping his fingers between her legs. Her hand strayed to the front of his underwear. He grabbed her wrist and pushed it over her head.

"Do I need to tie you up?" Her lips parted on a quick inhale, but he couldn't discern shock from arousal in the dimness. "I want you to lie here and let me touch you."

"What about you?"

"We'll worry about me later." He nuzzled her breast before kissing his way across the softness. He sucked her pert nipple into his mouth, and she arched. Was she even aware how sexy and inflaming her whimpering moans were?

He caressed down her belly, her legs spreading before he even reached her pubic bone. He slipped fingers through her wetness and groaned around her nipple, stifling a curse. The list of things he wanted to do to her was growing by the minute. He prayed this was the first of many nights.

She grabbed both his arms, her nails digging into his skin. Her body was taut, ready to break, and he raised his head to watch her. Her orgasm rolled through her with the wildness of wind during a storm.

Her hips bucked, and he pushed a finger inside of her, his erection throbbing in time with her body. Her head thrashed. The chant of his name was the most erotic thing he'd ever heard. The adolescent part of his brain fist-pumped and cued the Superman theme. The moment was definitely theme-music worthy.

Her body settled back against the mattress. He kept his hand between her legs. A satisfied humming came from her smiling lips. He leaned over and brushed his mouth across hers. Her soft breasts pressed against his chest. She curled a hand through the hair at his nape and dabbed her tongue against his lips. He opened for her, and the abandon of her kiss settled an ache around his heart. All of the protections she kept in place like a force field had vanished.

"I'd like to worry about you now." She trailed a hand inside of his underwear, fingers brushing the sensitive tip of his erection.

He stood and pushed his underwear off. Another gasp from her lips. Primal instincts blanked his mind of rational thought. He settled between her legs, braced his elbows on either side of her head, and swept his tongue into her mouth at the same time he entered her.

Pushing up on his hands, he drove himself deeper inch by inch until he was buried inside of her. Her squirms only heightened his pleasure, but he grasped onto a thread of his civilized self. "Am I hurting you?"

"No. God, no. Please, Nash." She rotated her hips, and he hissed a long, slow breath in and out through his teeth. He pushed to kneel between her legs and watched where they were joined, wishing again for more light.

He pulled almost all the way out and slammed back inside of her. Being civilized and gentle was lost to him. He grabbed her ankles and pushed her legs farther apart and up, his hips pistoning. The thunder and pelting rain urged him on.

He dropped an ankle, pressed a finger against her, and rubbed. He didn't slow his pace, a sheen of sweat popping over his shoulders. His body begged for release.

She cried out, her body pulsing. He thrust once more and let go. A mind-numbing pleasure rolled through him. His toes curled, and he fell over her, her body spread out, lax and supple and inviting. He ground his hips into her one more time, inciting moans from them both, before pulling out and rolling to his back next to her, his body weak and tingling. He couldn't move.

Best. Sex. Ever.

Without his body anchoring her, Tally's mind pinged from past to present. Doubts threatened to swamp her even as her body hummed like she'd taken a shot of liquor. She'd had the best sex ever with her best friend.

The boy whose sticky hand had held hers while they'd spent hours wading the river. The boy who had hugged her after her parents had died, imparting a measure of hope that she'd clung to for months. The boy who she'd thought had abandoned her but hadn't.

Her intentions had been to physically distance herself from Nash while attempting to salvage their friendship. Instead, she had done the complete opposite. The darkness was deep, the thunder receding and leaving a heavy rain in its wake.

She'd had sex before. Even what she'd considered pretty great sex. But she'd never been made love to, and for the first time, she realized there was a difference. Sex had never involved more than nerve endings firing. Pleasure. Physical release. Satisfaction.

The door they had thrown open required her to lay out her vulnerabilities and trust him. Required her surrender. She'd handed him the power to wound her. A power she'd kept close for too many years to relinquish after one bout of sex. The flash of insight was as potent and damaging as a lightning strike.

Panic washed through her. Part of her wanted to curl into his side, let his hands cast her worries aside as easily as he had her clothes, but her fears had come home to roost. She needed to be alone and work out what this night meant.

The longer she lay, the louder the primal part of her yelled. The air became oppressive, and her breathing grew shallow. She sat up, swung her legs off the bed, and reached around for her clothes. Panties first. Her bra was too complicated for her shaking hands.

"I'm assuming this means no spooning?" His voice reverberated in the room like distant thunder.

She startled and looked over her shoulder as she pulled on her jeans and T-shirt. He'd propped his head up on his hand and pulled the sheet over his hips, the white line stark against his solid, tanned chest. Her ability to see in the dark was nearly her undoing. Her fingers itched to pull the sheet away. She turned her back to him.

"Look, Nash, this was"—fun, amazing, heart-rending—"a mistake. Maybe. I don't know. Anyway, I'm not the cuddling type." Tears stung her eyes, but her voice was thankfully granite hard. She pulled her boots on, sans socks, and stood, casting a reluctant glance from the corner of her eye.

"I don't want you to go." His tone was testing, and like every other test in her life, she would fail.

"I gotta go." This time her voice cracked, and before he could make a move, she ran the same route as she had the first morning. Rain blurred her eyes and chilled her body. She slid into her car. A strange disappointment bled through the panic.

She was seriously screwed up if she expected—wanted—him to chase after her. Like he was the one with something to prove. The tears came even before she turned off his street, mingling with the rainwater dripping from her hair. It was an ugly cry, her nose running and her face splotching.

The state line seemed to represent more than a change in towns or states, it seemed a representation of her life. Nash was so close, yet they were separated by their experiences. Somewhere along the way, their paths had diverged.

She parked and walked to her apartment, her head down as she trudged up her stairs. All her worries and thoughts were on the man she'd left behind.

"Whose bed have you crawled from?"

Heath's voice startled her. Her keys skittered down two steps. He stepped from the deep shadows of an opposite doorway. Rain poured out of the leaf-clogged gutters like curtains leaving them cocooned from the outside world. She felt trapped.

"What are you doing here? Seriously, you are crossing into creepy stalker territory and it doesn't suit you."

"I want to talk to you. Let's go inside. You look cold." His eyebrows rose, a smirk lifting one corner of his mouth. She glanced down and crossed her arms over her chest, muttering a curse. How had she ever found his obnoxious half smile attractive? It was calculated and without a hint of real happiness. Not like Nash's easy grins.

"There's nothing left to say." She made a move, but he stepped in front of her.

A teeth-baring grimace replaced the half smile. "I want another chance with you. I'll do whatever, be whatever you need me to be." His tone and expression offset the words.

A couple of months ago, she might have given him another shot out of loneliness or weakness or straight-up stupidity. He wouldn't—couldn't—change for her, any more than she could change for Nash.

"I've moved on and so should you." She backed up a few paces to retrieve her keys off the steps.

A figure emerged from the sheet of rain holding her keys and shaking his head like a dog. Nash. Before she could stop herself, she grabbed his thick University of Edinburgh sweatshirt and pulled him to her like she was picking teams on the playground.

With a sense of calm, he handed her the keys, removed his glasses, and proceeded to dry them on the edge of his shirt, his gaze shifting between her and Heath the entire time.

"You're shitting me, right?" Heath gestured toward Nash but otherwise ignored him.

"Why are you acting like the two of us together is preposterous?" Nash's voice took on a slightly foreign lilt.

Tally looked heavenward.

"I could fucking break you in two right here."

"Do you always settle disputes by beating the crap out of someone?"

"It's worked for me so far." Heath stepped forward, stretching his neck in the universal signal for a beat down.

"How about we take it to the ring?"

Heath froze a second before rusty laughter burst out. "Are you serious?"

Nash shrugged. "Why not?"

"This is ridiculous. You two are not fighting over me." She grabbed one of Nash's biceps. It was rock hard, his entire body strung taut even though his voice had stayed nonchalant.

"I'll be in touch." Heath's sly half grin was back. "But I won't hold it against you if chicken out. I remember what a pussy you were in school." He disappeared through the sheet of rain.

"Are you insane? Heath hates you." Her emotional state deteriorated further. Now in addition to feeling like her heart was being sheared in two, she was overwhelmed with worry and anger.

"He's not my favorite person either." Nash stared toward the stairs.

She attempted to feed the key into the lock, but between the rain and her shakes, it slipped time and again. He came up behind her, wrapped his hand around hers, and pushed the key home. She made no move to twist the knob, their hands still joined.

His body was warm behind her, solid and comforting. "Why do you think what we did was a mistake? And, don't give me a bullshit answer." His breath wafted over her ear, inciting shivers.

Her superficial excuses crumbled. Their differences in education, his worldliness and her lack thereof, his ease with himself and her shame didn't matter. Not really.

"I'm scared." Her whispered words wavered. The past days and especially her decision to sleep with Nash clarified the heart of her fear. Nash had been right. Her dyslexia was an excuse to not take chances, to keep people at arm's length, to avoid letting anyone glimpse her insecurities. But, her true fear was something else entirely.

"Of what?"

"You'll hurt me."

"How am I going to hurt you?" Each one of his questions peeled back another layer of protection, uncovering a raw wound.

"You'll leave. Like everyone else." When the truth emerged, horror warred with relief, but there was no retreat. He had caged her in.

"Your parents?"

A tear streaked down her face. Please God, not now. She tried to quell the urge with a deep breath, but her lungs shuddered the air in and out, giving her away.

"Your brother?"

She nodded once. No matter that she understood the reasons, even sympathized, she couldn't shake the resentment that had taken hold when Cade had left Cottonbloom to make a life away from her and Sawyer. After depending on her big brother for so long, she'd felt abandoned and alone.

"And me too, I suppose."

She didn't speak, knowing the answer wasn't fair. The night she'd walked away from his aunt's house thinking he didn't want to be her friend anymore had left an indelible mark even the truth couldn't erase.

He turned her hand around the knob and the door opened. The blast of AC was uncomfortable on her rain-soaked, wrung-out body. He forced her inside like he was herding sheep. His heat left her. She half-expected to hear him leave, but the lock clicked and the chain rattled. His arms came around her again, his chin stubble rasping over her temple.

"What if sex screws up our friendship? What if you end up hating me? Or I end up hating you?" One question stumbled over the next.

"What if this ends up being the best relationship either of us has ever had?"

It was already the best relationship she'd ever had. There was nowhere to go but down.

"Was the sex not good for you?" he asked with a faint echo of her own insecurities.

A bloom of heat came over her chest, and she hoped steam wasn't rising from her clothes. "It was amazing, and you know it. But you can't tell me if Harvard or Yale or some prestigious school in Europe offered you a job, you wouldn't take it and run."

"First off, I haven't even gotten tenure at Cottonbloom College. Second, I wouldn't abandon everything here to chase a job. I wouldn't abandon you." His arms tightened.

A warmth that had nothing to do with his body pressed into hers calmed her internal turmoil. "Are you sure?"

"Woman. You have to learn to trust me. Just a little. Can we see where this goes?"

"I guess."

"Wow. That was pathetic, but I'll take it. Why don't you take a shower and warm up?" He dropped his arms and tapped her backside a couple of times to get her moving.

She stopped halfway across the den and turned around. Neither one of them had turned a light on.

"I'm not going anywhere." His words were a battering ram to her defenses.

She took her time in the shower. A sense of safety and contentment she'd hadn't experienced since before her parents died relaxed her. She'd assumed relationships were built on conflict and leaving and loneliness because that's what her recent experience had taught her. Perhaps she had to cast back to before, when her life had been as close to perfect as she could remember.

As she dried her hair with the towel wrapped around her torso, she closed her eyes. Her happiest childhood memories were populated by her family . . . and Nash. Always Nash. What would happen to her memories of him if things soured between them? Would they be ruined?

With her hair mostly dry, she slipped out of the bathroom into her bedroom. It was empty and the door closed. With shaking hands, she pulled on panties and a T-shirt, ready to rip the door open, her breathing too quick. She pressed an ear against the thin, cheap wood, the murmur of a TV coming from the den.

Two deep breaths calmed the irrational panic, and she stepped out. He'd taken his sweatshirt off and draped it over one of her kitchen chairs. She traced the red letters across the gray front with a finger. University of Edinburgh. She wanted to believe in him, in the possibilities that stretched into the future.

He was sprawled on her couch asleep, one arm thrown over his head, his face pressed into a red decorative pillow, a tassel mixing with his hair. His plain white T-shirt had a few damp splotches, his biceps and shoulders stretching the seams to the ripping point. The hem rode an inch up over his jeans, his stomach taut. It looked at least two sizes too small.

How could he look sexy and adorable at the same time? She grabbed his hands in hers and tugged, her destination her bed. He let out a sleepy grunt, but opened his eyes and stood up.

"Come on, Professor, let's go." She backed to her room, and he followed like a sleepwalker. He allowed her to undress him, first peeling his shirt over his head. Her fingers shook as she worked his jeans open. Disappointment bounced her stomach when the opened fly revealed a pair of dark green boxer briefs.

Even unaroused, the bulge in his underwear had her staring and swallowing past a lump. She finished tugging his jeans down before she could get distracted. He kicked them off and collapsed in her bed, pulling her down with him. She ended up facing him, pressed together from chest to knees.

He didn't move for a few minutes, but then his hand moved up under her T-shirt to caress the bare skin of her back.

"Please don't fight Heath," she whispered into the darkness.

"He'll never respect me nor let you go if I don't. Anyway, this fight has been a long time coming."

"What are you talking about?"

"He made going to school a gut-wrenching experience for me. I was too weak and intimidated to fight back then." He yawned, and his hand drifted over her backside and squeezed. "Anyway, I might surprise you."

If he was trying to distract her, it was working. Before her back could arch and rational thought left the building, she popped up on an elbow. "Look, I know you've boxed, and I saw you in the gym. You can pound a bag and jump rope, but Heath has trained with MMA-type fighters. He won't let you circle him in the ring and jab a few times, he'll take you down and choke you out."

"Fighting is the only language men like him understand." He hummed, yawned, and rolled to his back. "Duels date back since before the written word, you know."

"So men have acted infantile since the beginning of time?"

He answered with a soft laugh that trailed into the darkness. Adrenaline left echoes in her bloodstream, keying her up and making it difficult to drift off. Every time she did, the picture of a bloody, beaten Nash acted like a set of jumper cables.

Notching herself into his side, she lay her head on his shoulder, her hand over his heart. She measured time by the rise and fall of his chest, and somewhere in the darkness, sleep claimed her.

Chapter Fourteen

Her internal alarm pulled her from a deep sleep. She didn't want to leave her erotically charged dream. Not yet. Heat pooled in her belly and spread like wildfire. Her body was primed. The details were fading, but a naked, very aroused Nash had been involved.

Instead of dissipating upon waking, the need to climax coiled tighter. An appreciative rumble had her eyes popping open, her mind moving slowly, but finally moving. Dawn light fuzzed the room. A dark head was between her legs. A tongue lashed her; lips claimed her.

The jolt of reality versus dream should have squashed her arousal. Instead, she wanted to cry out in thanks. She drove her hands into his hair and fisted the strands inciting another rumbling moan. He cupped her buttocks, his hands big and warm and tilting her toward his mouth. She flattened her feet on the bed and pressed higher.

Nonsense words flew out of her mouth. Later she'd be embarrassed, but for now all she cared about was chasing her pleasure. It was a foreign feeling.

One of his fingers barely breeched her, tossing her into an orgasm so intense she wondered for a moment whether it was a dream after all. Finally, she became aware of the cotton sheets underneath her, the softness of his hair in her hands, his shoulders pressing against her inner thighs, her legs splayed to the side, her bones molten.

The bed shifted, and she opened her eyes into his. No glasses to dissipate the warmth. He was smiling and looking rather pleased with himself. And why wouldn't he be? His body hovered a few inches above her, his erection straining toward her like a divining rod.

"I've never been woken up that way."

"You were kind of asking for it."

She blinked a few times, her lassitude fading. "What?"

"You woke me up muttering something. At first I thought you were awake, but then I realized . . . woman, you've got a dirty mind."

She reached out and pulled at the sheet for protection, even if it were foolish at this point. "What did I say?"

He brushed the sheet away and trapped her wrists in one of his hands above her head. His body dropped over hers, the wet head of his erection on her belly. He nuzzled his face next to hers. "You were dreaming about me. Said my name while you touched yourself. Begged me to lick you."

"Ohmigod." She tugged on her hands, but his grip firmed.

"Don't freak out. I loved it and based on your reaction, so did you." His admission muffled her embarrassment, and her legs cut against his as he lay kisses from her ear to her mouth. "I dreamed about you too, Tallulah."

Every time he said her name in that husky lilty way, it was like an injection of sugar into her bloodstream, even as the feeling of his big body covering her was a flint to her arousal. "What did *you* dream about?"

"I dreamed I was taking you from behind. Hard and rough."

She was surprised . . . and even a little disappointed. It was a position that gave him the power. Although, she had no right to complain, considering he had made her dream come true. She could be just as unselfish for him.

"Let's make your dreams come true." She tried to inject tease into her voice.

A primitive growly noise vibrated his chest against hers, and he dropped his face to nip at her neck. After pushing back onto his heels between her legs, he helped her flip, and she assumed the position on her hands and knees.

She waited for him to take her. Instead he scraped his fingernails down her back from shoulders to buttocks, liquefying her knees. He gripped her hips, his fingers biting into her flesh a little harder than was comfortable, and pushed slowly inside of her.

He hummed. "That looks amazing."

Her breath stilled. He was watching them. She closed her eyes, jealous of his view. Her elbows quivered. "I thought . . . I thought you wanted it rough?" Her voice wasn't too steady either.

"Only when you're ready to handle it, and I don't think you are. Shall we get you ready?"

She didn't have the breath to ask how he planned to prepare her. He took one long slow stroke into her body. His hand delved in her hair and massaged her scalp. He tugged. Not hard enough to hurt, but hard enough to make her want more.

He wrapped one arm around her waist, while his hand continued to pull at her hair. Her body followed his directions until she was upright on her knees with his chest pressed tight against her back. His hands moved to her breasts, gently yet systematically driving her to the brink of insanity. She squirmed, still impaled on his erection.

"Touch yourself. I want you to climax again, this time

with me inside of you. Then I'm going to let loose on you, baby."

Where had Nash learned to talk like that? Suddenly she wanted nothing more than for him to let loose on her, knowing somehow that he'd make it good for her. She dropped her hand to between her legs.

With his lips at her temple and his hands on her breasts, an orgasm racked her body after an embarrassingly short time. Now he thrust but held her upright, his fingers joining hers, his touch rougher than hers, and that much more arousing.

He pushed her back over to her hands and knees, his hand around her nape and finally fulfilled his promise. He slammed into her, pushing her up the bed, and she urged him on with breathy encouragements, popping her butt up higher.

A roar accompanied his final thrust. She felt his climax not only in the bucking of his hips against her, but in the pulse of him inside of her. She reached back and grabbed his leg, holding him against her. He curled over her, chest to back, his weight diving her flat to the mattress underneath him.

Instead of rolling off, he threaded his fingers through hers and nuzzled her hair aside. "I could get used to waking up like that every morning. How about you?"

Of course she could. Her stomach churned like an out-of-balance washing machine. She squirmed to the side, not making much headway with his weight anchoring her. "I really should—"

"There's nothing you should be doing except lying here with me." He shifted off her but kept a big, warm hand pressed against her lower back. She didn't argue. Truth was she didn't want to leave him. He lay kisses down her spine and massaged her backside.

An indeterminate amount of time passed while she

enjoyed his touch. Languidly, she raised her head. The digital clock incited a mild panic. "Nuts! I'm going to be late." She sat on the edge of the bed, her knees weak and trembly.

"Can Reed open the gym?"

She had asked Reed to cover for her too often of late. "He closed for me last night so I could come see you. They'll be a line of people waiting to get in for their morning workout."

She attempted an air of nonchalance while she pulled on her standard workout gear but when she snuck a glance, she found him staring at her with a smile on his face. She smiled back.

He rose and stretched. He might as well be holding a neon sign reading BEHOLD AND SALIVATE. She did. He slipped on his boxer briefs, breaking her trancelike state.

"I'm going to be working on the gazebo later. Maybe you could bring me a Coke during one of your slow times?"

"Sure." Her voice cracked, and she cleared her throat.

They left her apartment together and met Ms. Effie coming up the stairs in her robe, holding a mug of coffee and a morning paper. The huge grin and not-so-subtle thumbs-up only flushed more heat into Tally's face.

Could things get any more awkward? Yes, they could. She backed toward her car. "Okay, so I'll see you later?"

His eyes narrowed, and he matched her step for step until she bumped into her fender. His arm came around her waist and brought her flush against him. "A week ago, I might have let you scurry away to your safe place to wonder and doubt and nitpick at what we're building. But, not after last night"—he dropped his lips to her ear—"and this morning."

"What are we building?"

"You still don't know? How about I leave you with a reminder."

Her lips parted on another question, but his kiss silenced her. His lips were soft yet unyielding. His kiss took but gave even more. His control surprised and aroused her. She wrapped her arms around his neck and anchored herself to him.

Her world seemed to tilt, her emotions veering off course. The only stable force was the cause of the chaos. She clung to him even as he threatened to wreck her. As his lips took hers in one drugging, sensual kiss after another, she realized no matter what, she'd never be the same. There was no use in protecting herself against something that had already happened.

He pulled away. An eternity had passed yet the sun still sat low, the orange light of dawn stretching across the sky. More than anyone, she understood how life could change in an instant.

"Now, then—" His thumbs caressed both her cheeks in hypnotic strokes. "I want you to promise me not to overthink things."

"I promise," she said as if truly hypnotized.

"You're going to come over to my place after you close up the gym. Bring everything you need for the morning."

Again, she nodded as if under his spell.

He kissed the tip of her nose and left her sagging against the trunk of her car. She was feeling the urge to run again, but this time straight into his arms. Instead, she watched him drive off and slid behind the wheel with a smile on her face. She was done fighting.

The next days and nights passed in a haze of happiness and lust. The days at the gym were long, and her nights with Nash even longer. They made love, but instead of hightailing out of his bed, she lazed in his arms while they talked about nothing and everything. Dawn kept sneaking in too soon, separating them.

The only contentious moments came when she brought up the fight with Heath. Responsibility weighed heavy on her conscience. If it wasn't for her, he wouldn't be putting himself at risk. He refused to discuss it. After a few days with no developments, she decided the men were all talk, which suited her fine.

Reed had volunteered to close the gym, so Tally and Nash could grab an early dinner. Tally was content to laze on the couch in his arms. She'd even convinced him to watch *The Bachelor* with her. He laughed as if it was a comedy and not a dating show. Halfway through, her phone buzzed. Sawyer's name popped up. "What's up?"

"Don't suppose you've heard from Uncle Del today?" The clang of metal sounded in the background.

She pushed up from Nash's chest. "No, why?"

"He hasn't been answering his phone. I'd run out there, but Cade and I are in the middle of a two-man job out at the shop. You mind checking on him?"

"Not a bit. I'll run out there now."

"Text me if you need me." A beep signaled his disconnect.

"What's wrong?" Nash had joined her on the edge of the couch.

"Uncle Del's gone incommunicado. He's probably fine, but now that he's older, one of us tries to keep tabs on him. His place is secluded. I'm going to drive by and check on him. Do you want to meet up later or call it a night?"

"I'll ride out with you unless you'd rather be alone."

Was this a test? She chewed on the inside of her cheek. Monroe's words came back to her. Nash wasn't judging her or laying a trap. "You sure you don't mind?"

"Of course not."

"In that case, we'd best take the Defender. The track to his place can get washed out in the summer."

They were largely silent until he pulled onto the parish highway. "Does he go incommunicado often? And, by incommunicado, I'm assuming you mean drunk."

A half smile snuck past her worry. "Once a year if that these days. A little more often when we were kids. It's why he could never hold down a job for more than a few months."

"How in the world did he take care of you?"

"He didn't. Cade took care of us. All of us. Covered as much as he could for Uncle Del, so the state wouldn't interfere."

"How so?"

"Uncle Delmar was officially our guardian. He tried, he really did. He hunted for us. Taught Cade how to hunt. Cade was afraid if the state caught wind, they'd split us up into foster homes." Tally fiddled with a string on the hem of her shorts.

He was quiet as they pulled up in front of Uncle Del's house. She could imagine what he saw. The ramshackle house spoke of poverty. Dark green paint flecked off buckled clapboards, a couple of car engines sat out front, exposed to the elements. Various other metal objects sprouted out of the ground like shrubbery.

The engine sputtered off, leaving a heavy silence. Tally opened her door, but paused when it was clear Nash wasn't following her. His hands were gripping the steering wheel, his knuckles white. The sounds of the river snaked into the cab on a breeze. Everything smelled different. Swampier and more verdant.

"You all lived here?" He gestured out the window, and Tally couldn't decide what emotion thickened his voice.

"Actually, we lived in a trailer past those trees." She pointed toward the copse of pines. "Cade tried to go to school and work, but he barely brought in enough to keep us fed and clothed. The mortgage on top of the funeral expenses was impossible. Selling out was the only option."

Moving from the comfortable middle-class brick ranch into the decrepit trailer had seemed like the beginning of a dark fairytale. Cade had tried his best, hanging the frilly, pink curtains from her old room over the dingy, taped-up window of the back bedroom she shared with Sawyer.

They only reminded her of everything she'd lost. Not long afterward, she'd stripped the tiny room of her old life and burned it all in a clearing in the woods. The smoke had brought Cade running, but he'd found her dry-eyed and resolute in her mission. He didn't panic or yell, just put his arm around her shoulders as her memories burned.

"You can stay in the truck if you want, Nash. It's okay." And it was okay. Because they were sleeping together didn't mean he had to deal with her drunk uncle and crazy ex.

She climbed the decrepit front porch stairs and pounded on the door, rattling the windows. If her uncle were on a binge, it would take more than a ladylike rap to rouse him. She tried again, this time yelling, "Uncle Delmar, you in there?"

No answer. The porch sagged another inch as Nash came up behind her. She risked a glance over her shoulder. His expression was serious, his brows drawn together. She jiggled the door handle, not surprised to find it unlocked, and popped her head inside. "Uncle Delmar?"

"In here." Her uncle's voice was soft but not slurred.

Nash stepped inside behind her, his bulk filling the small foyer. The interior was dim and she blinked, her Fournette eyes becoming accustomed to the dark quickly. Her uncle was sitting in the middle of his couch in the den. A stale, mothball odor emanated from the walls. She gave Nash another out, whispering, "You can wait outside."

He closed the door, casting them in deep shadows. "You don't have to manage him alone. That's why I'm here. For you."

His words shocked her into immobility. He brushed by her, laying his hands on her shoulders for a quick squeeze, before taking the lead. He stepped into Delmar's small den and knelt in front of him.

"It's Nash Hawthorne, sir. I'm here with Tally to check on you."

She leaned against the doorjamb. The pines filtered the light from the setting sun through a side window, providing the only light.

"Ah, Nash. Your mama was good people, God rest her soul." Uncle Del patted Nash on the shoulder.

"Yes, sir, she was."

"Your aunt too. Leora, sweet Leora."

Tally straightened in the doorway, exchanging a glance with Nash. She sat close to her uncle, taking his hand. "Are you okay?"

"I'm as sober as the preacher on Sunday, if that's what you're asking."

"You're not sick, are you? Sawyer said you weren't answering your phone."

"Nothing a doctor can help with. Feeling my age, I guess. Didn't much want to talk to anyone to be honest. I've been sitting here thinking, wondering how things might have been different."

She could feel Nash's gaze on her, but stayed focused on her uncle. The moment took on an importance she couldn't quantify. "Was Ms. Leora your sweetheart?"

His head fell back on the couch and he was silent, his eyes open, but unseeing. "We were going to get married as soon as my tour was done. 'Cept, my tour never ended. I kept fighting the Viet Cong even after I was home." He squeezed her hand and raised his free hand to the scars on his face.

"My aunt broke off the engagement?" Nash asked.

"I never blamed her. I wasn't the same man she'd fallen in love with. I turned into someone unlovable."

The despondency in his voice had her gripping his hand tighter. "You're not unlovable, Uncle Del. I love you."

His brown eyes glimmered and his lips relaxed, not quite smiling but the sadness in his face eased. "I don't know what I would have done without you kids over the years. Gave me something to aspire to." He patted her hand and her grip loosened. "Wish I'd set things right a long time ago."

"It's not too late." She'd told Ms. Leora the same. Did she really believe it? Had Nash turned her into a sappy romantic?

"What do you mean?"

"I have it on good authority that Ms. Leora still thinks about you too."

He sat up straighter, his hands curving over his knees, and looked down at Nash. "Does she?"

"I'm not sure exactly *what* she thinks about you, but she kept your letters," Nash said softly.

"My letters . . ." Her uncle shifted to the side and flipped on a lamp. The light banished the lingering despondency. His knee bounced with a restless tension. "What should I do?"

Her love life wasn't ripe with good examples. All she had was Nash. She caught his eye and said, "You could take her a bouquet of her favorite flowers."

"She was always partial to wildflowers. Is she still, Nash?"

Nash gave a slight shake of his head. "I'm not sure. I can't recall her having fresh flowers around much."

Her uncle pushed himself up. "I need to get gussied up."

"You're going over there right now?"

"I'm getting older by the minute. No time to waste." He shuffled toward the back bedroom.

Tally stared for a moment before shaking herself out of her shock. "I can't believe it. How will your aunt react? Will she throw him out? God, what if she crushes his feelings, Nash?"

"Either way, the two of them need closure. They've spent the last fifty years drifting on different rivers, neither one of them finding what they were looking for. But for the record, I don't think she'll throw him out. You didn't see her the day she was looking through that old box."

Energy born from anxiety had her falling back into old habits when she'd kept her uncle's place tidy. She tossed a couple of empty beers bottles and an empty bag of chips into the trash. Nash stood in the middle of the room, his hands stuffed into his pockets.

She moved to the kitchen and washed the few dishes piled in his sink. The water coming from the faucet was tinged with sulfur from the well. Bile crept up her throat. She'd come to hate that smell. Hated the way it clung to your hair and your clothes. Like the devil had moved in.

She opened drawers, looking for a dishtowel. She'd half-closed the bottom drawer when the contents registered, and she reopened it slowly. A white rubber band bound a roll of money. She thumbed through it. All twenties. An estimate put it at close to seven hundred dollars. Her stomach bottomed out.

"What's that?"

She dropped the money back in the drawer. Nash was

over her shoulder and she hadn't realized it. "It's a wad of cash."

Nash didn't seem to think anything unusual of the money, drying and stacking the dishes. A different sort of worry inserted itself. Her uncle did odd jobs all over the parish, even into the Mississippi side of Cottonbloom, but she couldn't recall him ever having that much cash sitting around. He lived hand to mouth.

The squeak of a door startled her. Her uncle emerged from his bedroom, and Tally couldn't do anything but stare. His hair was parted and slicked to one side in a style reminiscent of a bygone era. He wore the khaki pants usually reserved for Sunday mornings and funerals and a plaid button-down, a red bowtie at the collar.

"Do I pass muster?" He held his hands up and spun around.

"You look"—she searched for a word—"dapper." And he did.

He adjusted the bowtie. "It's a clip-on. You think she'll notice?"

Nash spoke up. "I think she'll be so surprised to see you, she won't care about your bowtie."

Tally and Nash followed him outside. Her uncle hesitated between house and truck. While he hadn't been the most responsible caretaker, he'd always been around to give hugs and tend to her bumps and scrapes. He'd believed in her and encouraged her when things at school had been their worst. She loved him. Even though she worried Ms. Leora would hurt him, Nash was right. Her uncle and his aunt both needed the closure.

She hugged him; the scent of his cologne couldn't mask the essence of the river that emanated from him. His rounded spine and knobby shoulders made her wonder how he'd gotten so old without her noticing. "Everything will be fine. Go get Ms. Leora some flowers and knock on her door."

Her uncle's arms tightened around her before letting go. The nervous smile on his face was hopeful, and he winked. "You two are welcome to hang out, but don't wait up for me."

She waved him down the track until he was out of sight. A deep breath of loamy, humid air was both comforting and disturbing. The tops of the pine trees swayed in the wind as if beckoning her. She weaved through the trunks, the white of their trailer flashing. Dimly she was aware Nash followed her.

The old trailer had seen better days when Uncle Delmar had hauled it into the clearing for them. Now it was straight-up dilapidated. Vines were crawling up the sides, pulling it to the earth. Ashes to ashes, dust to dust.

She turned around. Nash's gaze was on her and not the trailer. Without letting doubts and insecurities take hold, she walked into his body and wrapped him tight. His arms came around her, his hands making circles on her back.

She buried her face in his neck and breathed in his uniquely male scent of woodsy cologne and books. "Thank you for coming out here with me."

"So this is it, huh? Home sweet home?" His dry humor eased her melancholy.

She kept her head on his shoulder, titling her face to look. "In all its glory. Obviously, it wasn't in such bad shape then. Cade kept talking about moving us to an apartment in town, but when Sawyer left for college, things got even tighter. Cade was determined Sawyer wasn't going to come out of school saddled with huge loans. I knew he would work himself to death to send me too."

"Your family is amazing, Tally." The awe in his voice had her pulling back.

"What do you mean?"

"To lose your parents, your house—everything really—and to claw your way back up. Cade holds more patents than you can count, Sawyer is the parish commissioner, and you—"

"Own a gym. Big whoop-de-do."

"Sometimes I want to shake some sense into you. You started the gym from scratch. It's successful. You shortchange yourself all the time. Almost as if you want to get the hit in before someone else can knock you down."

She stared in his eyes. Monroe had told her the same thing, but hearing it from Nash made it impossible to ignore. "You're right."

"About what?"

She almost smiled at his shock at her easy agreement. "You're right about me not owning my success." She blew out a breath and wondered if this was how alcoholics felt at their first meeting. "I'm Tallulah Fournette and I'm proud of what I've built."

Nash's face lit with his smile. "That's my girl."

She didn't trust herself to speak, only wrapped her arms around his shoulders and pressed her lips against his neck. He wrapped her tight against his chest. She flicked her tongue against his pulse point. His skin tasted like sunshine—warm and a little bit salty.

"Have you ever had sex in your truck?"

His arms jerked. "Can't say that I have." His voice was hoarse but had the excited lilt of a boy offered a lifetime supply of candy.

"Is it not on your list?" She smiled against his skin, the stubble on his jaw tickling her. What would that little bit of stubble feel like against her breasts or her inner thighs? Need carved out a hollow place in her lower belly.

"It is now in the number-one position."

She laughed and turned her back on the trailer. They walked toward his truck, arms around one another. Before she stepped into the pine trees, she cast one last look over her shoulder. Her past seemed to cling to her like the vines slowly destroying the old trailer. But finally she felt them loosening.

Nash was good for her. He reminded her how to laugh, how to play, how to see the good around her.

The truck was bouncing through the ruts when he spoke again. "Where can we go?"

"There's an overlook a few miles down. Teenagers go there to mess around."

"You went there a lot?" The bite of animosity shortened his words. She could only assume it was motivated by jealousy. That shouldn't make her happy. It did. She turned to the passenger window to hide her smile.

"I went down there to smoke a little weed, drink some beers." She directed him to a secondary road.

The asphalt was crumbling along the edges, forcing him to drive down the middle. Trees encroached on both sides. A premature darkness covered them, but like switching on a light, they emerged onto the overlook, the sun not yet dropped behind the trees on the far bank. Warm orange light suffused through the cab, the effect surreal and magical. Compared to the stream behind their old houses, the river flowed by wider and wilder.

The overlook was deserted. He parked, rolled the windows down and turned the engine off. The subtle sounds of nature filled the silence. Crickets, cicadas, and bullfrogs weaved a harmonious song.

He shifted the seat as far back as it went and reached toward her breast. She hadn't expected him to pounce on her like a horny teenager and tensed. He pulled the tie off her braid, the end hanging over her right breast. Her nipple hardened at the subtle brush of his fingers. With one hand, he unwound the first few inches.

"Get on my lap." The command in his voice fired equal amounts of excitement and trepidation.

She scrambled over the console and straddled his hips, pressing her pelvis against his growing erection. He pushed her shirt up and over her head and broke the world record getting her bra off. The suddenness surprised her but before she could react, he tossed it to the floorboard.

"Geez, how much practice have you had undressing women?" Naked from the waist up and with his gaze roving her body with an intensity that was almost frightening, a protective instinct overcame her, and she covered her breasts with an arm.

He took her wrist, his hand big and strong and gentle. He could force her arm away, but he only held her wrist, his thumb caressing the underside. "I practiced with a bra on my pillow. After two grueling years of study, I got to put my honed skills to practical use my senior year in college."

Pride and playfulness wove the admission. A laugh snuck out of her. She'd forgotten for a moment, this was Nash. He was a different breed of man than she was used to. The sense of trust he inspired relaxed her. Only then did he draw her arm away.

He took a swift, shallow breath. His chest seemed to move faster.

She laid a hand over his heart. "Do you need your inhaler?"

A smile crested his face, and he took a deep shuddery breath. "My asthma is not what's stealing my breath. You're so unbelievably beautiful. Will you take your braid out?"

Tears burned up her eyes. She tilted her head back, letting gravity pull them back down. Was she seriously teary because he'd spouted romantic nonsense? She blinked. Dangit, that's *exactly* why she was teary. It was a forgone conclusion, she was officially a sappy romantic.

The tremble in her fingers slowed the process, but finally, she shook her hair around her shoulders. He shifted her on his lap, leaning her back over his arm. He nuzzled his face into her neck, kissing his way down to her breasts.

Her body was ridiculously responsive to his touch—almost embarrassingly so. Her nipples were already peaked and straining toward his mouth. The tickle of his stubble along the side of her breast shot fire through her veins.

She threaded her hands into his hair and forced his mouth to the tip of her nipple. "Quit torturing me."

"Beg me." His voice was rough and teasing at the same time.

"Please, Nash."

"Please what?"

"Please, I've wanted you all day. Seeing you work with your shirt off, your pants riding low. God, I wanted to climb on top of you. I'll bet half the ladies in town are going to dream about you tonight." It didn't matter they both still had pants on. The satin of her panties slipped against her as she ground herself against him.

He grazed her nipple with his teeth followed by the flick of his tongue, but she needed his mouth. Passion had burned away her pride.

"I dream about you every night, Nash. Dream about you taking me in every way imaginable." It was all the truth, yet somewhere in her head, her conscience hit a panic button. The alarms didn't have a chance to register.

He pulled her nipple into his mouth at the same time

his hand covered her other breast, pinching her nipple between his fingers. Blinding sensation shot through her body as her hips bucked into his. The relief of her orgasm held any regret at bay. His head fell back against the seat, his eyes closed. She scattered kisses over his face. Each slow grind of her hips against him sent another wave of pleasure through her.

Her body was draped over his, her face buried in his neck, his hand roaming her bare back and into her hair. Slowly, her body ceased its undulations against his and she stilled. Had she dry-humped Nash? Why couldn't she teleport like one of his superheroes? Or wipe his memory clean?

"Did that really happen?" His breath tickled the hair at her temple.

"I don't know why—"

He gripped her hips and pushed against her, turning her bumbling explanation into a gasping moaning of his name.

"If I'm not inside of you in thirty seconds I'm likely to embarrass myself in my pants. Get naked—now." He pushed her to the seat and worked on his zipper.

His command was easier to follow than trying to explain why she had no self-control around him.

Her shorts and underwear were off in record time. They reached for one another at the same time, and he pulled her back on top of him, taking her mouth in a kiss so devastatingly sensual, the buzz of pleasure hit her like a shot of his favorite single-barrel Scotch. She rocked her hips, this time nothing separated them, and she slid over him with the perfect amount of friction. Another climax hovered, ready for her to grab hold.

He maneuvered her hips up and fit himself at her opening, pushing inside of her a mere inch. "Look at me," he said in a guttural, rough voice.

With her hands gripping the back of his seat, she pushed back from him, her body begging for more but his hands holding her out of reach. She tossed her hair over her shoulders, a whimper of distress escaping. She felt feverish, ready to keel over if he didn't get inside of her. She rolled her hips, but his hands stayed tight.

"I love seeing you wild." The look in his eyes burned away any embarrassment or shame.

"I need more. Please, Nash, I need your big, hard—"

He slammed her hips down. As the rhythm increased, his fingers bit into the flesh of her hips. She welcomed the almost-pain. It centered her in the moment.

Her body got what it wanted, what it needed, what she had been begging for. Another orgasm ripped through her like an EF5 tornado, destroying every flimsy wall she'd tried to erect around her heart.

He muttered a curse and pulsed inside of her. She squeezed around him, echoes of pleasure cascading down to her toes.

His head was resting on the seatback, his eyes closed. She lay a hand on his chest, worried about an asthma attack, but his breathing didn't seem haggard or distressed, and his heartbeat thumped strong.

She cupped his cheek and ran her thumbs across his cheekbones and along the line of his jaw. He was handsome, but even more, he was kind. Why was she surprised? He'd always been different than the other boys. He'd never pulled her hair or called her names.

Instead, he'd taken her hand in kindergarten to show her a spider and explain how it was unfortunately nonradiated, so there was no chance of becoming Spider-Man.

She wrapped her arms around his shoulders and kissed him. Everything she couldn't say aloud went into her kiss. What if he'd never come back to Cottonbloom? What if the circle hadn't been completed? Would she have spent the rest of her life feeling incomplete?

But there was fear in the kiss as well. Fear of what the future held. She didn't believe in fairytales or his comic books anymore. Life was hard and sometimes tragic for no reason. If the Fates decided to rip them apart again, then it would happen. Her uncle and his aunt were a living testament. A sense of melancholy made her kiss him all the harder.

His lips came alive under hers, and his gentleness tempered her desperation. With his hands running up and down her bare back and with him still inside of her, he calmed her fears.

His soft T-shirt caressed her breasts and the zipper of his pants pressed into her calf. He hadn't managed to get his pants all the way off. She smiled against his mouth. The fact she could smile, even want to laugh, after the most intense sexual experience of her life steamrolled through her.

She loved him.

She pressed her lips harder against his to keep from saying the words aloud. It wasn't shock or fear or even happiness that sent tears like little pinpricks at her eyelids. It was relief. Of course, she loved him. How could she not?

Her profound, almost painful, vulnerability was offset by the safety he imparted with every look and touch. The urge to tell him stamped out any logical arguments. She pushed back from him. His head tilted and his hands stilled on her back. Expectation thickened the air. Her breaths came faster, and she wet her dry lips, ready to be truly reckless.

The sound of an engine getting closer was like a pin to

a balloon, breaking the sense of solitude. The whoop of voices out of opened windows carried through the evening air.

He pushed her off him and had his pants up and buttoned in two seconds. She yanked her T-shirt on, forgoing the complications of her bra, and shimmied her underwear and shorts back on.

He cranked the engine and had them moving even before her shorts were zipped. He looked over at her with his eyes bright with laughter. "Well there's another thing checked off the list. At the rate we're going, we'll get all this craziness out of our systems before the end of the month."

"Yeah, maybe." A rush of awkwardness shifted her away from him. His sperm soaked her panties, clammy and uncomfortable. It seemed nothing momentous had happened for Nash. He was still busy checking things off his list.

A black SUV broke the tree line, followed by a nineties-era sedan with rusted-out side panels. Nash waved a hand out the window before hitting the narrow, washed out road, leaving the teenagers to their mischief.

Thank the sweet Lord she hadn't said anything. Those rednecks deserved a thank-you note or cheese basket or something. There was no reasons for her feelings to be hurt. After all, she had been the one to suggest getting it on in his truck.

Despite the logic, her heart ached like Nash's punching bag. She banged her head against the headrest a couple of times.

"Imagine them arriving ten minutes earlier." He chuckled. "Would you have been embarrassed or kept on going?"

Under the trees, twilight had fallen. She stared out of the passenger window into the dark forest. Her hurt feelings morphed into anger. While she had gotten gooey with love, he'd been playing out his favorite internet video. "Of course, I would have been mortified. I'm not a porn star."

The truck slowed. "I was just teasing."

"I'm tired. Could you take me home?"

"What's wrong?" He stroked down her arm. She scooted out of his reach.

"I'm tired. That's all. The thing with Uncle Delmar and all our late nights . . . I'm tired."

"Tired. Right." They didn't talk on the drive back to her apartment, but his hands were tight on the steering wheel.

He didn't park but pulled up to the curb leading to the stairs. As her hand made contact with the door handle, he locked the doors, making her attempt useless. "What the hell, Nash? You want to role-play some prisoner-captive fantasy now? Maybe videotape it this time?"

"I'm not letting you do your thing and run away. Tell me what is going on in that beautiful, maddening head of yours?"

She wadded up her bra, stuffed it under her leg, and wished she could break the window and shimmy out like Daisy Duke. "You've become kind of, I don't know, important to me."

"You're important to me too. I thought I'd made myself pretty clear about that fact." Exasperation strung his words together.

"Back there, you sort of made me feel . . . trashy. Like all you were doing is checking things off some sex list you're keeping."

"There is no list. Never was. The only reason I agreed to the list idea was to spend time with you." He muttered a few choice words. "I want to date you. I want to be your man. Do I need to spell it out for you?"

She jerked around. "That was uncalled for."

Confusion flickered over his face before it hardened. He unlocked the doors and faced the windshield, his hands gripping the wheel so tight his biceps flexed. "How about you give me a call when you've grown up and decided not to sabotage anything good in your life?" His voice held an unfamiliar edge.

She fumbled with the handle before throwing the door open and hopping out. He peeled out of the parking lot before she'd even made it to the stairs.

Her tension ebbed into the darkness and left a simmering anger, but she wasn't sure if it was directed at her or him. She trudged up the steps and knocked on Ms. Effie's door.

Locks jangled and the door opened. Ms. Effie's hair was in rollers and she wore a pink terrycloth robe. "You look like someone shot your dog."

"I feel even worse. Is it too late for a visit?"

"'Course not. I was getting ready to paint my toenails and watch a Hallmark movie. Come on in."

Tally closed the door and took up her customary seat on the couch. Ms. Effie would have to start charging her for therapy soon. "Nash and I broke up. I think. He told me to grow up."

Ms. Effie shook a bottle of purple sparkly polish and stayed suspiciously quiet.

"Do you think I self-sabotage?"

"Sounds like someone's been watching too much Dr. Phil." Ms. Effie didn't look up from applying the polish to her big toe. "What do you think?"

Tally bit at her thumbnail. "I don't know. Maybe." She let the evening's events roll through her head. "Probably," she said on a sigh.

"So . . . grow up."

Tally waited, but Ms. Effie hummed an indefinable tune while dabbing on polish.

"That's it?"

The woman sat back in the chair and screwed the top on the polish. "Yes, that's it. If you want an adult relationship, you have to be an adult. Quit running away and making excuses. I heard the little exchange the other night with Heath. I was getting ready to call the police when Nash showed up. He's a good man, isn't he?"

"Yes." Her voice was barely a whisper.

"He treats you well?"

Tally nodded.

"The sex is good?"

"Ms. Effie!" Heat rushed into Tally's face. She reached for an AARP magazine and fanned herself.

Ms. Effie's lips quirked. "I'll take that for a yes. Do you care about him?"

Tally continued to fan herself and swallowed. "I love him."

"Then, darlin', grab him with both hands before he gets away."

The laugh that snuck out morphed into a teary-eyed smile. She lay her head against the soft back of the couch and closed her eyes. A tear trailed into her temple, but she didn't bother wiping it away. "What if he breaks my heart?"

"Walking away never knowing will hurt even worse down the road."

Ms. Effie's words resonated as clearly as Nash's had earlier. Her uncle's situation amplified the truth. She did need to grow up. Her focus had been on the success of her gym as if that could somehow compensate for her other perceived deficiencies.

But that's not how things worked. She had ignored the

festering stump of her emotional life while her gym flourished under the attention. Now that she was trying to have a normal, sane relationship with a normal, sane man, she was like a kindergartner learning the ropes of a new environment. She'd best learn quick before she lost him.

"You're right." She stood but rocked on her feet. Should she go now or wait? Maybe given a night, the hardness she'd sensed in him would soften, and he would be more forgiving. "I'll find him in the morning and apologize and lay it out for him."

Ms. Effie propped her other foot on the table. "Let me know how it goes."

After saying their good-nights, Tally walked into her empty apartment and flipped the light on. She saw the room through Nash's eyes. A brown water stain crept down one corner, and the edge of the shabby carpet was frayed. Most of her furniture was thrift-store finds from when she'd first moved in.

It no longer felt like a home, it felt like the vines pulling at the old trailer. She could afford a nicer place, but she'd always questioned whether she deserved one. Like she questioned if she deserved a man like Nash.

While she wasn't one hundred percent convinced deep down she did, she was like a molting caterpillar, another layer shed and that much closer to getting wings. She collapsed on the bed still clothed, and fell asleep. Memories, some welcome, some not, battered her dreams.

Chapter Fifteen

She awoke feeling as though she hadn't slept, her eyes grainy and her head stuck in the past. After sweet-talking Reed into handling the gym and cancelling her kickboxing class, she dropped to the floor and pulled a box from underneath her dresser. Her fingers left lines in the dust that had gathered on the lid. She wiped her hand across the top, turning the grayed-out flower print vibrant once again.

She wiped the grime onto the back of her shorts. How many years had passed since she opened the box? At least five, although she was always aware of its existence like a splinter dug too deep to remove. Was it the same sort of box Ms. Leora kept her keepsakes in?

She fumbled with the simple brass latch before flipping open the lid. An assortment of memories were stored inside. Pictures, poems, cards. Her family smiled up at her. She was maybe eight, her grin huge and open, her two front teeth gone, reminding her of Birdie. At eleven, Sawyer's hair flopped over his eyes, his stance relaxed, his smile already charming and too cool for the rest of them. Cade had hit puberty, his face taking on shades of the man he would become. As if he could sense the approaching tragedy, he stood strong and solemn.

Finally, she allowed her gaze to fall on her mother and father, taking them in as if they were one entity or maybe a matched set, not to be separated. Light and dark. Her father's ready smile had lightened her mother's more serious nature. Instinctively, she understood that they brought out the best in each other. Her mother had curbed her father's impulsiveness. Maybe without her, he would have ended up more like his brother Delmar. And, in turn, he'd made her laugh and dance.

Tally ran a finger over their smiling faces. Maybe it was a blessing they were taken together. Could one of them have managed without the other?

She put the photo aside and filtered through the rest of the contents, unfolding a newspaper article. The local paper had run a story on Nash when he left for college at sixteen—the town genius.

The picture they ran with the story was grainy, but she could make out constellations of acne on his face. His thick-rimmed glasses emphasized his too-big nose and made his eyes look small. His hair was shorn close like a brown cap. He hadn't been handsome, but now that she knew the grown-up Nash, she could see the promise in his strong jawline and high forehead. She could also see the remnants of the boy he'd been in the warmth and openness of his smile.

The picture she was in search of lay at the bottom, facedown. Her mother's loopy handwriting filled the white space—TALLULAH AND NASH, 10 YEARS OLD.

She turned the picture over, her fingers shaky. She and Nash sat criss-cross under the willow tree, huge grins on their faces, arms across each other's shoulders, each holding a Popsicle. She'd been as big as he was back then. Her hair was a tangled mess. Her mother forced a braid or ponytail when possible, but Tally had liked her hair free back then.

Nash's left knee was skinned, the scab dark on his tanned, spindly legs. She'd forgotten about his crooked bottom teeth. Somewhere along the way, he'd gotten braces because his smile was perfect now.

A sadness lurked around his eyes. She flipped the picture over. His mother had died when they were ten. This must have been taken the summer before, but she'd been sick for years.

She stared at the picture awhile longer. Would she step back through time if she could? Recapture the innocence staring back at her? Ask her parents to skip their date night? Or was she exactly when and where she was supposed to be?

Nash was *her* match. Her lost glove. The sugar to her salt. A sudden urgency had her changing clothes and tossing everything back in the box. Everything but the picture of her and Nash. She slipped it into her back pocket.

Her destination was his cottage, but instead of breaking up with him and hightailing it far, far away, she planned to hole up until she convinced him she was ready for more. Ready for everything.

Crossing the steel-girded bridge, she stopped short and turned down River Street. His Defender was backed up to the gazebo. She parked in the grass behind him and ran up. He wasn't there. She looked up and down the street, not seeing him.

She settled onto the bottom step to wait for as long as it took.

"I don't know, ladies." Nash pulled at his bottom lip and ran a hand over the quilt in his lap. Five of the Quilting Bee's regulars sat in a circle, their thimbles flashing.

Every single one of them, his aunt included, had a pair of magnified glasses perched on the end of their noses.

Mrs. Carson looked over the top of her glasses. "We weren't always old, Master Nash." The tease in her voice and the use of the childish moniker made him smile in spite of his desperation.

He had screwed things up. Even though he'd told himself time and again he had to take things slow and not spook her, he'd let his frustration get the better of him.

Her accusations that he was using her for sex rankled. After a poor night's sleep, he'd concluded his anger was a reflection of his fears. Maybe she was using him for a good time and nothing else. That didn't explain her freeze out after the hottest sex of his life though. Why did the woman have to be so confusing?

His mood headed further south when his dad had called out of the blue to invite him to lunch. He'd been too punch-tired and thrown off guard to come up with an excuse. He should be happy to see his dad, but after his mom had died, Nash had felt like an afterthought at best, a burden at worst.

"You can sleep with your pride, or you can work things out." Mrs. Carson's voice turned more serious. "Don't get to be our age still carrying around regrets."

Was his imagination or had Mrs. Carson's gaze flitted over his aunt?

"What do you think, Aunt Leora?" The can of worms he was opening should probably be kept nailed closed, but curiosity got the better of him. She hadn't said a single word about Delmar Fournette.

His aunt stopped her work, pulled her glasses off, and looked toward the front window. "Vera's right. If you love that girl, then don't let her go. I loved a man once."

The other women, Mrs. Carson included, kept at their

tasks, their gazes downcast, lending a strange sense of privacy between him and his aunt.

"The man in the picture?"

"Yes." His aunt's voice had taken on a dreamlike quality as if she were somewhere else. "He was a good man once. Maybe he still is."

"Then he didn't die in Vietnam?"

"No, but he came back different, and I was too stubborn to accept that things had changed. I wanted him to be the same carefree boy that left instead of the troubled man who returned."

"Was it Delmar Fournette?"

Dropping his name in the room shattered the sense of solitude. All the ladies turned toward his aunt to pat her hands or offer comforting words. Mrs. Carson slipped a plaid-quilting square into her hands to use as a handkerchief, but his aunt only chuffed a small laugh.

"I should have known it wouldn't take you long to guess after finding that picture. He hasn't changed so much, has he? Still a handsome devil."

Nash wasn't sure how to answer.

"I've been unfair to the Fournettes. Tallulah in particular, I suppose. She reminded me too much of Del and what I lost—or what I threw away. The older I get the bigger my regrets loom."

He nodded, a hollow ache for his aunt spreading through his stomach. So many years wasted when the man she loved was just on the other side of the river.

"I'm sorry," he whispered.

"I was twenty-two when he came back. I didn't understand what unconditional love was then. Too young and immature. Taking care of your mother was my penance, I suppose. I loved her right until the end."

Nash's throat tightened.

His aunt sniffed, put away the square, and picked up

her needle. A secretive smile came to her face. "He came to see me last night."

The women gasped in unison and broke out in magpie chatters until Mrs. Carson shushed them. "What did he want?"

"Brought me a huge bouquet of wild flowers. We sat on the swing and talked."

"About what?" Nash asked.

His aunt's cheeks flushed, her laugh girlish. "That's none of your business. And if I'm not mistaken, you have your own problems to deal with. Don't repeat my foolishness."

He stood up, the quilt falling from his lap. Even as his heart beat an urgent rhythm, he stopped to give his aunt a hug around the shoulders. The scent of hairspray and lotion cast him backward. "Thank you for understanding, Aunt Leora."

She patted his shoulder. "Go on, son."

Son. He held on a moment longer. He was out the door and jogging down the street when he spotted her car tucked in behind the Defender. Slowing to an amble, he jammed his hands into his pockets while his insides worked themselves into knots a boy scout would be proud of.

She was sitting on the gazebo steps, her legs bent and her chin tucked on her knees, playing with the laces of her shoes. She wasn't in her work uniform of spandex, but black cotton shorts and a purple T-shirt.

He blew out a long, slow breath, his hand wrapping around his inhaler, and said, "Hey." A sense of inadequacy turned him mute.

"Oh, Nash." She was up before he could unstick his brain. Her body crashed into his, driving him back a step on his heels. Her arms were tight around his neck, and he ran his hands up her back, feeling like he was in a dream. The worry and anxiety and self-flagellation of the night before melted under the heat of their bodies together.

Her lips moved against his neck, her voice muffled. "I'm so sorry. You were right. About everything. I do need to grow up and I do sabotage everything because I'm afraid of becoming too comfortable or, heaven help me, happy. I know it can all disappear in an instant. But the alternative is even worse."

It took a few seconds for her words to weave their way into his heart. "What's the alternative?"

"Not being with you when you're right here in front of me. Not being able to . . . love you." She ended with a questioning lilt.

"Hold up. Are you saying what I think you're saying?"

She pulled back. "What do you think I'm saying?"

He expected to see her usual defensiveness, but instead her vulnerability was written on her face like a stone carving. "You tell me." He was willing to give her anything and everything, but he needed her to give him this.

Her throat worked as if choking on the words. "I love you. You must know that. I always have, but it's different now."

"How is it different?"

"Because we're both grown-ups, and obviously, we're attracted to each other, but it's the same too."

"How so?" He knew he was pushing her past her comfort zone and rubbed his hands up and down her back to impart support.

"You make me laugh and protect me and make me feel . . . normal. I want to be with you. If you'll still have me." She bit her bottom lip as if waiting for him to pass judgment.

He cupped her face. "I'll have you, if you'll have me.

I'm sorry if I made you feel used or cheap last night, and I'm especially sorry for what I said in the truck. I shouldn't have—"

"Yes, you should have. I was running scared." She wrapped her hands around his wrists and tilted her face toward his.

Finally, it seemed, they were beginning to understand each other. He half-smiled and leaned in for a kiss, but stopped a hairsbreadth from her lips. "By the way, I love you too, Tallulah."

He swooped in before she could do anything but gasp. Their shared memories flavored the kiss, but a sprinkling of something new added a tenderness and a promise of new memories.

He broke away, breathing hard and wishing they were anywhere but in the middle of town. Preferably somewhere with a bed and air conditioning. He could sense the gazes of five women.

The devil on his shoulder—strike that, it had set up camp farther south—urged him to text his father to cancel their lunch. He wouldn't though. His sense of responsibility was strong. He supposed he had his aunt to thank for that.

He groaned against her temple. "I have to go to Baton Rouge to meet my father."

"I've taken the day off, I can come with you."

"You want to come with me?" He didn't want a witness to what was sure to be an emasculating, mortifying experience. *Please say no*, part of him begged.

"You came to Uncle Del's. I'm coming." In her tone was an immovable strength and in that strength, he found comfort.

"All right. You need anything or can you head from here?"

She grabbed her purse while he opened the passenger

door of the Defender for her. She snaked an arm around his neck and kissed him, her lips firm, the contact too brief. The meaning was clear. He could count on her.

He tooted the horn and waved at the ladies crowded around the front window of the Quilting Bee. They all waved back, and he suppressed a guffaw.

Tally scrunched down in the seat. "What will your aunt say?"

"Actually, she urged me to make things right with you. I was heading out to find you." He gave her a brief run-down on what his aunt had confessed.

"Do you think they'll start dating?" Her small smile was at once hopeful and incredulous.

"No clue. Aunt Leora actually blushed. And giggled."

Tally's response was laughter. They blew past the Cottonbloom Parish line on the way to Baton Rouge, and his thoughts moved from his aunt to the upcoming meeting.

His father was a mystery. People on the Louisiana side of the river often asked after him, giving a he's-a-good-man nod and murmur. Was he a good man? Nash honestly couldn't judge.

"How long has it been since you saw him last?"

"College. Last time we talked on the phone was right before my postdoc in Edinburgh. Otherwise, it's been sporadic emails."

"Family is tough. You know Cade and I hardly spoke for a few years after I graduated high school."

"I didn't know." The siblings' bonds had seemed un-breakable. When he'd been small, he'd envied Tally her big, protective brothers. "Why?"

"Because I refused to go to college. It would have been a waste, and Cade had already sacrificed so much for me and Sawyer." She shook her head and sighed. "He thought I was rejecting him or what he'd done for us. I had kept my dyslexia a secret for so long, I couldn't tell him. I wanted to pretend I wasn't a weirdo."

"I like weirdos. In fact, I'm a weirdo too." He slipped a hand around her shoulders and massaged her neck. She gave a little laugh and laid a kiss on the inside of his elbow. Goose bumps rippled up his arm.

"Everything is good now. Great, even. Maybe this is your father trying to form a relationship with you."

"He and I don't exactly have many common interests."

"I said the same thing about us, if you remember," she said dryly. "Anyway, you both have the river, right?"

His chuckle contained more sarcasm than humor. "Not sure how long we can discuss mudbugs."

"I'll be there to diffuse any awkwardness." Her hand roamed up and down his inner thigh.

"If you keep that up, we're going to find another back road and won't make it to Baton Rouge."

Her hand made a quick pass over the front of his pants before retreating to lay primly in her lap. "I'll try to keep my hands—and mouth—off until tonight."

His foot twitched on the accelerator, making them lurch forward. "Are you saying what I think you're saying?"

"You'll have to wait to find out, Professor."

He loved the tease in her voice. It hinted at the ease that was growing between them, and what their relationship could become. Soon enough, he parked the Defender on a side street a block from the restaurant. He grabbed her hand and stepped inside, his gaze pinging off the occupants. He didn't see his dad.

They took a booth and sat on the same side, facing the door. Nash checked his phone. No texts. He wouldn't have been surprised if his dad bailed. In fact, he would welcome the reprieve.

Tally put her hand over his, stilling his unconscious nervous tapping. "It's going to be fine. No worries."

His father had picked a casual Italian place close to the dock. A good portion of the lunch crowd wore uniformed shirts with their name embroidered on the breast. It seemed this was a gathering place for people getting off or heading in for their shifts.

The bell over the door tinkled. Cement shot through Nash's limbs. His father stood inside the door and looked around the room, his gaze brushing over Nash but moving on. He had aged. His hair had thinned and faded from brown to gray, and he looked rangier. He wasn't wearing the oil company's uniform, but jeans and a red T-shirt.

As if it belonged to someone else, Nash's hand raised and waved, drawing his father's attention. He was ensnared by his father's gaze. White noise filled the space between the buzzing conversations and the soft music.

Tally was on the outside and stood, a smile on her face and her hand outstretched. His father grasped Tally's hand in a shake, and they exchanged the trite greetings of acquaintances who hadn't seen each other in years. His father didn't give any indication he was surprised to see her there. Stuck inside the booth, Nash offered his hand next and held his breath.

In his memories, his father's hands had been stuff of legend. Huge and wound with strong tendons. Now, his hand was no bigger than Nash's, his knuckles gnarled and the skin thinner with prominent blue veins. His father slipped to the middle of the bench seat opposite Nash and Tally. Under the table, Nash groped for Tally's hand. She threaded her fingers through his. Her touch calmed him, made it easier to breathe. He didn't want to have an asthma attack in front of his father.

"You look good, Nash." His father fired first. "Finally got some muscle on you."

His lack of athletic prowess as an adolescent had needled his father. He'd wanted a popular, football-playing jock—like him. Instead, he'd gotten a skinny, comic book–reading nerd. That was a history that couldn't be rewritten.

"What's up, Dad?"

"I was surprised to hear you were back in the States. Figured you were done with us. You're teaching up at Cottonbloom College?" His father relaxed into the corner of the booth and set his arm along the back, shifting so he didn't have to make eye contact.

"Will be in the fall."

"Wished you'd emailed me or called or something earlier. A kick to hear about my son from someone else."

If Nash had to put an emotion behind the tone, he would've have picked hurt. "I didn't think you'd care."

His father's eyes narrowed as if he was flinching from a near hit. "What are you doing this summer? Hanging out?"

"Working on a research paper." An old defensiveness crept into his voice. His father thought reading books had been a waste of time and studying history even worse. In his father's eyes, the only worthy work involve copious amounts of blood, sweat, and tears.

"Nash is being modest, Mr. Hawthorne. He's going to write a book." Pride fired Tally's words. He wanted to lean over and kiss her right then and there.

"Something exciting or history?"

Tally huffed. "History *is* exciting."

Nash squeezed her hand hard enough to get her to turn. Not caring what his father thought, he kissed her, a simple brush of his lips over hers.

"So you two, huh?" His father pointed back and forth between them.

Nash nodded. "Yep."

A silence descended, and Nash wished the server would make an appearance. His father toyed with the knife and fork rolled in a paper napkin.

Nash chewed on his bottom lip before saying, "How's life in the Gulf?"

His father stopped fiddling. "They tell me I've gotten too old for the rig. Time to hang up my boots. I'm retiring." His father delivered the news like a diagnosis of terminal cancer.

Nash wasn't sure what was expected of him. Commiseration or congratulations. He settled on logic. "They can't force you out because of your age."

"I made a couple of mistakes. Everyone does sometimes, usually it's not a big deal, but they documented them, used them against me. It was either take retirement or get fired. Everything is automated now, and they don't need as many men out there."

"I'm sorry, Dad. That's terrible. What are you going to do?"

"Don't really know. That rig . . . after your mother died, it's all I had left."

Nash tried to summon the sympathy his father was after. He tried really hard. Instead, anger welled up from a place he'd hidden from everyone—even himself. He pulled his hand out of Tally's and leaned over the table.

"You had *me* after Mom died. You left three days after her funeral for that goddamn rig. It's like when Mom died, I died too for all you cared."

His father had paled, his face tinged gray, the deep grooves along his mouth standing in relief. The waiter chose that moment to approach their table with a smile pasted on his face. They put in drink orders, but Nash waved him away when he started reeling off the specials. Anything he tried to eat would get stuck in his throat.

Once the waiter was out of earshot, his father picked

the conversation up where they'd left it. "I loved your mother, Nash, I did. She was a sweet woman. Sensitive. I couldn't watch her die like that . . . slow and painful. I'll admit I was a coward to let Leora take care of her. And afterward too. It was easier to let Leora have her way with you. She had more to offer you than I did."

Slivers of truth intersected his childish pain, and his next lash was weaker. "When you were on leave, you were always itching to get back to the rig."

His father ran a hand through his hair, mussing the neat comb lines and exposing white scalp. Although he turned to face Nash, his gaze was focused somewhere over his shoulder as if looking into the past. "Look, I never meant to get married. Got your mom pregnant on one of my leaves. I did the right thing by her though. Never wanted a kid, but there you were."

Words injected like poisoned darts. Unwanted. Mistake.

His father's gaze finally slipped to meet his. "But you were sweet like your mama. Hardly ever cried. Smiled all the time. Soon as you could talk, you asked me questions like I had all the answers. But I didn't. Not hardly. You didn't have no interest in tossing a ball. Always had your nose in a book."

"I was a kid, Dad. You could have taken me for ice cream, taken me to the movies, taken me fishing. It wasn't complicated."

"You were some crazy smart prodigy. And, look at you now, a professor. I don't know nothing about all those dead folks you're so interested in. My life has been keeping the oil flowing. And now . . ."

Nash sensed his father was at a crossroads and looking for a sign. Part of him wanted to leave his father there, lost and wandering and unwanted. The waiter returned with their drinks.

"You could come up to Cottonbloom until you figure things out." The words felt pried from his mouth.

"You sure?" His father's eyes sparked. "That would be great. Do you have an extra bed or even a couch I could borrow for a couple of weeks? Just until I can find work."

Maybe there was justice in the world. Nash knew his smile contained more than a fair amount of diabolical glee. "Actually, I'm living in Aunt Leora's guest cottage, but she's rattling around in that old house of hers. I'm sure she'd be delighted to offer you a room."

His father winced, but nodded. "Not sure delight will be her first emotion. I respect her though. She took care of your mama until the end. For a while, I thought she'd be strong enough for the both of them."

"Aunt Leora's getting older and needs more help. That's one of the reasons I came back to Cottonbloom."

His father dropped his gaze to the table and rubbed his hands together. "I guess no one can outrun the years, but I'm not ready to be put to pasture."

An awkward silence descended. Tally said, "Nash loves to fly-fish, Mr. Hawthorne. Maybe he could take you out on the river sometime."

Nash cast a side-eye glance toward her.

"I didn't know you still liked to fish, son. What kind of bait do you use?"

Now that they had tread into one of man's sacred subjects, the conversation flowed and the tension ebbed. Nash pulled out his phone to share pictures of one of his fishing trips in Scotland. As he flipped through the pictures, a photo of a crypt under a northern English church flashed.

His father touched his hand. "What was that?"

Nash flipped back. "It's thought to be the final resting place of one of the Knights Templar." He zoomed in on the stone carving along the lid of the coffin, pointing at various elements and explaining their meaning. Sometime during the lecture, his father had sat back in the booth and crossed his arms.

"Dang son, you nearly got me excited about some old dead guy. You really love this stuff, huh?"

"You find pumping oil miles out of the ground exciting. I find dead guys exciting."

"All right. Show me more." The slow nod his father gave seemed to hold a deeper acceptance than a simple affirmative.

Nash didn't stop to examine the childlike satisfaction he got from explaining each picture to his father. Maybe his father was humoring him, maybe he was attempting to mend the years of distance, maybe he really was interested. Nash didn't care.

By the time he'd finished, their drinks were empty and the waiter was sending them unhappy looks. The three of them slid out of the booth. Nash threw a bigger tip than the waiter earned on the table.

His father had always seemed larger than life and intimidating as hell. Now, they stood eye to eye, and Nash had at least thirty pounds on him. They walked into a damp inferno and stopped on the sidewalk. Nash took a deep breath of salty air. He preferred the loamy, swampy air of Cottonbloom to the salt. Always had.

"I should probably give Aunt Leora some warning else she might pass out on the front stoop. When do you want to head up?"

His father looked in the direction of the ocean, even though it wasn't visible from where they stood. "Nothing keeping me here. How about I come up tomorrow? That too soon?"

A frisson of shock rocked through Nash. His father had no one. "Not at all."

His father rocked on his feet. "I guess I'll see you

tomorrow, then? Hope I'll be seeing more of you, Tally."

"I'm sure you will, Mr. Hawthorne." Tally offered her hand, but his father pulled her in for a half hug.

"Your parents were good people. I was too lost in my own grieving to offer you much back then, and I'm sorry for it. Call me Jack, please."

"Thanks, Jack."

His father stuck his hands into the front pockets of his jeans and smiled, backing away a few steps before turning and walking down the street. Nash stood there until his father disappeared around a corner.

"Wow, that was interesting." Tally's ironically given understatement made him chuckle.

"Not at all what I expected."

"It's good though, isn't it?" She weaved their fingers together as they walked to his truck.

"You think?"

"It's a second chance, Nash."

They climbed into the truck and he cranked the engine, but didn't shift immediately into drive. The air conditioning barely made headway through the scorching heat inside. Strangers walked past them, each one with their own stories of heartache to tell or secrets to keep.

"When your mother died, you lost both your parents, didn't you? Just like me. I didn't realize . . ." She shifted toward him and traced her fingertips over the tattoo on his biceps.

He caught her hand in his. "He was alive. Out there. I teetered between wanting to make him proud and wanting to give him the finger."

"It was nice to offer him a place to stay."

"Even if it was with Aunt Leora?"

Her lips quirked. "Even so. Seems to me she's softening with the years."

"Thanks for coming with me."

"It's what a girlfriend does, right?"

Something flared between them, something he wasn't sure he could define, something that instilled fear and joy. He jerked the shifter into drive and got them headed toward home.

They didn't talk much on the trip back to Cotton-bloom. He didn't ask, and she didn't protest when he drove them to his place. They were finally on the same page of the same book.

She took his hand and pulled him up the stairs to his loft bedroom. She slipped his glasses off and set them aside. He pulled his shirt off and tossed it to the floor like a white flag of surrender.

He went for her shirt, but she batted his hands away while she leaned in to press her face into the hollow of his neck. Her lips tickled the soft skin under his ear. She was being sweet, too sweet.

He unwound her braid, tangled his hands in her hair, and tugged her head back. The kiss he gave her was a command and a plea. After the tumultuous meeting with his father, he craved simple and uncomplicated. He would make it up to her later.

He went after her shirt again, but she dislodged his hands. Her kiss-reddened lips were parted, and she looked as if she wanted to say something. Instead, she dropped nips and kisses along his jaw and neck, trekking slowly south to his chest. Only when her hands tugged the front of his pants as she fell to her knees did he comprehend her intent.

"You don't have to—"

She palmed him over his pants, his half-hearted protest forgotten. The shorts dropped to his ankles. He toed his shoes off and kicked the shorts aside, leaving him only in underwear.

Like the morning that had burned itself into his memory, his erection was pressing and prominent. Too lightly, she skimmed her fingers down the length.

"I've dreamed of you like this . . . on your knees in front of me, but I always wake up feeling like an insensitive jerk." Even as he said the words, he was wrapping her long, dark hair around his hands.

Her gaze shot up, a spark of humor in her eyes. "Don't you get it? *I've* dreamed of doing this ever since that morning." Her voice dropped to a whisper. "I want to make you happy."

She didn't give him a chance to respond. She pulled his underwear down and wrapped a hand around him, nuzzling her lips around the tip. Closing her eyes, she opened her mouth.

He tried to hold still, but instinct took over and he pumped his hips, his hands tightening in her hair. A small amount of awareness lurking under his primal need kept him from pressing too hard or deep. She opened her eyes and cast them upward. Their gazes met and held. His hips stilled.

It was if a picture had been taken, freezing them in the intimacy. Her eyes huge, her face flushed, her hair wild. His needs shifted. He pulled out of her mouth and scooped her to her feet, bringing her body into his. His underwear slipped down and he kicked it off, completely nude while she was dressed. But not for long.

He kissed her, long and deep, wrestling with her shorts. They fell away. Her shirt followed his across the room, the purple landing on top of the white. He undid her bra with one hand and peeled it off. With every piece of clothing he removed, the more impatient he became.

The raw emotions clawing to escape required pacification. He pushed her backward until her knees hit the mattress, and she plopped down. He continued to maneuver her body across the bed until he was between her legs.

He was poised to take her when he noticed the tear trailing along her temple. He swooped to kiss it away, the salt muting his single-minded intent. "What's wrong?"

"What if I don't know how to do this?"

Instinctively, he knew she wasn't talking about sex. He settled his forearms on either side of her head, his brain having difficulty locating words that were more than one syllable. "We'll figure it out."

The tip of his erection brushed the center of her and his hips jerked.

"But what if I'm not as good at it as you are?"

A laugh of surprise and desperation spurted out. "It's not a competition. It's . . . an exploration. Like we used to explore the river together."

"We're not kids anymore."

"Trust me, I know." He circled his hips against her, his erection finally pushing inside of her an inch. He captured her gasp with a kiss. One firm stroke buried him deep. She tore her mouth away, her back arching.

Each stroke stole another sliver of rational thought until words were lost in the fog of his building orgasm. Yet, it was indefinably different this time.

He wanted to close his eyes, lose himself in the physical, but he didn't. When she climaxed, his name fell from her lips. He kissed her silent, his pelvis grinding into hers one last time as he followed her.

He wasn't sure how much time passed before the kisses she peppered over his shoulder and neck revived him. He rolled off her to stare up through the skylights at the clear night. She scooted away, and he raised his head enough to see her cute backside disappear into the bathroom.

Not good at it, she'd said. He almost laughed again.

Not only was she the most amazing lover he'd ever had, but now that her walls were crumbling, her sweetness flavored everything.

When the water turned off in the bathroom, he repositioned himself in bed, propped up on the pillows. He half-expected her to ask for one of his T-shirts, but she slipped under the covers naked and fused herself to his side, her head on his shoulder.

It was early yet, and he wasn't ready for sleep to end their day together. The revelations and drama had him keyed up and only one thing would calm him.

"Can I read to you?"

Her hand stilled where it had been tracing patterns on his chest. The grenade he'd launched sat between them. "There's something I want to read to you. May I?"

She turned to her back and scooched up the pillows, pulling the sheet to her neck. "It's okay. You can read while I . . ." Her gaze swept the room.

"Lie here and enjoy it? Look, this is not to make you feel uncomfortable or whatever. This is something I want to share with you. Will you let me?"

She shrugged, her reluctance palpable. He trotted down the stairs to retrieve the book he had in mind. It had been years since he'd read it, and it took a few minutes to locate it in the bookcase.

He walked back into his bedroom, flipping through the book like they were old friends kept apart too long.

"Do you always walk around naked?"

He glanced up. Her eyes were huge and focused below his waist. She clutched the sheet to her chin like some horrified maiden. This reaction from the woman who'd gone down on him not a half hour earlier made laughter pour out of him.

He slipped back in bed but didn't bother to cover himself. Affecting a thick Southern accent, he said, "Why

Miss Fournette, you have already been well and truly compromised."

"If you do not cover yourself with a sheet, sir, I shan't be able to control my unladylike urges." Her Scarlett O'Hara voice was threaded with enough husky promise to make his blood run faster.

He leaned in for a kiss but flipped the sheet over his hips. Her arms circled his shoulders, the sheet falling to her waist. Before her soft, perfect breasts could distract him, he pulled the sheet to her chin and retreated. "Enough of that, you wild, wicked woman."

He crossed his feet at the ankle and turned to page one, smoothing the paper.

She stopped him before he even got a page in. "Hold up. This is a kid's book."

"It's Harry Potter. It's for anyone who has ever felt abandoned. For every misfit. I can't tell you how many times I read it. Afterward."

"After your mother died?"

"And after I lost you," he whispered before focusing his attention on the book.

Chapter Sixteen

His voice wove a spell around her. Not in a way that put her to sleep, but in a way that transported her. After a time, she forgot to worry about her dyslexia and the huge leap they'd taken together and relaxed. She closed her eyes, but her brain absorbed the words like a good rain after a long drought.

It took a few heartbeats for the silence to register. She opened her eyes to find him looking down at her. "I thought you'd fallen asleep."

She popped up on her elbows. It seemed strange to see him and the stacks of books and the moon through the skylights. "No. Not at all. I was . . . in the story."

A slow grin warmed his eyes. "You like it?"

"It's amazing and so is the way you read it. Your British accent is really good."

"You won't mind if I read to you again sometime?"

"You kind of have to. I need to find out what happens, don't I?"

He flipped the lamp off and rolled toward her, tucking her into his body, but making no move to make love to her.

"They've made amazing leaps in therapies for dyslexia, you know."

She stiffened, but he didn't allow her to pull away. "How would you know?"

"I looked into it. There's a center—"

"I went there once to ask about their programs, and it was a bunch of eight- and nine-year-olds. It's humiliating enough already without having to sit next to a kid who eats his boogers."

The rumble that vibrated her cheek was distantly humorous. "How about a private session, then?"

"I don't know."

"I could teach myself the methods behind it and work with you."

His persistence, even if it was in her best interests, rubbed her like sandpaper. "Leave it. You're my boyfriend, not my teacher. Anyway, you said you don't care if I can't read *War and Peace* with you."

"It doesn't affect the way I feel about you, but is it wrong that I want you to experience the joy I've found in books?" She hesitated and he pounced. "I'm going to look into options and I want you to keep an open mind. Okay?"

She nodded. She really did want to learn to read better and faster. It wasn't the work it would take to overcome her dyslexia that had held her back, it was the humiliation of being nearly thirty and having to ask for help with something the average third-grader could do.

The next morning, Tally slipped into the Defender for a ride back to her car. Although it was probably her imagination, her neck heated with the thought of his aunt watching. No matter what Nash had said, she wasn't convinced of Ms. Leora's one-eighty turnaround. The woman was probably waiting for her to screw up so she could jump out with an "Aha!"

They spent as much time as they could in each other's company over the next week. Ms. Leora welcomed Jack Hawthorne with equal amounts of trepidation and optimism. Tally continued to expand her plans for the senior program and to solidify her small part in the festival. Sawyer reviewed her signage and advertisements, making corrections as needed. As many times as she reviewed it, she always misspelled or dropped a word.

She and Nash spent the weekend together except for work, and she even went to church with him and Ms. Leora, although she made Nash sit between them. While it was all-around tense and unenjoyable, she considered church with Ms. Leora a necessary evil if she was going to be with Nash. The looks she received from female members of the congregation varied from incendiary to welcoming, depending on their age and marital status.

Afterward, she sank down in the passenger seat of the Defender and kicked her shoes off. She couldn't wait to get back in her jeans and T-shirt. "I'm glad that's over." They passed the street to his place. "Hey, you missed the turn."

"Listen, I've got some stuff to do this afternoon, okay?"

His voice was distant, distracted. A jumble of rocks slid through her body to congregate in her stomach. Something was wrong. She'd caught him staring off into nothing several times over the weekend, but she'd put it down to Charlemagne. Maybe it wasn't some dead guy. Maybe it was her. Had she done something wrong?

She forced a smile. "Sure. I've got stuff to do too."

He pulled into her lot and didn't bother parking, just idled at the steps to her apartment. She grabbed her shoes and pushed the door open, but before she slipped out, he grabbed her wrist. "I'll call you later. Promise."

She glanced over her shoulder, his gaze ensnaring

hers. Regret and an apology for what he was leaving un-
said hung in the cab. Was this a passive-aggressive way
of trying to distance himself from her? Were they getting too serious, too fast? Of course, they were. The same
worries plagued her, but she had put her trust in him.

"Sure. Call me later." She twisted out of his grasp and,
holding her shoes to her chest, ran up the steps and into
her apartment in time to watch him drive off.

She changed out of her Sunday dress and wandered
her apartment. Ms. Effie spent Sundays with her son and
his family. Cade and Monroe were probably doing something that would give the preacher a stroke, and Sawyer
went fishing every Sunday after church.

The last days with Nash highlighted how lonely her
existence had been before him. What would she have
done on a Sunday afternoon before Nash? Watch TV or
head to the gym to work. Real exciting. She flipped
through the channels.

After watching an entire sitcom and realizing she had
no idea what it had been about, she threw down the re-
mote and grabbed her keys. On autopilot, she drove to
town and parked. She walked down the sidewalk to the
gym, kicking a rock along with her. She stopped. Unease
rippled down her back, making goose bumps pop on her
arms in spite of the heat.

Reed's truck was parked a few spaces ahead, and if
she wasn't seeing things, so was Heath's SUV. Although
his Defender was nowhere in sight, she could sense
Nash's presence. She ran the rest of the way. The shades
were all drawn, but she could see the glow of fluorescent
lights. She tried the door, but it was locked. She dug into
her purse for the ring of keys and fumbled them out.

Her hands trembled from a combination of fear and
fury. If what she thought was happening was actually happening, she was going to kill someone. Preferably Heath.

But Reed and Nash were a close second. A triple homicide.

She threw the door open. No one even noticed her. Heath and Nash circled each other in the ring. Jack Hawthorne and Reed had their backs to her and Bryce, Heath's butt-kisser, was yelling encouragement from the opposite side. It was a standard square boxing ring with ropes and not the octagon-style of the MMA. At least Heath couldn't back Nash up against a wall and pummel him.

Nash bounced on his toes and threw a few jabs, one snapping Heath's head back. The men were feeling each other out. Heath was a bruiser and lumbered, heavy on his feet. He wasn't as tall as Nash but thick muscles and tattoos roped his chest and upper arms. His legs were short by comparison, giving him a low center of gravity and an almost inescapable ground game.

Nash was leaner, and moved with an ease and grace that was dancerlike. His punches were crisp and quick. If the match was decided on style points, Nash would take it. Heath was the bull and Nash the matador.

But Nash didn't have the kicking or ground game to compete with Heath. The differences between boxing and MMA-style fighting were like sharing tea with the Queen of England versus grabbing a beer with your drunk uncle. One was civilized and one wasn't.

Nash's fist snaked through Heath's weak left-side defense. His head popped back and forward like a bobble toy. He shuffled a couple of steps to the side, dropping his defensive stance altogether. Touching the rising red welt on his cheekbone, Heath worked his guard in and out of his mouth.

Tally wanted to yell at Nash to take advantage of Heath's surprise, but Nash only stood back, bouncing on his feet, and smiled around his mouth guard. Too much a gentleman. Like a bull being hit with the first of the spears, Heath charged him.

The slap of body against body and the grunts of two men as they grappled for dominance filled the gym. She rushed forward and grabbed Reed's shoulder.

He spun, muttered a curse, and had the good sense to look sheepish.

"If you weren't irreplaceable, I'd fire your butt right now."

"Good to know you value me as an employee."

"Doesn't mean I can't *kick* your butt."

"That's it, Nash." Jack's voice popped her attention back to the ring.

Nash had put a few feet between him and Heath. He worked a combo, one fist blocked Heath's punch while the other grazed his cheek. But it was the same one Nash had hit earlier, and Heath winced backward.

This time Nash advanced, landing several body blows and a nice shin kick that smacked of kickboxing not traditional boxing. Heath retreated and held up a hand as if calling the match. Nash straightened and turned his head toward them, catching sight of her for the first time. His eyes widened and his hands dropped.

Heath barreled forward, not as fast as Nash, but fast enough to catch him off guard. He grabbed Nash around the chest and threw him down, landing on top of him and snaking an arm around his neck. Reed jumped to the mat and pulled at Heath's shoulders while Nash struggled under his weight and pushed at his arm.

Tally's limbs liquefied and her scramble into the ring was clumsy. She banged her head against one of the padded metal rope hooks on her crablike crawl to Nash. Reed had wrapped an arm around Heath's neck trying to pull him off, but the man seemed possessed.

She jabbed Heath in the eye since his crotch wasn't in

striking distance. Cade had taught Tally how to fight dirty, and she wasn't as principled as Nash.

"Fuck me!" Heath rolled off Nash, covering his eye.

Nash gasped for air, his legs kicking as if he could inflate his lungs with them. Tally looked to Jack and reached out a hand, urgency straining her voice. "His duffle. Hurry."

Jack slid the bag across the floor of the ring. Tally grabbed it and riffled through it, finally locating his inhaler in a side pocket. She fumbled it to his lips, but his mouth guard was still in place.

A memory of making each other laugh by covering their smiles with sliced orange peels bubbled to the surface. She wasn't sure whether the sting of tears was for her past or present with this man. She yanked the guard out and tossed it aside. His eyes were open and fixed on hers. He covered her hand with his and helped guide the inhaler to his lips. They pumped it together.

His breathing eased. She stroked her hands down his face, and he caught her wrists pressing her hands against his cheeks. A small cut over his left eyebrow oozed blood, the eye already swelling. Heath might have gotten a few body shots in, but otherwise, Nash escaped relatively unharmed except for the near choke-out and asthma attack.

"Are you okay?" she whispered.

"I think so." He pushed up and let his head hang between his knees for a moment before saying, "I've been better, but I've been worse too."

Now that she was reasonably assured he would live, anger superseded her worry, although she wasn't sure who to direct it at.

She spun around and stalked to the other end of the ring. Heath had a hand pressed to the eye she gouged but fixed the other eye on her with unadulterated hate.

"Get out. Now." She almost hoped he argued with her so she could call the police.

Heath rose, his shoulders hunched, his face jutting forward. She recognized his attempt at intimidation. He dropped his hand. His eye was bloodshot and puffy. "I would have gotten a choke-out if you hadn't poked me in the eye. And don't even try to pretend that wasn't on purpose."

"Damn straight it was. You appeared to concede the fight right before you tackled him. That would get you disqualified in any professional match, which is why you'll never make it. Not to mention, you aren't good enough and never will be. This was a once and done. No rematch. And no winner."

"This ain't over." He pointed his finger like a parody of a movie villain and affected a redneck tough-guy accent when she knew darn well he'd grown up in a squarely middle-class neighborhood on the Mississippi side of the river.

She was tired of feeling inferior to him when she wasn't. Nash had given her that. "You know what? It finally is, Heath. If you text or call or come within twenty feet of my apartment or this gym, I'll get a restraining order. Grab your stuff and get out. And good luck finding somewhere else to train."

Jack herded the two men to the front door, and Tally threw the bolt as soon as they were out.

"That fella was your ex?" Jack side-eyed her.

"I broke up with him months ago but he wouldn't leave me alone. Nash thinks if he can beat him up like a third-grader on the playground, he'll leave me alone finally."

"I hate to break it to you, but I think you're just a piece of this puzzle. He knew that fella when he was a kid, right?"

Jack's face was stern, his skin brown and rough, long

grooves carving his cheeks. Years of being battered by the ocean air had taken their toll. Yet she could see traces of Jack in Nash—the nose and the set of his jaw, stubborn and determined.

"Nash was picked on. A lot. I guess nowadays you'd call it bullying," she said softly.

"Sometimes a man has to put his own past to rest before he can move on."

His words resonated in the briar-filled patch she'd nurtured inside of her own heart.

Nash shuffled toward them. Reed was behind him, holding his gloves. She unlaced Nash's helmet, pulled it off, and finger combed his sweat-dampened hair back. Next she ran her hands down his torso. None of his ribs seemed to be cockeyed, and he didn't wince at her touch. She trailed her hands back up his chest and touched him close to the cut above his eyebrow. "You might need a couple of stitches."

He grabbed both her wrists and dipped his face, but she didn't meet his eyes. "I'm fine. Nothing that a couple of days without getting punched won't fix."

"What if you have a concussion?"

"I don't, but if it makes you feel better you can wake me up every hour tonight." His crooked smile held a sexual tease she was in no mood to acknowledge, much less return. She tugged her hands free.

Now that she was assured he wasn't seriously injured, she released the reins on her emotions and shoved his shoulder. "For someone so brilliant, you are an idiot."

"Look, I—"

"How long have you two been training?" She pointed back and forth between him and Reed.

Reed had the good sense to step behind Nash to avoid her gaze.

"Not long." A hesitant hitch in Nash's voice signaled

he realized he was stepping into a minefield. "How did you know?"

"You threw some kickboxing moves in there. When and where?"

"Now and again."

"Here?"

"After hours or at Reed's place on his time off while you were working."

"You didn't say anything."

"I knew you wouldn't like it."

"So you decided *not* telling me was the way to go?"

He sighed. "Look, I'm sorry." Impatience turned the apology trite.

"You don't sound sorry."

Nash's hand tightened around the strap of his duffle, and he leaned forward. "Do you get how miserable Heath Parsons made my life?"

"You and Reed went behind my back to train for a fight you knew I did not approve of. You lied to me." Emotions vied for dominance—anger, fear, love. She didn't want him to see any of it.

"I didn't lie. Not exactly. You stopped asking." It was a weak excuse and by his tone, he realized it too.

She took a step closer and jabbed a finger at his chest, her voice dropping. "You kept secrets from me, Nash. And I'm supposed to trust you?"

"I didn't want you to worry." He pulled his bottom lip between his teeth, a complicated range of emotions crossing his face. "I needed to do this. Can you understand that?"

She would try to understand it later. Maybe. "Since you opened the gym, you can lock it up, Reed. I'm outta here."

"Tally—" Nash extended a hand.

She didn't acknowledge him, but pushed through the door and strode down the sidewalk. He didn't follow her.

She slowed as she approached her car. A lone figure stood on the riverbank, looking over at the Mississippi side of Cottonbloom. She continued on until she was standing shoulder to shoulder with Sawyer. Maybe he could help sort out this mess.

"Look." He gestured toward a three-foot square track of green stems denuded of their blossoms. "Regan has gone too far this time. She knows why I planted these flowers. What they mean."

The anger and hurt in his voice took Tally aback and took the focus off her problems. "What do they mean?"

"They're for Mama," he said so softly she almost didn't hear. "While you were out playing with Nash, and Cade was in the garage with Daddy, I would help her with the flowers."

Even though Sawyer reminded her forcibly of their father, he'd been a mama's boy. Maybe for the same reasons their father and mother fit together so well. Tally and her mother had been too much alike, reticent and serious, to be confidants.

They longer they stared at the carnage, the more something niggled at her.

"I'm going to lay into her." He puffed up with a big breath and took a step.

The something that was niggling snapped into place. She caught his wrist. "It wasn't Regan. Lordy, I think it was Uncle Del."

He swiveled his head toward her, even as the rest of his body strained toward the footbridge. "What?"

She gave Sawyer a brief rundown of her and Nash's discoveries regarding their uncle's love life and added, "He asked Nash whether wildflowers were still Ms. Leora's favorite."

"Wow." He ruffled the hair at the back of his head. "I guess that lets Regan off the hook." More than simple relief lightened his words. She studied her brother, but couldn't discern how he felt about his ex-girlfriend. "What're you doing out here? Working on the gym's part in the festival?"

His question stoked her anger. "Heath and Nash went at it at my gym without telling me."

"Was Nash hurt?"

"No, but Heath fought dirty, and he could've been." Sudden tears clogged her throat.

"Heath is a d-bag. You don't know how many times I wanted to take him in the swamps and dump his ass."

"You never said you didn't like him."

"I was afraid if I voiced my disapproval, it would have only made you like him more. I'm glad you finally saw past his bad-boy act to the jerk underneath. You deserve a nice guy."

She didn't say anything. What was there to say? She rubbed the corner of her eye hoping Sawyer wouldn't notice her unusual state of upheaval. Fat chance. He pulled her into a hug. Cade had been her rock growing up, but Sawyer had been her teddy bear. Always there with a shot of much-needed optimism and enthusiasm.

"Nash is a nice guy." His chin moved to the top of her head.

"He knew I didn't want him to fight, but he did it anyway. Behind my back."

"All right, stupid about women, but he cares about you." A smile was in his voice.

"I'm really mad at him right now."

"Daddy used to go fishing when he and Mama had a fight. You remember?"

She pulled out of his hug. "They never fought."

"They tried not to do it front of us kids, but they fought, all right."

Her memories skewed. She didn't doubt Sawyer. Of the three of them, he was the most intuitive about other people. "What did they fight about?"

"Money. Family. The usual. Daddy would disappear for a couple of hours in the boat. Mama would bake. By the time he came home with a cooler of fish, a pie or cake or cookies would be in the oven and they'd kiss and make up. It's okay to be mad. Doesn't mean you have to stay mad forever."

"Why aren't women beating down your door?" She was not asking rhetorically. Her brother was good-looking, considerate, and nice. Why weren't the women of Cottonbloom staking a claim on him?

"Who says they're not?" He squinted at the blue sky.

She hung out at his place enough to know they weren't. Maybe he'd cycled through all the available women. Or had Regan Lovell ruined him so many years ago?

Before she had the chance to ask, he said, "I hope this incident isn't going to affect the exhibition fight for the festival."

She made no effort to disguise her eye roll. "Is the mudbug festival all you can think about?"

"I'd prefer you refer to it as the crayfish festival. Mudbug might turn off the city folk we're trying to attract through our quaint slice of Americana here."

"You're going to make me wear overalls and go barefoot, aren't you?"

"Would you?"

The hopeful tease in his voice drew a small smile to her face. "The exhibition is still on. Talk to Reed about it if you want." She backed away.

"Where are you headed?" He was back to sounding worried.

It was as if their daddy was looking down on them. "To the river."

Sawyer hesitated as if he wanted to say more, but nodded and let her go, pushing his hands into the pockets of his shorts.

She was mad at Nash, mad at herself, but mostly she was disappointed and hurt. It had taken a lot for her to trust Nash. And, she did—had. Did. She still trusted him and loved him, but knowing Nash had not been upfront with her was painful.

But could she really judge? She had hidden her dyslexia, the seriousness of Heath's stalking, her loneliness from everyone. Shame had made her bury her secrets. Had Jack been right? Had the need to eradicate old shames driven Nash to fight Heath?

She parked at the end of the dead end street and took the path to the river. It had been a long time since she'd sought solace from the river. She dangled her feet over the side of the bank, but the water was too low to reach with her toes.

How could they leave the past behind them and focus on building a future when the past surrounded them?

The river flowed. The water, sparkling and new; but the banks, muddy and rife with exposed roots, were unchanging. Perhaps, that was the point. Not to leave the past behind, but to shore it up until it was strong enough to support the future.

"Hi there."

Tally startled. Birdie popped out from behind a tree in shorts and a T-shirt with a rainbow-colored unicorn across the front.

"How do you do that? Do you have a network of underground tunnels?" Tally asked, only half-joking.

A perplexed expression came across the little girl's face. "No, just walked up. You were thinking hard and didn't hear me." Birdie joined her on the bank. "Whatcha thinking about? A boy?"

"Maybe." Amusement bubbled out of the stew of emotions upsetting her stomach, but she kept her response confined to a twitch of her lips.

"Is it Nash?" Birdie felt no such compulsion and gave her gap-toothed grin. The white jagged edges of new front teeth were pushing through her gums.

"Maybe." Tally flashed the girl a smile before her amusement faded back into uncertainty. "We had a fight."

"'Bout what?"

"About a fight, actually. A different sort of fight."

"I heard Mr. Nash was planning to beat up some man at your gym. That what you're talking about?"

Tally cocked a leg up on the bank to face Birdie. "Where'd you hear that?"

"Heard Daddy say. Apparently everyone is talking about it." Birdie sounded so adultlike that Tally suppressed another smile. "Daddy hoped Nash won. Did he?"

"Neither one of them won, but Nash played by the rules, the man he fought didn't."

Tally had accepted that Heath Parsons was the kind of man she deserved. That her dyslexia was some penance she had to pay instead of a hurdle to overcome.

No longer. She deserved more. Better. Not just in her love life, but her life in general.

She'd worked hard and turned her gym into a thriving business. She had two brothers who loved her and friends who cared about her. And Nash. No matter how childish she considered the grudge he held against Heath, she understood it on some level, because wasn't she being just as childish about her dyslexia?

"You're a cool kid, Birdie. Do you know that?"

"Yeah." Birdie nodded. "I know."

Tally laughed so loud a pair of birds flew out of the trees across the river and the plop of frogs escaping to the water sounded below their feet. "You could be president, you know. Don't let anyone tell you that you can't. President Margaret Thatcher sounds good."

"I like it too." Birdie grinned. A whistle cut through the trees. "There's Daddy. We're going to town to get Mama a birthday present."

Birdie took off like a wild animal through the trees before Tally had a chance to even wave. She hoped the little girl never lost her attitude that anything was possible. Somewhere between her parents' deaths and her struggles in school, Tally had lost sight of the endless possibilities. Nash had helped open her eyes, but it was up to her to explore them.

A plan took shape as she stared into the flowing river. A plan she needed to implement on her own.

Chapter Seventeen

The week passed in fits and starts. She stayed busy, but Nash was never too far from her thoughts. The gym had been her only focus for years. Besides Ms. Effie and Monroe, she hadn't developed relationships outside of her business. Or hobbies, for that matter. The gym had been her safe, comfortable place.

Her first order of business was to hire someone trustworthy to help her and Reed cover the early openings and late closings, so they could both have more time off. If her expansion plans had to be pushed out, then so be it. Or maybe she'd take Cade at his word and accept a loan.

Jack Hawthorne pushed through the doors with a smile. They shook hands before Tally gestured him around to the working side of the front desk.

"Can't tell you how much I appreciate this. It's slim pickings out there for a man my age." He smoothed a hand over a crisp blue button-down to equally crisp khakis, his jitters obvious.

"Believe me, you're doing us a solid." She booted up the software that managed the memberships and payments. While the program loaded, she glanced over at Jack. "How's Nash feeling?"

"His head is fine, but his heart ain't doing so good. He's tearing himself up about you. Not sure what to do."

"He knows where to find me."

A troubled look flashed over his face. "That's what I told him."

If Nash didn't man up by the end of the week, she'd seek him out. But for now she had other things to focus on. "Now then, how are you with computers?"

The next hour passed with Tally teaching him the ins and outs of the system. While he told people Nash got his brains from his mama, the intensity he focused on each task reminded her of Nash.

While Reed showed Jack around the gym and explained the daily routines, Tally called to set up an appointment with a reading specialist for the next afternoon. The lady on the other end showed no surprise or shock or dismay that an adult was calling, and it settled the nervous rolling of her stomach. Taking charge felt good.

With the last of the evening crowd gone, Reed and Jack were completing the closing checklist. The bells over the door jangled. Tally looked up from the reading center's brochure.

Ms. Leora stood in the doorway, wearing a dress and low heels, her pocketbook held in front of her like a shield.

Shock held Tally in place a few beats longer than was polite. "Ms. Leora, good evening." She came around the desk and gestured the lady farther into the gym, but Ms. Leora remained planted, her gaze scanning the floor. "Nash isn't here, if that's who you're looking for."

Ms. Leora took a couple of shuffling steps forward, stumbling on the edge of a rubberized mat. Tally caught her arm, steadying her.

"Is Jack here?" She sounded flustered.

"He's in the back. Let me—"

"Wait." She clamped Tally's upper arm, her hand cool and soft. "I'm sorry for everything, Tallulah."

Ms. Leora's eyes were the same soft, encompassing brown as Nash's. Tally had never noticed. Years of regrets and resentments seemed to melt like cotton candy left in the sun.

"It's all right." She patted the hand still wrapped around her arm.

Forgiveness was easy to find. Maybe it was because she was no longer playing a victim to her own life. Maybe it grew from the love she'd discovered through and in Nash. Maybe it was true that time healed all wounds. All she knew for sure was that sides had shifted. The river no longer separated her from Ms. Leora. Their love for Nash and Delmar united them.

Ms. Leora grabbed for her hand and squeezed. "I'm worried about Nash."

The warm fuzzies turned frigid. "What's happened?"

"I overheard Nash on the phone. He and that man might be fighting again tonight. I thought he might be here."

"Why is he doing this?" she muttered between clamped teeth. Louder, she called, "Jack. Reed."

The two men walked from the storage area, their heads close, laughter trailing faintly to them. It dried up when Jack noticed Ms. Leora. He quick-stepped toward them. "What's going on? It's Nash, isn't it?"

Ms, Leora's hands tightened on her pocketbook, the patent leather squeaking. Tally pointed at Jack. "Apparently, your son has set up a rematch with Heath. Either of you know about this?"

Reed mouthed a curse and ran both hands over his hair while Jack shook his head and said, "I had a feeling something was going on, but no, he didn't mention it."

"To me either," Reed said. "Told him to steer clear of Heath and his crew."

"If not here, where would they go?" Tally asked. The four of them exchanged glances, but no one had anything to offer.

Tally slid her phone out of her back pocket and hit Sawyer's name.

"What's up, Sis?" Sawyer's voice was teasing but tired.

"Do you know anything about Nash and Heath having a rematch tonight?"

"Nope. Haven't heard anything."

She rubbed her forehead. "Any ideas where they would go? Another gym, maybe?"

"Sit tight. Let me see what I can find out." He disconnected, and Tally tapped the phone against her chin. Without anyone having his back, things might end very badly for Nash. Hadn't he learned the hard way that Heath didn't follow the rules?

Her phone buzzed, and she bobbled it before regaining control and hitting the button. "Tell me you found something out."

"I did." Her brother sounded grim, which threw some wood on the anxious fire making her muscles twitch. "Get down to my place. We'll have to take my truck."

"They're out in the swamps?" She tried to massage the lump out of her throat.

"Not quite that dire, but we might need four-wheel drive."

"On my way." She hit the red end button.

"I'm coming with you," Jack said.

"Reed, can you lock up and then walk Ms. Leora to her car?" Tally was halfway to the door.

"Tallulah." Her name quivered out of Ms. Leora's throat. "Will you call and let me know?"

Tally almost gave the woman a hug, but settled on

patting her shoulder. "I will. He'll be fine. I'll make sure of it." The confidence in her voice felt false.

She and Jack made the drive to Sawyer's farmhouse in relative silence. She parked by the willow tree and ran up the steps.

Sawyer met her on the porch, truck keys in hand. "Let's hit it."

He and Jack exchanged brief greetings while they piled into Sawyer's truck. She took the middle, straddling the gearshift. "Where are they?"

"A track of land out in the boonies where we used to have bonfires and party in high school."

"You mean out behind old man Benson's cotton field?"

Sawyer side-eyed her. "How would you know?"

"Puh-lease. I'm surprised we didn't run across each other at some point or other."

He harrumphed, but amusement superseded any disapproval.

They were silent the rest of the way. The truck rocked back and forth through washed-out ruts, the headlights illuminating recent tracks of other tires. She gripped the edge of the dashboard. Heath and his buddies could gang up on Nash and pulverize him. Who would stop them? She scooched on her seat as if she could move them along faster.

Dim light shone through the trees. The bonfire outlined a dozen or more people milling around and a wall of backs on one side. Yells carried on the air. Sawyer pulled to a stop along a row of mud-splattered trucks. As soon as feet hit the ground, she ran.

By the time she squeezed through the wall of backs, she was out of breath from exertion and fear.

Nash and Heath circled one another, both bare-chested, bare-knuckled, and with no protective gear. Someone was going to get seriously injured. She'd taken one step into the clearing when hands grabbed her upper arms and pulled her back into the wall of bodies.

Jack and Sawyer stood on either side of her, each with the grip strength of a bear. She twisted her arms. "Let me go. We have to stop this."

"We'll stop the fight if it gets out of hand. But Nash has something to prove. To you and himself," Sawyer whispered close to her ear.

Heath went on the offensive first, lobbing a fist toward Nash's face. He swerved and the hit glanced off his ear. She pulled forward again. "But—"

"No buts." Sawyer firmed his grip. "Let's assume I understand men a bit better than you do. If Heath or his crew try anything, I'll pull my Cottonbloom Parish commissioner card and break it up."

"You will not. Nash would never forgive you for busting in to save him."

Was Sawyer right? Was Heath a demon Nash had to wrestle on his own? It was like her dyslexia. Nash may have shoved her in the right direction, but she'd had to locate the courage to make that call to the center. Heath represented a shameful part of Nash's past.

Nash's foot slapped against Heath's calf, a red welt rising. Heath went in for a takedown. Nash sidestepped out, but Heath laid a couple of body blows before Nash could put distance between them.

Tally closed her eyes. She couldn't watch Nash be hurt. Even though Heath might be a demon from his past, responsibility weighed on her. If she hadn't dated Heath, if she had only reported his creepy stalking to the police, if she'd been stronger, then would Nash be in a darkened field fighting him?

The answer was a resounding "maybe."

"Time."

She opened her eyes. Bryce had stepped into the

clearing and laid a hand on each man's shoulder. Was that it?

"You each have one minute."

Heath and Nash retreated to opposite sides of the makeshift ring. Tally ran toward him.

He did a classic double take. She ran her hands up and down his sides, but nothing felt out of place. "Ms. Leora came to see me."

"Was she mad?"

Tally made an exasperated sound while she checked the side of his head that took the first jab. It was too dark to tell much, but he was at least in one piece and talking. "She was worried. Same as the rest of us."

Sawyer and Jack pushed in behind them. "Hey, Dad." Jack and Nash exchanged a half hug, and he and Sawyer exchanged a fist bump.

Tally propped her hands on her hips. "I suppose this is why you've been avoiding me all week."

"Didn't want to lie to you. Didn't want to worry you either. Figured we could talk things out afterward."

"What if you get seriously hurt out here? What then?"

"I can hold my own." Both defiance and resentment hid poorly in his words.

She was either with him or not. She either accepted his need to prove himself or didn't. She circled a hand around his damp neck and planted a bracing kiss on his lips.

"Okay, listen. Your strength is your boxing skills. Heath's is his grappling. If he gets you on the ground, you're toast. He'll choke you out. But he tends to drop his left hand, especially as he tires. You might sneak some good jabs in."

"Why are you helping me all of a sudden?" He sounded more bemused than suspicious.

She leaned her forehead against his, so only he could hear her words. "Because I don't want to see your handsome face messed up, Professor. And because I love you and understand you need to do this. Even if I think it's crazy and adolescent."

His lips parted and her gaze dropped to his mouth. "I love you too. Will you be waiting after it's done?"

"No matter what happens, I'll wait." Nerves pinged through her body, making her feel electrified and numb at the same time. "Where's your inhaler? Just in case."

Nash fished it out of a duffle at his feet and held it out. She clutched it tight to her chest like a talisman.

"Let's go, asshole." Heath bounced on the balls of his feet in the middle of the clearing, the bonfire's light giving him a devilish glow.

Nash gave her one last look and circled toward Heath. She didn't want to watch, yet couldn't tear her gaze away. Sawyer slipped his hand around hers, and she gratefully hung on. The fight proceeded with a series of jabs and parries. The longer Nash stayed upright, the better chance he had of winning.

Heath retreated and Nash followed, kicking at his shins. Heath didn't try to defend against them. A tingle zinged up her spine. She had observed Heath train enough to recognize a trap. She opened her mouth and croaked a warning. It was lost in the calls and yells of the mostly male crowd.

Heath made his move, pulling Nash first into a clinch and then moving to hang on his back, his arm tucked under Nash's chin. Tally closed her eyes. It was a matter of seconds now. She counted to ten.

The crowd roared. Sawyer dropped her hand and yelled encouragement to Nash. She opened her eyes to see Heath on his back, gasping for air while Nash bounced on his feet and rubbed his neck.

"What happened?"

Jack wore a grin. "Nash flipped him all the way over his back. Where did he learn to do that?"

Tally blew out a slow breath. It was Reed's signature move. The man was getting a raise. And a big hug.

Bryce stood to the side, looking lost. Sawyer stepped between the men, putting a hand on Nash's shoulder. "I'm calling it. Hawthorne is the winner."

Whoops and the buzz of conversation drowned out the night sounds. Money exchanged hands. Men crowded around Nash, pumping his hand or slapping his shoulders. No one seemed upset Heath had lost.

Nash emerged from the crowd a dozen feet away, and their gazes met and held. She took a few steps back and turned to walk past the line of trucks to a path that led through dark woods to the river.

He caught up with her halfway down the path, the sound of the river snaking through the trees. She kept walking until the water came into view.

"Do you feel better now that you've beaten Heath?"

"I do."

His brief, honest answer had her searching for words. "This fight had nothing to do with me, did it? Not really?"

Tally's voice was flat, unemotional. She'd told him she still loved him during the fight, but how hurt and mad was she? One thing he'd promised himself was to tell her the truth, if he got the chance. She deserved that much.

"I've been thinking about the reasons all week."

"Did you make a list?" This time sarcasm weighed the words.

He had to tread carefully, and in the dark he couldn't read her expressions to know if he was on the right path. "It wasn't even Heath I was fighting out there. It was myself. I couldn't come to you until it was finished."

"What do you mean?"

"I had to prove to myself I wasn't the same weak kid who couldn't stand up for himself. Once I threw the challenge out, I couldn't back down. It would have been like all those times in high school. The logical side of me knows that sounds crazy. I'm done being scared of someone or something from my past." He ran his hands through his hair and leaned up against a pine. The bark bit into his bare back. "I hope you can understand that."

"Are you going to start looking up all your high school foes and challenging them to a fight in old cotton fields?"

The lilt in her voice made him think there was hope. "Like some caped crusader? Not a chance. But Tallulah, you're wrong about one thing. This was about you too."

"How so?"

"I had to prove to myself, to you, that I deserved you."

His name came to him on a whisper. Leaves crunched as she approached. He didn't move until her hands touched his sides. He wrapped his arms around her and hauled her close, his face in her hair.

"I have an appointment with a reading specialist tomorrow." She leaned away from him.

"I'm glad." And, he was, but the sudden veer of the conversation left him confused.

"I had to prove I deserved you too." She sling-shot his words back at him.

Her admission absolved him. From the outside, people might wonder what bonded the two of them. Inside, however, they had imprinted on each other too many years ago to count. No one else on earth understood him like she did. He cupped her face, wishing he could see her better. The wind had picked up around them, gusts shushing the leaves like ocean waves.

"You know it doesn't matter. You don't need to prove anything to me." He skimmed his nose alongside hers.

"You didn't need to beat up Heath to prove anything to me either, but I get it. Because I'm going to deal with my dyslexia mostly for me, but for you too."

"We deserve each other, don't you think?"

"I love you, Nash." She'd seen him at his best and worst, his strongest and weakest, and she loved him.

"I love you too, Tallulah."

Her weight fell into him. A franticness overtook the sweetness of the moment. Their lips went in search of each other, meeting with desperation. Heat sped through his body, lighting his nerve endings like sparklers. A soft rain overtook the wind, and droplets worked themselves through the trees, skating down his shoulders and back.

The taste of salt on her lips cast the moment in different tones. He brushed his lips across her cheeks. "You're crying. What's wrong?"

"I'm sad that we were apart for so long."

"It was less than a week. I didn't want to—"

"Not that. I'm talking about the years and years I lived without you." Her whispered words spoke of sadness and regret and what-ifs they couldn't change.

He gathered her close, his heart aching for her. For them. He'd missed her too. More than he thought he could bear some days. He'd lived with the hollow place in his heart for so long, he hadn't realized until he'd come back that she was the missing piece.

"Maybe we had to be apart to realize how much we needed each other."

"I think a couple of months would have been more than adequate. Not two decades," she said, obviously not ready to give the universe such an easy pass.

"We both had mistakes to make before finding each other." He kissed the tip of her nose. Past pain would always be there, but Nash was less concerned about it now. Now was the time to look to the future. And the future was full of laughter and love with this woman. "You needed to date some losers so you'd appreciate how awesome I am."

"You're not *that* awesome." She huffed, but her tears were gone and a small smile tipped the corners of her mouth.

"Maybe not, but you turned out perfect. What other woman would be okay with my comic book obsession or T-shirt collection? When I saw your Superman socks, I knew I'd always loved you and would love you forever."

She threw her arms around his neck and pressed her mouth close to his ear. "You know, if you ask me nice enough, I would wear a Wonder Woman costume for you. And, if you're really nice, I'll let you take it off me."

"That'd better be a promise."

Standing by the river with a soft rain making music in the leaves, he felt the moment shift. His words meant more than silly bedroom games and were weaved by elements of their past and future. "It's a promise."

Epilogue

Tally left the gym in Jack's capable hands to mosey over the footbridge to where Nash was trimming out the new gazebo. She'd poured two glasses of ice tea she'd brewed especially for him the night before and transferred into a gallon jug.

He straightened from hammering a decorative scalloped wooden lattice below the rails. Lifting his T-shirt, he wiped his face. His bare chest incited lurid fantasies involving him naked, his pleasure in her hands. How many laws would they be breaking if they made out on the newly finished gazebo floor?

He took a glass. "You're not going to give up until you convert me back, are you?"

"Hot tea is unnatural, Nash." She grinned.

He killed half in a dozen gulps without coming up for air. "Okay, I'll admit, that's refreshing. Thanks."

They sat side by side on the gazebo steps, the roof shading them from the noonday sun. Green shoots of grass showed in the charred ground. The resiliency of nature always astounded her. People seemed so fragile in comparison.

"What kind of deep thoughts are going on over there?" Nash asked.

She took a deep breath and met his warm gaze and smile. He loved her and she loved him. It had only been a few days since their declarations on the river, and although they'd spent as much time together as possible, time was fleeting. She wanted more with him. "I know it's kind of soon to be talking about this, but do you want to move in together?"

His smile crumpled. Not into a frown exactly, but everything about him had tensed. "Are you sure?" He sounded as if his breath had been taken away—and not in a good way.

The old Tally would have backtracked, made excuses. Along with finding Nash, she'd found a new type of courage over the past month. Not the kind needed to climb water towers, but a courage that ran deep.

"I don't want to waste another minute of my life. I love you. I want to go to sleep and wake up next to you. I want to laze in bed with you and make love to you whenever I want. But if you're not ready for that, I can wait until you are."

She blew out a long, slow breath and waited. He stared at her, his breath wheezing in and out.

"Ohmygod, are you having an asthma attack?" She popped to her knees in front of him and pulled at his pockets in search of his inhaler. He never failed to have it on him.

He grabbed one of her wrists, stilling her hands, and pulled the inhaler out. Seconds after taking a pump, his breathing eased. He pulled her closer, using the hand he held captive and pressed his lips against hers.

"I would love to move in together. I wanted to mention it, but I was worried I'd scare you off."

"I'm not scared anymore. I trust you."

He cupped her face, his thumb stroking her cheekbone. "I trust you too, Tallulah Fournette. I guess the only question is your place or mine or somewhere altogether different."

"I've thought about it a little. My apartment isn't anything special, and while I'll miss Ms. Effie, I'll see her at the gym now that I'm teaching the senior classes. Your place is small, but I like it. Plus, your father and aunt are right there."

"Exactly, my father and aunt are *right there*." His eyes widened in emphasis.

She giggled. "I know, but you and your dad are finally getting to know each other, and I think your aunt would be lonely."

"I don't know, Delmar is making regular appearances. She might want me and Dad gone." He paused and played with her fingers. "How about we stay at my place temporarily? Until we can build something bigger. I'm already scouting land along the river."

"Are you serious?"

"I already told you, I'm a professor. I'm always serious." His smile belied the point.

"Which side of the river?"

"Land is cheaper on the Louisiana side."

"Nash, that sounds perfect."

He kissed her again, this time slow and sweet. Time ceased to have meaning. He lay back and took her with him, his body hard, his lips soft. A moan snuck out.

A throat cleared. Tally's eyes popped open to find Nash wearing a similar deer-in-headlights look.

"I . . . uh, didn't mean to interrupt." Regan sounded both embarrassed and interested.

Tally scrambled off Nash, pulling at the spandex of

her workout shirt. "You're not interrupting." The polite response shot out of her mouth even though they all realized Regan had interrupted.

"I didn't see you at first, and then . . ." Her apologetic grimace seemed sincere. "I wanted to check to see if the gazebo would be ready by this weekend."

"Why?"

"Thought I might invite a band in to play Saturday night." Regan's expression turned from apologetic to scheming.

"Our side is having our normal block party Saturday night with my uncle's bluegrass band." Tally's eyes narrowed. No matter what Nash had said, the woman was as slippery and deadly as a cottonmouth.

"Well, considering you never invite anyone from Mississippi . . ." Regan held her hands up.

"Everyone is invited. It's implicit. Monroe had a blast last time we had one."

"She was only there because—" Regan squinted toward the footbridge.

Tally shifted. Sawyer strode toward them. Energy crackled around him. As he got closer, she could see the tight set to his jaw and his uncharacteristic frown. The sight of Regan applied flint to the anger stiffening his movements.

"You've taken things too far, woman!" His voice was so rough and cutting, Tally flinched even though he was obviously not addressing her.

The target of his fury took a step back, into the shadows of the gazebo. Sawyer kept barreling toward them as if he planned to run Regan into the ground. She grabbed one of the square columns of the gazebo as if bracing herself for impact. He stopped three feet shy of her.

"I promised on my parents' grave I had nothing to do

with burning your gazebo down." He jabbed his finger in her face.

Regan had paled, her usual bravado absent. "I believe you."

"Then why did you do it? Or have someone else do it? Lord knows, I can't imagine you out in the river getting your hands dirty."

"I have no idea what you're talking about, Sawyer." She wrapped her hand around his finger and pulled it down.

Tally stayed still as if any movement would draw attention, but Nash squeezed her hand, and she looked over to find a question in his eyes. She gave a small shake of her head and a shrug.

"*Someone* took wire cutters to at least fifty crayfish traps last night. Not only did good, hardworking men lose their harvest, but now we might be short for the festival."

"Are you accusing me?" There was outrage but also surprise in Regan's voice.

"Who else? You want to get back at me for the rabbits. Tit for tat? And I know you still think I'm an arsonist." He gestured toward the rebuilt gazebo. "But this was taking it too far. You've caused grief for several families. How long have you been planning this little retaliation?"

"I want to win the contest and the grant money, and I'll admit to doing some not very mature stuff, like painting your wall. But, I wouldn't deliberately destroy someone's livelihood. Surely you know me better than that."

"You were awfully quick to judge me when the gazebo was burning. Let me see your hands."

"Why?" Regan balled her hands and tucked them behind her back.

"To check for blisters."

Regan harrumphed. He grabbed her forearm and

pulled her right hand around. Taking her hands in both of his, he examined them.

"See? Nothing." Regan's voice was breathy, and she tugged. For a few heartbeats, Tally wasn't sure if Sawyer was going to let go.

"Fine. So you got someone else to go out and sabotage me out of spite."

"In the shock of the moment, I did think you were involved with burning down my gazebo, but I know you're not an arsonist." She laid a hand on his arm. They stared into each other's eyes for a long moment.

"To be honest, I have a hard time picturing you cutting a bunch of traps. Or even hiring someone to do it." A large portion of his aggression seeped from his voice. "You like your revenge in your face and warm rather than under-the-table sneaky."

Regan crossed her arms. "Thanks. Really favorable character analysis there, Sawyer."

Nash cleared his throat, and everyone turned in his direction. "Seems to me someone doesn't want either festival happening."

A numb wave passed through Tally in spite of the heat. The roll of cash in her uncle's drawer snapped into her head. Could he be involved? She couldn't imagine him sabotaging his own nephew. Plus, all of those crayfish harvesters were his friends. Where had that money come from?

Regan and Sawyer continued pointing fingers at various members of their respective communities, their arguments buzzing like white noise. Nash took Tally's hand and whispered, "What's wrong?"

Forcing a smile, she nudged her head toward the warring exes. She didn't want to put Sawyer or Regan on the warpath. Not until she talked to her uncle. "I'll tell you later. Promise. After I move my stuff over to your place."

The warmth that flared in Nash's face turned her fake smile into a genuine one. He curled his hand around her nape and pulled her in for the sweetest, hottest kiss of her life.

Read on for an excerpt from Laura Trentham's next book

Till I Kissed You

Available in August 2016 from St. Martin's Paperbacks

Chapter One

Regan Lovell ran her hands up the shifting muscles of her lover's back, lost in a state of wonder. The rhythm of his thrusts progressed from slow and steady to wild and erratic. It didn't take long. He moaned softly in her ear, his hot breath sending shivers through her body.

It was done. She'd lost her virginity to Sawyer Fournette.

While it hadn't been the out-of-body experience the romance novels she'd read in preparation would have her believe, it had been magical in its own way. She clasped her knees around his hips and wrapped him tight in her arms, his body sagging over hers, his breathing ragged.

Her mother would be horrified she'd given up her virginity at all, much less at eighteen, before she could use it to barter for a doctor or a lawyer at Ole Miss. She expected Regan to get an MRS degree, just as she had done thirty-odd years before.

But what would send her mother into an early grave was who she'd lost her virginity to. Her mother deemed Sawyer a Louisiana swamp rat and considered Regan's fascination with him a phase. A means to rebel against her parents and their expectations, and that's all.

What her parents didn't know, or couldn't accept, was that Regan had dreams and ambitions and a heart of her own. It wasn't a phase or a rebellion; it was love.

He stirred against her, his sparse chest hair tickling her breasts. She crossed her ankles around his backside, holding him inside of her. "I love you, Sawyer."

He pushed up on his elbows. "I love you too, Regan."

"Forever?"

"And ever." The humor and love in his voice were honestly more satisfying than the sex had been.

"Even after I eat too much barbeque and get fat and my hair turns gray and I lose my marbles like Nana Rosemary?"

"Even so." He kissed the tip of her nose, and she smiled at their game.

Other more immediate questions clawed at her chest. *Will you love me after we go our separate ways for college? Will you love me even though prettier girls will try to lure you away? Will you wait for me?*

He wiggled his hips free and dropped to her side in the bed of his brother's old pickup truck. She looked down her body, but everything looked the same, not that she really expected this final crossover into womanhood to leave a visible mark. She was irrevocably changed but not in a way her mother or her friends could pinpoint.

Now the sexual haze was clearing, she became acutely aware of her nakedness. Subtle rustling while he disposed of the condom had her biting her lip and reaching for the edge of the threadbare quilt as cover. Was there a bloodstain like she'd read about in books?

Cooling air wafted over her. Through the arms of the pines, twilight cast shadows that shifted with the breeze. The river was close enough to serenade them with bullfrog croaks but far enough to avoid the worst of the bugs.

Citronella candles burned on the tailgate, keeping the mosquitoes away. She closed her eyes. The scent of the candles mixed with the pines and Sawyer to form an intoxicating blend she'd never forget.

Sawyer stripped the corner of the quilt away and blanketed her with his body. His expression was a mystery. He alternated between a too-mature seriousness and a boyish playfulness, leaving her unbalanced.

His everyday life was far removed from the plush elegance of hers across the river in Mississippi. But that's one reason he drew her. He was different, exciting, and had more depth than all the boys in her school combined.

There was more to him than sports and parties. With him, she wasn't afraid to talk about things that interested her—not cheerleading and beauty pageants, but world events and politics. He didn't laugh when she laid out her dreams even though she wasn't yet out of high school.

He believed in her.

"Did I hurt you?" He brushed her hair back from her forehead.

"A little. You were bigger than I expected."

His laughter made her smile. It always did. "That was the perfect compliment."

"Was it? Well, it's the truth. Not that I have any basis for comparison, but I'm sure yours is the best." His chest rumbled against hers, the vibrations electrifying her toes and fingertips. "Was I . . . okay?"

"Ah, baby, you are everything I've dreamed about and more." His lips tickled her ear, but she needed to see his eyes. See the truth or lie. She cupped his cheeks and forced his face up.

Nothing but love shone from his face. The kiss he gave her was sweet and retained a hint of the innocence they'd entrusted to each other that night. She squeezed her eyes to shut off the spigot of tears that threatened. His weight pressed her down into the ridges of the truck bed, not that she planned to complain. She would stay all night under him if she could.

She would love Sawyer Fournette forever.